Danna

One day you'll be on these pages.

Thank you for everything

The Blood Runs Darker

Billy McLaughlin

E: billymclaughlinbooks@gmail.com
F: facebook.com/billymclaughlinbooks
T: twitter.com/bilbob20

Available:
Invisible
Lost Girl
In the Wake of Death
The Dead of Winter
The Daughter
Krampus
Fractured
Four
The Blood Runs Darker

Download: Author.to/bmb

Thank You

Here we are again. Meeting on Book number 9. Even as I say it, I can't believe it. It's been a little tricky getting here. A year ago, this was almost finished in a completely different guise. The intention was only ever to make slight tweaks to the layout of the plot. Once you've prodded that beast, it's difficult to get away from it. So, this story now exists with only a snippet of what it was originally about. It's made for an interesting journey.

I've lots of people to thank as usual. My husband Will who is eternally supportive and patient as I hole myself up at the kitchen table for hours and days on end. To Lola & Ted, our fur-babies who keep me company in the days that lead to the final product. To all the family, friends, work-friends, colleagues, online book family and the many people who buy or download the book, I want to say an enormous thank you. It's difficult to put into numbers how many of you reach out to me through reviews, messages or demands for another book. Just know that I appreciate it every time and, if I look a little sheepish, it's only because I can't believe just how many of you there are.

You have all been so patient waiting on this book. Someone reminded me the other day that it's been 16 months since, 'Four,' was released. It hasn't seemed that long. Let's hope that once you've enjoyed this one, you'll spur me on to write another.
I hope this book finds you all safe and well and taking care of each other.

xBilly

Prologue

Debra Mullen ran as fast as she could.

Moonlight reflected on thick ice, sub-zero temperatures quickly freezing up the falling snow. Her heels crunched as she moved quickly, fearfully, sweat clinging to her under arms as she pulled the magnetic foil cover from the windscreen and threw open the door.

She looked back. Just once. Long enough to know she had escaped. Tears streamed, the inside of her thighs aching, bruising forming at the top of her legs. It wasn't the kind of sex she was used to. It wasn't what she had come here expecting.

Light flickered in her eyes as she glanced in her rear-view mirror. She saw a door behind her close, heard the echo of it slam like a gunshot in the dark. Twisting the key in the ignition, the car sparked to life and she thanked god her trembling hands hadn't caused the car to stall.

She could feel her heart pounding in her chest as she hit the lock button on her car doors. She heard the click as she secured herself inside the vehicle. She slammed her foot down on the clutch, her shaking hand pulling at the gear stick and the car was ready to go. As she did, he suddenly appeared at her side.

Debra screamed. The steering wheel shuddered.

'Open the door.'

He was banging lightly on the window. Not the tap of a man desperate to harm her. That didn't make her feel any better.

There was no time for her to compose herself. She knew she couldn't stay there and gather her thoughts. She had to get away.

He banged harder on the window, causing the

door to shake and the glass to vibrate at her side.

'Just let me go,' she shrieked. She forced her right foot onto the gas and pulled the car away. It juddered in the snow, kicking up a storm of flakes behind it so that it caused the man to go down on one leg.

He roared in pain but didn't stay down long enough for her to feel eased.

She looked back and saw he was simply staring at her disappearing car.

As the car bolted over black ice, she saw the landscape of the city laid bare before her. Lights forged an orange hue that rose into the white dusky sky. It calmed her enough that she managed to re-gain control of herself. She couldn't drive down the country road in the state she'd fled the hotel in.

Debra flicked the button on the car radio. She didn't want company now. Music would soothe her though. Her car was gliding now, throttling through three inches of white fluff. She could scream for what she had gotten herself into. She should have known better.

Up ahead, she saw the twist in the road. It had come too late though. She wouldn't be able to navigate her way round that bend at the speed she was now going. Panic rose, but there was no time for that either. She twisted the steering wheel, saw the double set of lights of the oncoming car too late to avoid them and let out a sharp shrill scream.

The cars collided head on, the shattered glass giving invite to the falling snow and the bonnet of Debra's Volkswagen flying up as her car tumbled on to its side. It slid into a ditch that was much deeper than the snow had suggested. She had stopped screaming, allowed the accident to happen because it was already underway. She wasn't sure why she felt so calm though she suspected the pain hadn't hit yet. Her car stopped, the wheels still spinning, causing a backdraft of snow to fly at the other vehicle.

As she leaned up towards the door, she wondered if she could free herself and climb out of the top. Her seatbelt wouldn't free though. It was only when she pulled at it that she felt the liquid soaking into her dress. She looked down, saw the charcoal stain seeping through. It was then she felt the pain. A large triangle of glass had wedged itself into the centre of her chest and was now causing her to bleed. She began to fret, running her hands across the sharp edge. She suspected pulling it out would only inflict more pain and cause more damage.

Debra heard a man's voice then. Someone was calling for her. She didn't recognise it, so she knew it couldn't be him. She wanted to call out for help, but she simply felt too weak. She threw back her head, felt the rise in her throat and hooded her eyes as her head began to throb.

Her last thought before losing consciousness was her husband and how he might feel when he learned of her betrayal.

1.
Ten weeks later

Detective Brian Houston felt the deep etch of sadness when he wondered if his career was over. He heard the light snore of a sleeping baby and wished he had gone straight to his superiors with the envelope. Wouldn't that open a can of worms? Not to mention endanger his brother's life. He absently flicked the hard edge of his hair and watched the black clouds gather over the far away hills. If only he knew what he was setting himself up for.

When he was sure Gaby must be sleeping, Brian poured the letter onto the table and resisted the urge to scorch the entire thing. That wouldn't make the problem go away. It would only destroy the evidence that he was being blackmailed at all.

A gust of wind sounded outside, and he watched as the newly dressed trees began to wave against its push. Nightfall had arrived, a full moon appearing from behind a dark cloud. Spring may have been on its way, but nobody had told the skies.

Brian exited from the side door of their cottage, its quaintness almost contradicting the nasty taste the letter had left. Now stuffed in his pocket, Brian hoped that closing the door and starting the car would not wake either Gaby or Eva. His mood was bad enough without getting short shrift from his wife about waking the baby.

The drive from the wooded village to the abandoned quarry at the back of Milton Carter hotel was quick but not without its perils. The roads were lit only by the faint moonlight which disappeared when a turn in the road, a rising birch or a drifting cloud created a shroud. Brian, usually held up by nerves of steel, found the tension deepening until his forehead painfully creased and a trickle of sweat tore down his back. He had twenty minutes to get there, letter in hand and face down whatever retribution awaited him.

He wanted to laugh at the ridiculousness of it. A man who believed in the law, creeping out to defend himself against an act that he barely felt responsible for. Gaby had told him to turn it in. Her advice had been strong and unreserved. She wanted him to go to his superiors. Anything else, he would have. Something filled him with dread about the tone of the letter and the threat to his brother's life. He wasn't taking any chances. He would deal with this himself. Just as the blackmailer had advised.

The hotel rose into sight. It's white turrets at each end twisted up and created a far more grandiose silhouette than it deserved. The hotel itself was currently closed and undergoing a refurbishment that was supposed to marry with the promise of new tourism in the nearby village of Loch Achray.

Brian and Gaby hadn't been so fortunate to afford a house in the new money rises along the surface of the loch. Instead, they lived in the modest two bedded cottage that was centred between the new village and the old nearby town. He liked it though. He'd grown up in one of the housing schemes in Falkirk and wanted to raise his children in a safer environment. Right now, nothing felt safe to him.

He drove up to the hotel grounds, parked the blue Navara on the side-skirts of the building. The quarry was tucked behind an avenue of trees. He stood in the wind, midnight approaching and wondered if his blackmailer was here yet.

'You came,' called a voice from behind a

shadow.

Brian snapped his head round, his heart taking a slight leap. He hadn't even made it to the quarry. 'What do you want?'

The blackmailer stayed just concealed enough that no matter how Brian squinted, he couldn't see the man's face.

'Your neck in a noose.'

Brian felt a chill. He suspected it was more than a veiled threat. He knew what he was being accused of. 'This crap,' he said, pulling the letter from his pocket. 'I don't know what the hell you're talking about. I haven't done what you think I have. And if you think you'll get any money from me, I've got a mortgage that I'm over my head in, a recent wedding to pay for and a new baby.'

'I don't want your money,' chuckled the shadow, shaking his head. 'I think you know exactly what you've done. Otherwise you wouldn't be here alone.'

'Call me curious.'

Only when the blackmailer moved closer to him was Brian able to make out part of his face. He looked younger than he sounded, not as creepy as his letter or his voice might have suggested.

'I don't care about your brother or your drug deal on his behalf. That's not what I'm interested in.'

There was something malevolent about the speech, an underlying threat of something much more sinister than Brian had thought.

'I didn't do any drug deal on my brother's behalf,' insisted Brian. No matter what Jamie Houston had done, Brian would always defend him. He would also protect him as much as he could. It was difficult to protect someone who was now holed up in prison for attempted murder. Brian was telling the truth when he said he hadn't done anything on his brother's behalf. He suddenly understood that his blackmailer had misinterpreted the entire situation.

The sound of something shifting behind him caused Brian to suddenly turn. His eyes darted to the side and he found a breath stalling in his throat. 'There's someone else here.'

Silence.

'No, just me.'

As Brian turned back, the silhouette was now upon him. The approach was so sudden he couldn't even have prevented it if he had moved much faster. He brought up his arms to defend himself, but it was too late. Suddenly he felt something loop over his head and then nest around his neck. Brian's eyes widened, panic heating his cold terrified face. 'What are you doing?'

The blackmailer's breath deepened. He was now so close to Brian that they were almost skin to skin. Then he brought his leg round behind Brian's calf and took the weight from Brian's body.

A moment later, Brian felt himself lifted from the ground. It happened so fast he couldn't think. The faces of Gaby and Eva flashed through his mind and he found himself ready to scream. In terror, he brought up his hands to the nylon rope now tightening round his neck. It was already too tight for him to catch a real full breath. So, he settled for short sharp one's that would tide him over until the blackmailer cut him down. His legs were flailing wildly as he realised, he was floating a foot above ground level.

In the distance, silence continued to envelop the world, but the wind hummed a melancholy tune. Brian couldn't find his voice now, not even to scream. He dared not to think of his wife now as he realised, he might not be coming down at all. He couldn't bear to think of her sad face knowing he might never see it again. So, he wrestled with the rope until he felt himself weaken and his windpipe begin to tighten.

The blackmailer stared as he moved round Brian's hanging body. 'Don't worry, I'll take care of your little girl for you,' he said, followed by the echo of a sinister laughter.

It only caused Brian to writhe more. He wasn't quite there yet. Maybe if he was just angry enough, he might snap himself out of the noose and fall to the ground. It might just be enough to give him a fighting chance. When he'd calmed himself enough for a morsel of a plan to form, he caught a deep breath. Then he saw something silver glint.

The blackmailer brought up his arm so quickly that the blade was a mere blur.

Hope died as blood splattered from the first slash. Hanging had been painful enough and he wasn't even dead yet. The second, third and fourth slash to his face caused him to gurgle as blood trickled down his chin. The moon appeared just in time for Brian to catch a real glimpse of his killer's face. Suddenly, he recognised him. The identity of his killer would die with him and there wasn't anything he could do. Brian allowed his eyes to close, one last breath escaping from inside his burning neck. Then, he dangled until unconsciousness finally freed him of the pain.

*

Gaby was sure she'd heard her husband's car start up. It must have been a few minutes ago but she hadn't been quite ready to open her eyes. Three-month-old babies had that effect on a person. They hadn't been blessed in the way she'd heard other parents speak about. Eva, despite Gaby's love for her, was a nightmare. Now, when they finally did get some sleep, she almost felt as if she were living through a sleep paralysis. Still, she was certain Brian had gone out.

She rose from the bed, listening to the light breeze on the roof of the house. Shadows of dancing branches broke the eerie stillness and she wondered if Brian had been called to work. He hadn't seemed himself recently, not since that stupid letter had arrived. Still, it seemed to have been a hoax and was now suitably discarded into the bin. At least that's what she hoped for.

Eva stirred as Gaby stepped into the hallway. She was glad now she had allowed Brian to persuade her into buying the various little gadgets that allowed them to monitor Eva. Gaby never wanted to be one of those paranoid mothers who couldn't go half an hour without checking on the baby or phoning every twenty minutes from a girl's night out. She wanted to relax and enjoy motherhood but still enjoy the other things that being in her twenties allowed. The monitors had soothed her post-natal anxiety though and she'd come to terms with hearing Eva's breathing, sniffling and coughing in every room of the house.

She switched on the kitchen light, saw Brian's half eaten meal still on the table and untouched glass of water on the sink. She knew the late calls and long hours were part of his job and she had tried so hard not to allow it to irk her. Still, she had often wished he had chosen a profession that didn't involve all those things and the worrying nights. There were lots of things he could do. He wouldn't hear of it though.

He'd gone into the academy at the age of twenty-one and had never looked back. Besides she wouldn't have met him if he hadn't been a policeman in the first place.

Gaby popped a pod onto the coffee machine and slipped a cup under the nozzle. Tonight's drink of choice would be de-caffeinated because she didn't want to squander her few hours of sleep whilst Eva rested. She pressed her back against the sink and ran her eyes along the yellow checked wallpaper. She longed to strip it off and modernise the house because looking at these walls only reminded her, she'd given up a city life to move to this little country flavoured nook. Not that she regretted it. She would have gone anywhere for Brian. Sweet, generous Brian; the only man she had loved and who had loved her with such equal fervour.

A smile at the thought that he'd hopefully be home before she woke again. Gaby took a sip of her coffee, carried it back to her bedroom with her and slipped under the duvet. A few more sips before she pushed the mug to the back of the bedside cabinet. She wrapped her arms round her breasts and took sight of the baby sleeping a few meters away. How she adored that child. For a moment, all the sleepless nights forgotten, all the labour pain eradicated from her mind, Gaby felt elation. Her life was perfect right now. She couldn't imagine anything coming along to change that. With that thought to soothe her, she drifted into a dreamless slumber.

2.

The voice came through, masked by some contraption that was designed to hide his identity. Yet, his words were clear and concise. 'I'm going to kill someone.'

Dave Hawthorn groaned silently and adjusted the mouthpiece. It was going to be one of those days. He'd barely taken a sip of his first coffee this morning when he took a call from a woman unable to get her parrot down from the top of the fridge. Now, electro-voice had decided to phone in a prank. 'Can I take a few details?'

A chuckle. 'Why not? What would you like to know?'

Dave levered himself up on the arm of the chair and reminded himself this was better than the last job he was in. 'What's your name?'

The mechanical voice cackled. 'You can do better than that.'

'Alright,' sighed Dave. 'How about giving me your location?'

The laughter thickened, more threatening now. 'Well I'm not standing on Blackpool fucking tower.'

A trickle of dread. Dave didn't mind the calls from the suicidal or the hysterical. He could deal with those. He considered himself a master in the art of negotiation; a hangover from his days working at a car dealership. These types of calls though, they made him nervous. He hated not knowing what he was dealing with. 'Sir, can you tell me if you have any real intention of harming someone. Or yourself?'

The voice on the other end fell behind a deep breath. 'I've no intention of harming myself,' he replied.

A momentary silence fell between them.

Dave leaned forward, tapped on the keyboard and eyed the phone number. One previous call. Which meant they had called the service once before. 'Someone else?'

More silence.

For a moment Dave wondered if the caller had hung up but he could still hear the airy static on the other end of the line. 'Can I ask if you have a real plan to hurt someone?'

Dave looked up and saw the eyes of two colleagues falling on him. What bordered on tedious for him seemed to be the holy grail of staff room excitement for some other staff. He shifted uncomfortably in his chair, moved closer to the screen and prepared to lower his voice.

The man on the other side of the line drew out the pause, clicked his tongue theatrically and snorted. 'Victim? That's a very loose term. I don't believe anyone in this world is a victim. We've all done something to someone. Wouldn't you agree, Dave?'

A breath caught in Dave's throat, a chill tickling his spine. The caller knew his name. Had he said his name at the beginning of the call? He couldn't remember. Swinging round in his chair, Dave waved for the attention of the newest team manager, Jason Barr. He watched as Jason lifted his finger, indicating he'd be there in a moment before turning away. Dave returned to the static line. 'Is it someone you know?'

The line went silent again, this time the static faded and Dave wondered if he had been the victim of a hoax. Victim? He played back in his mind what the caller had said about victims and found himself increasingly disturbed by such a thought. He waved for Jason again. 'Hello? Are you still there?' Panic set in, not quite a full attack, but enough to send an ache through his gut.

The static returned. 'I'm here, Dave. Now, here's what I want you to do. Don't draw attention to yourself. Stand up and take off your headset. I'm going to give you some instructions which I want you to follow very carefully. If you don't do as I say, you can kiss your beautiful wife, Lizzie goodbye.'

*

Detective Inspector Rosie Cooper still found herself adjusting to the silence. It was a different world here. A world she could probably get used to if not for the fact she had to brave the cold. She had only experienced the low end of Autumn and the skin-beating winter. Now, early Spring threatened an incline in temperature but not enough for her to stop missing London.

Rosie pushed the photo away and scolded herself for obsessing over it. She thought she had moved on, left that part of her life behind but here it was, rearing its ugly naked head once more. She looked at his abs, his tough grip, arms wrapped round her like he was trying to shroud her from the camera. Why had she let it happen? *Stupid, stupid, stupid!*

She clocked the time and gave herself a psychological shake. Time to shower and drive to work. The five-minute drive to the station was pleasant enough, short enough she could enjoy the sight of the loch that her house sat on. She had bought Crystal Ridge in a mind fog. No thoughts on how she would keep the place warm when there was four inches of snow clamouring up the glass exteriors. No concerns for how she would conceal herself to the passing world, assuming anyone but her neighbours would pass. The house was stunning though. Worth the four hundred thousand pound she had sunk into it.

She could still remember the first time she'd seen it; a glass rock at the centre of the newly built village that snaked round the deep waters of Loch Achray.

She'd been happy here at first. It had been a haven away from everything that had driven her out of her life. Until the envelope arrived a few days ago. She had only told one person, her father of where she was going. He would never betray her. He would lay himself down in front of oncoming train for her. Yet, here they were. Her humiliation packaged into an A4 envelope from an unknown source. Someone from her old life had found her.

She placed the photo back in the drawer, peeled away the resentment that now grew for its probable sender, and stomped up to the shower. If she didn't think about the picture again today, her mood might improve. Though, not if the persistent vibration of her phone had anything to do with it. Rosie suddenly became aware of it when she was about to enter the shower. Having already dropped her underwear, she reached for a towel and wrapped it round her bony frame.

'Detective Cooper speaking.' As soon as she heard the dulcet tones of her chief, Martin Wall she knew it couldn't be good news.

'I need you to get over to the Milton Carter hotel.'

'What now?' It didn't seem that long-ago Rosie was outside that hotel for a fatal car accident. The hotel wasn't even open yet and here she was, being called there again.

'I'm sending you on this, Rosie because I know you'll handle it with dignity. A few of the guys are out there already. They're after blood and I want you to keep a handle on this.'

Suddenly, she felt a surge of panic spread through her. 'What is it, chief?'

She heard the gulp. Or was it the restraining of a sob?

What could have happened there that would cause the uniforms to react like that?

'It's Brian,' he whispered. 'He's been found hanged.'

Rosie gripped the phone, repeated the words to herself whilst trying to work out who Brian was. 'Brian who?'

What sounded like an angry scoff travelled down the phone at her. 'Our Brian. Brian Houston. The Detective you've been working with for the past six months.'

Rosie stopped moving, let the wave of shock pulse over her. She had heard the words, but she couldn't relate them to Brian. Not her partner, the man she had befriended since her arrival in Achray. She pushed the phone against her ear and didn't even realise a slight pain had now developed on the lobe. 'What happened?' She finally found her voice; a shaking quiver that wasn't quite her own.

'I've not been able to get a single bloody answer from that lot over there. They're hysterical. Some of these guys have been friends with Brian for years. I need you to calm them. Get to the bottom of what's happened. I would go myself but,' he froze right then as if he couldn't quite find the justification.

Rosie understood. She had lost a colleague once before and it was devastating. There weren't words strong enough for the loss. The force was a family, just like any other. Good eggs, bad eggs, rotten eggs that she couldn't quite help falling in love with. Brian was one of the good ones. 'It's okay, chief. You have other things you need to do. I'll handle it.' How? How was she going to calm those country brutes down? There was only the finest line between their upholding of the law and their willingness to drag someone down a dark path and give them a kicking. She didn't agree with it, but she knew it happened.

Hanging up the phone with trembling hands, Rosie forwent her shower, walked to the wardrobe and pulled out a blouse that didn't need ironed. She slipped into grey pressed trousers and a matching jacket. Then, she scraped back her curls into a tight ponytail and sprayed some dry shampoo on her hair.

Brian was dead? It couldn't have been suicide. A new baby, a lovely young wife and a career that even she would one day be envious of. Why would he do that? She told herself it couldn't be, particularly when the chief himself had said the other police presence were going crazy. Whose blood would they be after if Brian had taken his own life. That didn't make sense, which left her with the only conclusion she could suitably come to.

Her friend and colleague, Detective Brian Houston must have been murdered.

3.

Grey Carter watched the back court of his hotel become a crime scene. It wasn't the only time blue flashing lights had lit up the pale white walls. He had already had to delay the opening of the hotel due to the long winter and the overwhelming grief he had not expected to experience.

He felt a chill on the back of his neck, a hangover probably from the shock of finding a dead body hanging from one of the back arches. He hadn't recognised the face until he overheard one of the uniformed officer's saying his name. He had witnessed the explosion of grief right there. Grey had never experienced such a reaction to loss. Not even when Debra had died. Even she hadn't managed to shake whatever humanity he had to its core.

Grey had watched with great interest as a crime scene was erected. He had seen such a pathway to preservation before. Only once. When he was fifteen years old. It wasn't something he thought of often, certainly not something that had left any great impact on him.

He'd watched as they'd cordoned the area off with yellow ticker tape. His own grounds were now off limits to him. The body had been taken down with such delicate consideration that Grey was sure they must have contaminated some of the evidence. A tent, pale white was erected before a plain clothed officer adorned PPE and began a walkthrough of the perimeter.

A photographer in full white plastic clothing now leaned in on several items that had been numbered with yellow plastic markers. Grey couldn't quite see from the upper floor what was being photographed but he could see the intensity of the flashes that were capturing those images. It was like something from a movie.

He saw the grey Volvo arrive and a familiar figure emerge. God, even from up here she was stunning to him. He had imagined more than once running his fingers down her body and touching her neck with the tip of his tongue. He'd never allowed his imagination to fertilise beyond that because, on the few occasions he'd met her, she'd looked at him with the disgust probably reserved usually for a mass murderer.

He grabbed the pack of cigarettes from the table and decided to head outside. He knew he wouldn't be allowed to enter the crime scene and he didn't particularly want to re-visit the body of the victim. What he'd already witnessed was bad enough.

Grey was just exiting the side door of the kitchen when a young woman approached him.

'Excuse me, sir. Do you work here?'

Grey turned and saw she had a notepad in her hand. 'Are you with the police?'

'No,' she said, wide smile and battering eyelids that she must have used to charm lots of interviewees.

'Then, get off my property. And take your friends with you' He lit the cigarette in his mouth and moved towards a path that led down to the quarry. He ignored the young blonde woman's pleas and the calls from the other reporters. He wasn't giving anyone a statement. He didn't even want his hotel named in all of this. He wanted guests because of the stunning overhaul he had given to a backwater motel, not because of a ghoulish interest they had in re-walking crime scenes.

Silver smoke passed his eyes, black lashes

blinking above his chiselled jaw. His hair had been shaved into the wood of his lightly bronzed skin. His muscular right arm wore a series of colours that twisted into a skull tattooed onto his shoulder. On the left arm, a still-life python slithered down his skin, black split tongue rushing towards a red back spider that had been needled into the side of his fist.

He knew he'd be a suspect. It had happened on his grounds. If common sense applied, it made him unlikely to be the killer. Which meant they would doubly suspect him. After all, he hadn't had the most pleasant exchange with the dead detective. The questions would come. He knew that. That's why he wasn't speaking to the media. He knew there was a common belief that those who threw themselves into the path of a murder investigation quite often had something to hide. Hiding in plain sight, as it were.

Grey was prepared for the moment Detective Cooper would approach him. He'd worked on his answers for hours. He needed to keep himself out of it. He had the grand opening of the hotel in three days and there was no way he was allowing another delay. For now, he gave a gentle wave to Detective Cooper and disappeared for a short walk into the woods.

*

The cameras were still flashing when Rosie navigated her way through the personnel. She hated this part of her job. It was so tedious. When people watched these TV shows about forensics, it was all edited to look exciting and dramatic. A crime scene was rarely any of these things. Generally, it was searching for a needle in a haystack, hoping everybody had done what they were meant to and hadn't missed anything that might initially seem trivial.

Rosie walked towards the tent with the

trepidation of a new detective on her first crime scene. She could see two of the uniformed officers on the periphery, shaking their angry heads and vowing to find the killer. She understood their motivation. Rosie had been there herself once when her first partner had been gunned down on a busy London road. She'd been just as fused as they probably were now.

'You guys okay to be here?' She was standing a few inches away from them now.

'We wouldn't want to be anywhere else,' replied the elder of the two.

'I imagine this has been very traumatic for you both. If you need to speak to me, I'm here. Right now, I think you should both go and get yourself a coffee and calm down.'

The vocal one shrugged. 'A coffee won't help. I'll be seeing Brian's face in my sleep.'

Rosie saw the anguish in his face and wondered just how bad it must have been. She'd never seen a hanging. It was one of the very few traumatic things she hadn't seen. What else was there? She could see in their faces that there was something much worse than she was expecting. Finally, she prepared herself mentally and turned towards the tent. The examiner was emerging from the tent, thin grey hair floating in the wind.

'Must have been traumatic death,' he said as she approached. He gave her a short wave and introduced himself. 'Michael McKinney. I'm with the PF's office. I'm guessing you're Detective Cooper.'

'You've been forewarned,' she said, smiling at him. Rosie moved through the gatefold of the tent, saw there was still personnel in there and tried to prepare herself for what she was here to see. She forced her eyes to turn, everything in her head telling her to run away. Finally, she saw him. She gasped, held back the urge to vomit and turned away. 'Someone did that to him. Why?'

Nobody in the tent spoke. How could they? Nobody had any answers yet.

'Do you know how long he's been dead?' She gulped as she asked the question.

'Several hours. I would also say he was probably close to death when that happened to his face. There are blood splatters but there's not a lot of spillage after the fact.'

Rosie stepped back out into the tarmac of the hotel car park. 'Did anybody find anything suspect? Are there are any cameras? What is Grey Carter saying about it? I noticed he's off on a wander. Can we get him back into the hotel? I have questions for him?'

The older of the two uniformed police officers shifted. 'I'll go get him.'

Rosie moved away, headed for a bench on a nearby grass patch. She wanted a few moments alone to contemplate, to register what she had just seen and try to make some sense of it. The urge to weep pressed against her but she wouldn't do that. Not now. Not whilst she was being asked to hold the team together. There would be angry recriminations. Accusations would fly. She would have to deal with Gaby, his lovely wife and deliver this terrible news. Gaby would already be wondering where her husband was.

Sitting on the bench, cold fresh air cooling her flipping senses, Rosie let out a deep sigh. This was going to be a hard one. Not only would she have to deal with the investigation, she'd also have to support

Gaby, who'd become quite a friend to her in the past months. She would also have to support the officers in her division who were already gearing up their pitchforks for inevitable revenge. Why had the chief chosen her? Why not get Glasgow division up here? Hadn't he noticed the budding friendship between Rosie and Brian? Chose to ignore it, she thought, indignantly.

Once she'd ensured everybody had their tasks; walkarounds, evidence gathering and documentation, Rosie returned to her car and turned on the engine. She couldn't bear to watch those two young men skulking round doing nothing. She also wanted to take a moment to think about how she would deliver this news to Gaby. She threw her head back, the bun in her hair pressing against the back of the leather seat. It was hot in this car. She was thankful for a change that the wonky heating was serving a purpose.

From the corner of her eye, she saw him approaching. She'd recently heard a word to describe him that she'd never heard before. Once she knew what it meant, Rosie completely agreed. 'Gallus,' was the word. She watched him saunter to the window and then she rolled it down.

'You wanted to speak to me?'

She turned off the engine, heard it die a second behind the turn of the key, then she stepped back out of the car.

'Yes, I do. I want to know where you were last night and this morning. I'd also like to know if you heard anything unusual. Lastly, why don't you have any cameras? I heard you've spent half a million on this refurbishment and you don't have a single CCTV camera set up. I find that very bewildering.'

4.

Dave was grateful for the quiet roads as he raced from the southside of Glasgow along the M8 and off at the old fruit market. The car must have grown wings because he'd never known it to do this speed. He'd never had to race home to save his wife before. The whole time he envisioned Lizzie at home, running up a brand-new design and looking at him incredulously as he burst through the front door.

In five years, the estate he and Lizzie had bought into had thickened from a row of houses to spirals of houses that were all different twists on the same model. None of the houses looked particularly different until people saw inside. Which made Dave wonder if he and his wife hadn't been the victim of mistaken identity. In any case, he felt queasy, swallowing back the contents of his breakfast before they erupted onto the dashboard of his car.

He found himself eyeing the time. *11.37 a.m.* Perhaps he could still call the police and ask for help. He might even get one of his colleagues. Didn't the police always look after their own? He envisioned two police cars racing to his house. High alert for a woman sitting at her kitchen island working through her latest clothes designs. How stupid he would look? How angry everyone would be with him for wasting their time.

However, she hadn't answered her phone the twice that he had called.

He rallied through the main roads of Gallowgate and up towards the East of Glasgow. In the distance, he could see the last remaining high rises of the city, now emptying in preparation for their very own demolition. It wasn't a comforting sight. The towers of poverty once the stain on city life, now brought down to reveal an empty and soulless sky.

Finally, the terracotta roof of his house appeared. Where it should have offered him just a flicker of comfort, it heightened his anxiety until he was certain he might pass out and crash his Hyundai. Nearly there now. He'd soon know if the call had been a hoax.

But the man with the strange voice had known his name. How? Why? In his mind he hadn't given out his name.

He took a sharp right turn into his road, causing an oncoming car to almost veer into the side of a lamppost. The man shouted an obscenity, but Dave didn't hear it. He was too focused on the house at the end of the road. The one with the dark blue door that he'd come to know as the gate to his castle. A few seconds later and the car was screeching to a halt in the brick driveway.

'Lizzie,' he found himself shouting as he threw open the car door and rushing towards the house. The question in his mind all the way over was why someone would target him and his wife. He wasn't involved with anyone he shouldn't be. To his knowledge, his wife wasn't either. Beads of sweat dripped past the little crevices at the side of his eyes as he frowned in a myriad of confusion and anger.

He found himself shouting again, louder this time. 'Lizzie?'

Silence.

He ran to the kitchen, expecting she might be working on something with a set of headphones on. Perhaps she hadn't heard him. He didn't need to look far to know something had taken place. Broken glass lay on scattered sheets of drawn-on paper, now sodden and damp from whatever contents had been in the glass. Dave knew instantly the call hadn't been a hoax.

As if to complete his newfound terror, a mobile phone rang behind him. It wasn't a ringtone he recognised. It certainly wasn't his and he suspected Lizzie hadn't changed hers. He approached slowly, eyeing the contraption as if it might fly up and lunge at him.

It had been left here deliberately, he suspected. A way of connecting with him that wouldn't be traceable. These kidnappers were real, and they had been in his house. Now they had his wife.

Dave reached out with a shaking hand, snapped up the handset and answered the call.

'Good man.' That voice again. Still veiled behind whatever voice changing app or machine they were using.

'I've called the police,' said Dave, instantly regretting it as soon as he said it. In his panic, he had hurtled out whatever words he thought might help save his wife. *Stupid!* He wanted to kick himself.

'No time for liars today, Dave. You haven't called anyone. Otherwise Hermes would already be delivering your wife's body parts.'

Dave spun round. Was he being watched?

'There's no-one there. Not in the house anyway,' chuckled the strange voice.

'What do you want?'

'Just your neck in a noose. Don't worry, there's plenty of time. I don't want you to underestimate the danger your wife is in. Now, if you're in any doubt about how serious we are, I want you to consider how I managed to get through to you directly in a place as secure as your centre. I want you to imagine how the call I made to you was completely untraceable. Now, imagine what it might be like for you to phone a colleague or a friend and ask them to listen back to that call and find that it doesn't exist.' The voice paused. 'Now, have I got your undivided attention?'

Dave ran his fingers across his eyes and rubbed at the bridge of his nose. He brushed sweat back into the soft quiff at the top of his forehead. Blinking frantically through his dark lashes and catching a glimpse at the pallor of his skin in a nearby mirror, he caught his breath and grunted. 'Yes,' he finally whimpered.

'I will know if you've called the police. I will know if you do anything to compromise your wife's safety. Even just an eye roll at a stranger in another parked vehicle might result in her untimely death. Now, as it is, I'll keep her alive until you get here if you play ball. Do you understand the gravity of what I'm asking you, Dave?'

Dave stepped into the lounge and stared through the window. He could see the open door of his car at the front of the house and he could see Mr Fenton across the street waving at him. He waved back slowly and wondered if there was a way to get a message to the old man. Might as well put the old man's infuriating nosiness to good use.

'I wouldn't think about it, if I were you,' said the kidnapper, either reading his mind or watching him from some unknown corner.

Dave felt exasperated. There was no reason for him and Lizzie to be targeted like this. 'What do I need to do?

A snicker from the other end of the line. 'Glad we're on the same page, Dave. Go out to your car, disconnect your phone from the Bluetooth and bring it into the house. Put it on the table where I can see it.'

Dave's eyes darted round the room. He had been aware the kidnapper had been able to see some of his movements. There must be some cameras strategically placed around the hall. He didn't have time to search. Nor did he want to give the kidnapper any reason to harm his wife. He dashed to the car and fumbled with his phone.

Thirty seconds later, having disconnected from the Bluetooth in the car, he returned to the house and held the phone in the air. He returned the kidnapper's handset to his ear and ran his tongue along his drying lips. 'What now?'

The hallway felt different now. Not safe like it did before, but like an entrance into a world Dave didn't recognise or feel safe in.

'Put the phone on the table where I can see it. Take your wallet out of your pocket and take twenty pounds out. That should be enough for you to top up petrol if you run low. Dump the wallet and anything else you have in your pocket on the table. The only thing you should take to the car with you is the money and my mobile phone. Got it?'

Dave emptied his pockets, suspecting he might not even have twenty pounds in his wallet. He dumped some loose change and his lunch receipt beside his mobile phone and stepped back. Luckily, he found a ten-pound note and two fives. He looked round himself again and waited for the kidnapper to speak.

'Good, now we're ready to go. Drive back to the fruit market. It's closed today so there shouldn't be many people around. It should take you approximately eight minutes. I'll give you seven. If you're not there by the time I call you back, you don't need to go any further. I'll have chopped off your wife's head and thrown it into the deep water. You understand?'

'Please, don't hurt her. I don't even know what we're supposed to have done.'

The kidnapper sighed, speaking more firmly this time. 'Do you understand, Dave?'

Dave spun round once more, trying to catch sight of whatever contraption now allowed the kidnapper to spy on him. 'Yes,' he yelled, frustration catching up to him.

'Good, now get on your way. You've already wasted half a minute.'

When the line went dead, Dave rushed back to his car and quickly reversed out of his driveway. He checked the clock again and raced back to the main road, praying that the traffic lights would be generous today. In his mind, he rolled over the words again and again. Lizzie's head would be discarded into a river or a lake somewhere and he'd never find her. He felt as if someone was reaching up from his gut and pulling him down. He would trade places with Lizzie in a second. Yet, he didn't know why he was trading places with her. He was honestly dumbfounded that he and his wife had been targeted. That didn't matter now. He had six minutes to get to his next destination. No time to try and play guessing games with a psycho.

*

Spring may have arrived, but a new frostiness had developed outside the Milton Carter Hotel. Grey had already wandered into the maze at the end of his garden and found his way back out in record time. A few weeks ago, he'd almost decided to give up on the hotel but now he had gotten on top of everything and realised that no woman was worth throwing his life away for. Not even a dead one.

Detective Cooper had worked the room. Well, essentially it was outside, but she'd made her way round every member of personnel and given them a list of their duties. Not even the evident horror in her face could tear her away from the task at hand. Then, she approached the media. Where Grey had been short and dismissive, she was working them as if they were avid autograph seekers. Greetings were exchanged, gentle smiles and light handshakes that were followed by little titbits of information that told them nothing. Tomorrow, they would run headlines that looked sensational until they realised, they'd been played by a seasoned pro. That detective was a wily one, delivering just enough information to draw in witnesses but without giving anything away.

Grey waited patiently. In fact, he was almost enjoying himself. If the inevitable but irritating presence of the police could bring anything, it was the fact that the lead detective would look better with her clothes on his bedroom floor. He would never forget their first meeting. They'd danced dangerously between curt lines of questioning and the raised eye of flirtation. It had left him wondering if there would ever be any other reason to see her than the death of someone on or around his premises.

He knew she liked him. It wasn't the giggling adoration he had once enjoyed in his twenties. She'd eyed the litany of images needled to his muscular body and probably wondered why someone would turn their own body into a carved canvas. Then, she had taken a backseat when Detective Brian Houston had waded in with his own questions. Grey had noticed it then. The awkward glances as she sized up his face. Bronzed skin framed by the lining of his cropped black hair. The meeting of their eyes; her emerald pupils in oval arches catching his wide baby blues that dragged away her stare from his sullen pout.

That had been ten weeks ago. Much had happened since then and it had gotten to the point where he wasn't sure he would see her again. He wasn't sure he even wanted to. Other things were afoot for him now. Yet, here she was, befallen by tragedy and doing her best to remain the stoic and professional leader. It only increased his admiration for her.

Of course, none of this would have happened if the murder of that officer hadn't taken place. Grey wasn't a particularly empathetic person. He also wasn't averse to the destruction of anyone who might stand in his way. The hanging had seemed particularly gruesome though.

Grey leaned towards the crispy bark of a waving fir. The hoods of his eyes dipped just long enough to cover over those fantastic blue eyes that sparkled in the sunlight. When he opened them, he could see Cooper walking towards him. He could see that measured stiff upper lip that the English were so renowned for and he wondered just how steely her shell could be. What she had just witnessed couldn't have been easy.

He stepped out from underneath the tree, the shape of his head catching a ray of sunshine that only further browned his skin. 'It can't be easy to calm all of them down and stay focused. Not after seeing that.'

The expression on her face might have remained still but her body language was telling an entirely different story.

'Can I take you inside for a drink. I'm guessing you need something to settle your nerves.'

She looked like she might argue, throw some smart retort but she must have thought better of it. Her shoulders lagged. 'Okay, that would be good. Maybe you can answer some of the questions I asked over a coffee.'

'I don't know how much help I can be,' he lied, before escorting her through the side kitchen door.

5.

Adam Mullen didn't know why he continued to torture himself. It had been two months since his wife's funeral and the news of her death had been followed by thunderbolts of devastating revelations. The investigation into an apparent sexual assault had quickly been bedded when he, and the police had learned of her torrid affair. The bruises on her legs hadn't been forced intercourse but the result of some liaison she'd welcomed in the wake of her obvious dissatisfaction. The only person who appeared to be happy with news of the affair was Adam's mother, who had been nigh on incapable of containing her superiority.

He gripped the edge of each page of the photo album with sheer ferocity. He had never known anger until the day the police had arrived to tell him Debra was dead. Now, anger was the only thing he felt. Had she been the sole contributor to his pain and despair he might have found it in himself to forgive. Now, he stared at the three figures in the wedding picture; himself, Debra and his best man, Grey. Two of the most important people in his life committing the ultimate betrayal.

Adam slammed shut the book and watched a cloud of dust fog the basement when he threw the album to the floor. He could hear the doorbell now. He could also hear Gracie, his four-year-old daughter shouting that there was a man at the door. He kicked past the photo album, took the stairs two at a time and feigned a smile at his little girl as he rushed to the front door. He hadn't been aware until now but there were tears and they had already reddened round the outline of his dirty fair eyelashes.

A silhouette shifted impatiently on the other side of the stained-glass door.

Adam peered round the small window and tried to identify their visitor.

The man smiled. He was at least four inches taller than Adam, fine chestnut coloured hair neatly styled above oak coloured eyes and a chiselled jaw line that probably took ten years off him. He wore a grey Calvin Klein suit with a silk red tie that lent a striking edge to his otherwise staid look. He was smiling directly at Adam.

The younger man on the inside of the door hadn't realised he was staring. He could hear Gracie chattering behind him as he contemplated moving away from the door. He wasn't in the mood for visitors today, but life had to go on. Especially with Gracie now centred on his every move. Her little button nose was virtually twitching with inquisitiveness. Adam turned to her and ushered her into the lounge. Nobody who had arrived at his house recently brought good news. He didn't expect that to change now.

'Good afternoon, are you Adam Mullen?'

Adam wedged his foot behind the door, opening it just enough for them to exchange a conversation. 'That's me. Can I help you?'

'You're Debra Mullen's husband?' The smile hadn't wilted completely, though the man's eyes had narrowed gravely.

For Adam, the mention of his wife's name brought flutters to his heart. Even now, anger fuelling his very existence, he still couldn't truly hate her. No matter what she had done.

Perhaps Debra's only crime had been one of unhappiness. His mother had already berated him, scolded him like a child for blaming himself. If his wife was cheating with another man, his mother had boomed, it wasn't because of his inability to keep her happy. It was her inability to stay faithful that was to blame. Adam wanted to believe it. He still hadn't gotten there yet. 'Who are you?'

The man leaned towards the door. 'Can I come in?'

Adam wrapped his hand tightly round the door handle and pushed his foot in slightly. Nobody was coming in here until he knew who they were. It was now his sole responsibility to keep Gracie safe. Nothing would stand in his way of that. 'No! I don't have a clue who you are. How did you know my wife?'

'I didn't,' whispered the man, looking slightly awkward. He held up a police identity badge. 'I'm here about the ongoing investigation into her death.'

Adam's eyebrows rose. When he'd first been told the investigation had been closed and they weren't pursuing any other avenues, he'd called that station more than a dozen times. 'I didn't know there was an ongoing investigation.' He opened the door slightly, just enough for the man to peer inside.

'Sometimes it's in the interest of the family not to be given too much information. Particularly when it looks likely to be an accident.'

Adam stared back and saw Gracie linger apprehensively in the lounge doorway. He turned his head slowly, sizing up the man now loitering just inside his hall.

The man cut a menacing shadow as he blocked out most of the sunlight. The snarl in his voice leaned towards intimidation. Yet, he had shown his identification and he came bearing information that

Adam was sure he'd want to hear. Finally, he relented. 'Okay, you can come in. I'd prefer it if you're careful what you say in front of my daughter, though.'

'Of course,' whispered the Detective.

Once inside, Adam watched his new arrival peruse the room. Were all Detectives this nosy, he wondered? He sent Gracie to the kitchen. 'Sweetheart, get yourself a biscuit from the jar on the table. I'll be through in a few minutes.'

Both men watched her slowly skulk off.

'So, what new information do you have for me?'

'It's not easy, Mr Mullen. Your wife was working on some project at the Milton Carter hotel. Is that correct?'

'I believe that's correct. Though, I didn't know that initially. She was going there when I was at work.' The deceit only confirmed what he already knew. Lies had been told and there was no other reason for it than an affair. 'The hotel is owned by my friend, Grey Carter.'

'Friend?' Silence remained where a snigger should have been placed.

'He's my oldest friend. I've known him since we were five years old.' Adam wasn't hearing anything yet that justified entry into his house.

'Would you say he's loyal to you?'

Adam rolled his eyes. 'In many ways, yes.' He felt the urge to laugh now. Loyalty was a dirty word. Adam would never trust again because those closest to him, even his parents in some ways with their incessant belittling of his choices, had betrayed him. Adam sighed. He'd never felt more alone. 'When I was thirteen years old, Grey saved my life. I was cornered by a group of teenagers who wanted to take my wallet. One of them had a knife an inch from my face. I might have been slashed half to death if it wasn't for Grey.' Of course, Adam had paid Grey back in spades. He would never discuss that, though. That would be one betrayal too far. Not only of Grey, but of himself.

The detective sat down on the sofa and made himself comfortable. It looked like he wasn't in a rush to go anywhere. 'Sounds like a good friend.'

'When I bought my first house, he gave me five thousand pounds for the deposit. That was nine years ago. I've still not paid him back and he has never asked. I would never have been able to get this house if it hadn't been for him.' Adam felt weak for defending Grey, but all those things were true. Even if the other side of the coin was that Grey was a lying narcissist.

'Can't be easy then to realise that he's destroyed your life. Sometimes the very people who you trust the most are the ones who destroy your life with the most ease.' The detective wore a sorrowful gaze that indicated he knew more about loss than Adam might have suspected.

Adam turned to see Gracie wandering round the next-door dining room with a doll in her hand. She didn't seem much interested in the adult conversation next door, which relieved Adam immensely.

Finally, the detective leaned forward and began to deliver the information he'd come to share. 'Your wife wasn't having sex with Grey Carter.'

Adam waited for a smile, laughter, indication that this was a sick joke. When it didn't come, he fell into the chair. It wasn't exactly the revelation he was expecting. 'What?'

'There was nothing consensual about what

happened to your wife, Mr Mullen. She was certainly with him. She was there for exactly the reason she would have said she was there.'

The world appeared to slow, just for a second. His breath deepened. The man sitting before him began to shudder as if he would evaporate right out of Adam's vision. 'Nothing consensual?' It wasn't really a question, though. He was trying to make sense of what he'd just been told.

'Absolutely nothing,' said the detective, dramatically. 'We're certain now that what happened to Mrs Mullen was assault. Sorry to say I believe Grey Carter raped your wife.'

*

His hand was stinging. He hadn't expected the wife to throw such a fit. In the weeks he'd been watching her, there had always been a daintiness to her. He'd come to know her quite well. Yet, when she'd fought back, he'd been taken quite off guard.

He thought of the policeman. His body would have been discovered by now. It was true that killers often returned to the scene of the crime, inserted themselves into the crowd in order to fulfil some perversion of their character. There wasn't time for that now. He only had three days to do all that he had planned.

The identity of the policeman would be all over the news soon. It wouldn't take long for his father to make the connection. He could face the wrath of a police force. In fact, he rather relished it. His father? That was a different story.

He turned the van off the paved road and into the side of an old battered house. It was the last remaining house of its kind; thatched roof above wooden walls and single glazed windows that had mostly cracked in the worst of the winters. Trees formed a cave over the top of the house so that it was mostly concealed from prying eyes. The perfect watering hole for someone hiding in plain sight.

As he stepped out of the van, ignoring her groans in the back he was met by his mirror image. Two men, completely identical but with entirely conflicting agendas. He saw himself in the side mirror and snarled. His eyes were dark and heavy, sleepless nights spent planning what was about to unfold. The only thing that told the two of them apart now was the gristle on his face was concealed by a balaclava.

'Larry, what are you doing here?'

The other man peered in the back of the window and saw the bound and gagged woman wrestling against her knots. 'Pretty.'

He hulked towards the back of the van, threw open the doors so she was within his reach. He pulled at her feet and dragged her gently towards him. Then, he threw her over the side of his right shoulder and carried her towards the house. She wriggled wildly, her last defence before she found herself locked up in his hovel.

Then, he finally spoke to her. 'Don't worry,' he whispered, his masked face turning towards her. 'There's plenty of time before the fun really starts.'

6.

Dave parked his car in the wide-open grounds of the Glasgow Fruit market. The grounds were mostly abandoned on weekdays, so it was an obvious choice to draw him here. Nobody would hear his wife's screams, and nobody would see if he and his wife were being attacked. Not for the first time, Dave wondered how many people were involved and why they had targeted him and his wife. It's not as if they didn't live honest lives.

Dave checked the clock. He was here in the nick of time, the seconds slowly ticking towards the moment where he suspected all would be revealed. He looked at the old mesh windows at the top of the building and the abandoned land round him. He was minutes from his house and links to the entire central belt, yet he felt as if he was in the grounds of a remote abandoned warehouse where he was about to be killed, execution-style.

A gust of wind blew against Dave's neck. Or maybe it was just a chill on his skin. He had gone over it all in his head. The last thing he'd said to Lizzie before leaving for his shift this morning. Then the text message he'd send her at break that she hadn't responded to. Had she already been taken then? That was hours ago now. How long ago had she been snatched from the safety of their kitchen. Hadn't any of the neighbours seen anything? How can a woman be taken from a busy estate in the middle of the day and nobody notice?

The phone rang in his hand. Dave brought it up and stared in fear. He looked round the entire car park, the only sign of recent life being the piles of boxes near the far end exit. Was he being watched now? Only one way to find out. He answered the phone.

'Your wife isn't there.' That voice again, disturbing and disguised by whatever contraption or app the kidnapper had used.

'Where is she?'

A broken cackle; cruel and sadistic. 'You didn't think it was going to be that easy, did you? We just wanted to make sure you weren't followed and that you'll be obedient like the fucking dog that you are.'

Dave felt his fingers tighten some more; the taste of anger almost thick in his saliva. 'You've got the wrong people,' he bellowed.

'Don't waste your time. Or your wife's. She might have so little of it left. Now, I want you to get back in your car and do exactly what I say. If you behave as you have so far, I might even make it quick and as painless as possible.'

Dave shuddered. 'Where am I going?'

'Good man,' drawled the voice in his ear.

Dave turned the key in his ignition and slammed shut the door.

'Drive thirty miles north until you reach the village of Achray. You've got one hour to get there. Once you get to the new Welcome monument at the entrance of the village, I want you to pull in at the first turn-off and park there. I'll be in touch. Don't dawdle. Don't call anyone and don't be late.'

The line died.

Dave threw the phone onto the passenger's seat, slammed down on the accelerator and raced back to the spindly road that led to the motorway. He'd been to Loch Achray once, but it hadn't been so much a village then as a road wrapped round a lake. There had been some holiday homes, more like cabins really. He didn't know much about it, only that there was a development scandal a few years back when a group of animal lovers had threatened to blow up part of the development to protect the wildlife.

As he weaved in and out of traffic, he heard back that crispy disturbing voice and wondered how frightened Lizzie must be. The car juddered and he found himself mulling over the words. The kidnapper had said, 'We.' He'd heard it clearly. They weren't working alone. Which meant this wasn't the act of one deranged kidnapper. It was an organised hit. How else had the kidnapper managed to get through directly to him in the contact centre? How had they managed to take Lizzie in broad daylight? How had they managed to wire up cameras in his house so swiftly that they were able to track his every move. He heard the slight increase in his heart rate and realised that so far, he had underestimated the situation. What if Lizzie was already dead? With that in mind, he slammed down harder and felt the car judder as it screeched off into the far-right lane. He had an hour to get there. He had to use it wisely.

7.

Rosie watched the scramble of people at the corner of the building as the door slammed behind her. Detective Kevin Wallace was also present, having recently transferred up from Glasgow division.

She turned to face Grey Carter as he carried a silver tray on the flat of his palm and lowered it gently onto a table. Rosie had always been impressed by silver-service waiting. She had been a waitress herself in her late teens and had never quite mastered the pomp of it. Instead, she was forever dropping glasses and putting the plates down at the wrong patron. It was surprising to her that she'd even passed the academy considering how bad her nerves had been at that age.

She felt her heart surge as Grey sat directly opposite her. She had to stop thinking about him in that way. Her bad decision making was what led her to this place in the first place. She noticed his deep-set eyes landing on her. Was that how he had lured Debra Mullen into bed, she wondered? A married woman who was seemingly willing to throw her marriage away for a cad with no sense of responsibility. Or was she judging him too harshly?

'Let's start with where you were last night?'

'Not here.'

Rosie had never been fussed on the game of verbal fencing. She liked to know a spade was a spade. Somehow, she suspected Grey was anything but a spade. 'Where?'

Detective Wallace remained quiet, leaning forward only to sweep up a steaming mug of coffee.

Grey watched him without turning his head then returned his focus to Rosie. 'Does it matter? I'm not involved in the death of your colleague.'

'Then why won't you tell me where you were?'

His lip arched up slightly, his flaring nostrils the only indication he was at all nervous. 'I was staying at my flat in Glasgow. That's where I live. I spend my days here getting prepared for the opening later this week but I've no desire to become some creepy motel owner that lives up in the tower.'

Rosie tusked. 'When did you come back here?'

Grey's eyes then darted from Detective Wallace to Rosie. 'This morning.'

Rosie smirked. 'How early?'

'About half six.'

'So, that would mean you would have to leave Glasgow at approximately five o'clock. Why so early?'

'Why not? I'm an early riser. I get up, come here to use the gym and I get to miss the morning traffic. It's a win-win.'

Detective Wallace licked his lips, took another sip of the coffee and remained in silence.

'Okay, when did you discover the body?' Rosie was finding it increasingly difficult to say his name. It felt odd to be referring to her friend as a body. She also didn't relish the moment where she would be going to the Houston house to tell his wife the terrible news. If the small-village tittle tattle didn't get it there first.

'I found him at approximately eight-thirty.'

'That's two hours after you said you arrived here. Your car is parked at the side of the building. Did you not come in the way you brought us in?'

'No,' he snapped. 'I came in the front way as I often do. I have a smoke outside, watch the sun come up and then grab the mail if I haven't been here the day before.'

'That's your ritual?' Rosie felt her face tighten. She cleared her throat and allowed her expression to soften.

'Do you plan to live here?' Detective Wallace spoke now, awkwardly slamming the mug back onto the tray.

'I'm not sure,' said Grey, shrugging. 'I might do one day. Then again, I'm hoping to be so busy that there isn't a room here for me.' He snorted slightly, his upturned lips returning as he drew his eyes away from Wallace.

'Did you know immediately who he was?'

'Not immediately. Well, you've seen his face. Hardly recognisable to you either, I suspect.'

Rosie, desperate not to break in front of Grey, swallowed back a mouthful of saliva. Or was it tears. She couldn't be sure now.

'I assume you have CCTV,' said Wallace, possibly attuned to Rosie's growing anguish.

'Actually, not yet. My investor is sorting all of that out. It's being installed next week. I'm afraid my cash flow has run away a little.'

'You must have spent a pretty penny here,' acknowledged Wallace.

Grey's temperament altered slightly then. The sly expression faded, and his chest seemed to puff up. 'Anyway, I hope you catch the killer quickly. As I said, I've got an opening this week. You can imagine a murder wouldn't be good for business.'

Rosie teetered on the edge of saying out loud what entered her mind then. However, she seemed to find at least a modicum of self-control. Either Grey Carter was incredibly naïve to the fact that murder would bring the vultures by the bus load or he thought he was double bluffing them.

Rosie stood then, returned to the window and saw another car arrive. She was no longer clear on who was with the investigation and who was here for the feast of the media.

'Is that all?'

She turned back to Grey. 'For now.'

'You know where I am,' he said sharply, rubbing the python on his arm. 'I don't want the opening of my hotel to be upstaged by the presence of police.'

Yet, Rosie wondered if that wasn't exactly what he wanted. She walked briskly to reception and noticed just how much of an overhaul the place must have been given since she was last here a couple of months before. She stopped and held her hand up to stop her new colleague.

He spoke first. 'Do you think he had something to do with it.'

'No,' she quickly replied. 'There's plenty of ways of disposing of a body. Hanging it from your own property for the world to see doesn't seem to be a sensible way. I am curious though.' She was staring over the top of the marble reception desk.

'What?'

She nodded. 'All this money to refurbish what used to be a dilapidated school and you don't even fork out for a decent CCTV system before opening night. There's something odd about that.'

8.

He closed the lock on the metal chain and heard it click. It had taken twenty minutes to calm her enough to secure her ankle. Now there was time to step back and enjoy her for a moment. She wasn't the usual type that he went for. There was something very homely about her, something that might remind him of a schoolteacher he had once loved. He could picture himself peeling her skin without spoiling her at all, the blood darkening and falling like drops of scarlet bulbs into the cracks in the floor.

He felt the erection push against the inside of his jeans. He couldn't allow himself to become excited by her. Not yet. She had to remain exactly as she was. The detective had been surplus to requirements. Untouchable, really. Yet, he couldn't let him off the hook. This couple, though, they were to remain in one piece until everything was in place. That left the man angry and frustrated. He simply pressed down the lids of his eyes and glowered.

After staring long enough that she was becoming visibly distressed, he walked down the mouldy old stairs and locked the loft door at the bottom. He would enjoy her from a distance for now. Watch her scurrying like a frightened squirrel as she tried to break free, unaware that he could see her every move.

Then, he heard his brother's voice.

'You know you're not allowed to touch her, don't you?'

He nodded slowly, vacantly. It was like looking at himself. He had never felt comfortable with it. Larry, forty minutes older than him, was identical in every way. It was like staring into his own self and that had always sent pressures of rage through him.

Why had he been born that way, sharing himself with someone else who probably knew his every desire and thought. That was irritating beyond comprehension. The fact that Larry was always at his side was doubly infuriating.

Larry smiled, pushed his stemmed glasses up his face and stepped back. 'I'll let you get on. I know you've got things you need to take care of. I'll be here when you need me.'

The man turned as his twin disappeared down the stairs. He entered the room that lay directly behind him and switched on the monitor. He could see her writhe against the lock. It was almost devastatingly beautiful to watch. Yet, he couldn't focus on that now. Something else was beginning to itch. That was the problem. No matter what he was told, when those violent tendencies came to call, it was an itch he simply had to scratch.

*

Rosie watched the chief place himself front centre of the evidence room and tug awkwardly at his tie. He'd looked close to tears since she'd returned from Milton Carter. In this much brighter light, she could see the ironing streaks on his ageing black suit. He looked every inch like he'd fished out old threats from a dusty wardrobe to attend a funeral. There was no funeral yet, but he was no less solemn in his delivery.

'If there's anyone unable to do this, I want you to speak now. What I can't have is for any of you to get halfway through this investigation and then allow your personal feelings to get in the way. No conviction will stick if it's found that we didn't follow process.'

The room remained in silence, mostly because no-one was at the place yet where they could speak constructively. Anger and grief hung heavily in the air; corrosive and blistering through the atmosphere.

Rosie's thoughts weren't on revenge though. She thought of Brian and his wife Gaby, the first to welcome her to their home when she arrived in the village. Rosie had never known life outside of London. She'd become a police officer, as her dad had hoped when she was in her early twenties. She'd loved the thrill, embraced the bright lights of such a career in the capital. It had filled her with a dread she didn't recognise when she'd had to give that up to move here to this small backwater. Brian and Gaby had made it almost bearable.

She thought of Brian's acerbic wit; a sharp sense of humour cocooned inside a man who looked a little too bookish and nerdy for her. Her first impression had been wrong, and it didn't take long for him to bring down her iron steel guard.

'Brian Houston is one of our own,' continued the chief in his usual bombastic style. 'It's never easy when one of our own is taken. The first instinct is revenge. I won't have that on my clock. I want justice for our friend. I want it clean and neat and for the courts to do their job without interference. Am I understood?'

Some quietly nodded their head, and some groaned an affirmation, but nobody fully committed to his orders. She suspected he already knew they wouldn't. Even in his own pompous face, he wore the searing anger that belied the flat delivery and emotional detachment. Rosie appreciated his attempt at professionalism, but she imagined that stripping away the surface might reveal his true anguish.

'Detective Cooper, I want you and Detective Wallace to head up the task force. You're the newest to the team so I think you can remain the most detached. Would that be a fair assumption?'

Rosie pressed her lips together and shook her head quickly, though she felt a little stung by the suggestion that she barely knew Brian. They'd become thick as thieves in the few months since she had arrived. Had he not been watching their budding friendship?

Rising from the seat, Rosie moved to the whiteboard and ran her finger from the picture of Brian in life, the gruesome picture of his death that she hadn't been fully able to look at yet and she couldn't quite find the correlation between the two. The picture of the rope that had noosed round his neck was particularly macabre though the most disturbing image was of his face. She feared she would see it in her sleep and that knowledge crept up her back in tiny beads of sweat.

'I was a good friend of his dad's, you know. My boys played football with him. Not two miles from here. Lovely lad. His brother's a different kettle of fish. Always up to no good. It wouldn't shock me if it's payback for something he's done.'

Rosie didn't reply. She knew nothing about Brian's brother and wasn't about to start playing guessing games.

'I'm good at playing the politician,' he continued. 'Away from here, I'd love to kill this fucker with my own bare hands. But I'm a man of my word. I want them to throw away the key. Don't mistake me. I know you and he became very friendly very quickly, but I've also watched your work ethic in the time you've been here. I've only got one question for you. Are you up to the job?'

She knew she didn't cope well with failure and

she certainly didn't like to show weakness. She turned to him, taking the opportunity to turn away from the photos on the board. 'I'm up to it. I'm going to catch whoever did this. Just as you asked, fairly and squarely and I'm going to enjoy watching the courts hang him out to dry.'

9.

For one brief idiotic moment Dave considered pulling over. It wouldn't be long until the kidnapper was back in touch. If only he knew the real end game, the reason for his wife's kidnapping and then maybe he could take back a little of the power.

He weaved quickly through the traffic, honking impatiently at the driver of a yellow Honda who pulled in ahead of him. Still, his mind was more focused on the reason that he and Lizzie had fallen prey to kidnappers. They barely had a penny to their name. Lizzie had done little by way of work since last year so Dave was carrying the bills. Anyone who looked at their bank statement would probably be more inclined to offer them pity funds than hold them ransom.

His car sailed through a patch of rain as sunshine fell behind silver clouds. Silver droplets were brief but dripped down the window just enough that the wipers sprang into action. Dave wondered if work would be trying to get hold of him. He'd departed so quickly, without explanation that perhaps they'd sense something was wrong. Dave wanted so badly to call the police, but he knew he'd risk any chance Lizzie had of being saved if the police sirens went wailing into that village. Her safety was paramount.

Dave felt his heart pulse, a tightening of his chest bringing to head a slight ache. 'Don't have a panic attack now,' he muttered to himself, pulling his car one lane to the right and racing along at ninety mph. If only he knew Lizzie was still alive. Perhaps the kidnapper would allow him to speak to her, even if only to know she was alright. That might calm him down. For now.

He thought of all the traumatic calls he'd ever dealt with; people in distress, those who had been in accidents, the poor unfortunate souls trapped in abusive lives they were too afraid to escape from. There had been times where he'd had to log off his phoneline and disappear into a cold lifeless bathroom to ward off the harrowing things he'd had to listen to. The one thing that allowed him to remove himself was the knowledge that when he logged off for the last time at night, he was leaving it behind and returning to the safety of a warm home and loving wife.

Until today.

He had forty minutes to get to the monument at the entrance of Achray. Still, Dave wondered why there? Why a village most people didn't know existed? He couldn't think of any reason they would be taken there.

The mobile phone in the passenger's seat beeped quite suddenly. Dave pushed his foot down to break suddenly and did the unthinkable. He checked his mirrors, made sure no one was watching and grabbed the handset. No message. It was just the phone telling him that there wasn't much battery life left. Ahead of him the horizon was now tinged with a fiery red. Today might be dusking soon but the sky promised another day tomorrow. Not a particularly bright one should anything happen to his beautiful Lizzie.

A message flashed across the phone revealing there was only ten percent battery. It was at that moment he suddenly remembered. He'd had just enough foresight to remove his sim card from his own handset when ordered to disconnect it from the Bluetooth. His mobile phone was at home where he'd left it, but the sim card would still be at the bottom of his pocket.

He swung the car across three lanes, pulled into the hard shoulder and brought the car to an abrupt standstill. There wasn't much time. He ran his finger down the side of the mobile phone, searching for the cavity that would hold the sim. His fingers darted more frantically, time calling on him to hurry. Finally, he was able to remove the existing sim card. He reached into his pocket and found his own sim card. He wasn't sure if it would even match the network linked to this phone, but he'd taken it out when disconnecting the phone from the car Bluetooth. Now, he inserted it into the handset and waited for the phone to come to life.

He thought of Lizzie once more, the promise he'd made to always keep her safe. A marriage vow he was now failing on. He could hear her now saying that she could look after herself. She was tough and level-headed. Dave hoped that would be enough to keep her safe for now. He wouldn't allow himself to cry in the knowledge that she was in peril. Right now, he had to get moving. The phone was finally alive. Five missed calls appeared on the screen. His boss had probably been trying to reach him. He didn't have time to explain now but he did need his help.

'Hello,' came a voice as he dialled the number that would connect him to Jason Barr.

'Jason, it's Dave. I need your help.' He hadn't realised how breathless he sounded until he began to speak.

'Dave, where the hell are you? I thought you'd had a toilet emergency. We've hunted the building, rang you *and* your wife several times. You can't just have everyone worrying like that.'

'I'll sort that later. I need your help. My wife is

missing.'

A sigh from the other end of the line. 'What do you mean missing?'

Dave slammed his curled hand against the side of the door. 'She's been kidnapped. Someone called in to the service and claimed Lizzie was in danger.'

'Where are you now?' Jason's voice deepened, his own sense of urgency catching up to Dave's.

'I'm on my way to Achray. Do you know it?' He didn't wait for an answer. 'Listen, I need you to go back and look at the call. There's already a previous call from the number and I wonder if they've already called into the service.'

Silence fell upon the line for a moment before Jason spoke again. 'If your wife is genuinely in danger, I think we should let trained police officers handle it.'

'No,' snapped Dave. 'No police. The last thing I need is for sirens to come wailing in behind me. If this bastard is serious, they'll kill her without giving it a second thought. Just go back to the original call, will you? Find out what you can.' He looked at his watch again. Another minute had passed. 'Jason, I know you don't know me very well. Speak to anybody else who has managed me before and they'll tell you I'm not someone who panics or overreacts.' He could almost taste the desperation as it passed his lips. He needed Jason to believe him. It was his only hope. He didn't have time to make another call or try to reach out for help. Who would he call anyway? He, and Lizzie lived a lowkey life that mostly circled round each other. There wasn't an army of friends waiting to rush to their aide.

Silence fell on the line and Dave found himself checking the screen to see if they were still connected. He was about to speak when he heard his boss speak.

'Okay, I'll sit on it for now. But if these guys mean business, you're going to need help. Is this your own mobile number you're calling from?'

'Yes.'

'How far are you from Achray?'

'About three quarters of an hour, I think,' replied Dave.

'If I've not heard from you in an hour, I'm calling it in. If I call you and you don't answer, same thing. Once you know the location of where you're going, either call it in to me or message me. You got it?'

'Got it,' said Dave, trying not to lose control.

'Alright, kiddo. Hope your wife turns up safe and sound.'

Without further exchange, Dave ended the call and quickly made the switch back. He dropped the phone into the cup holder and swung back onto the motorway. As he looked at the clock, he took a deep breath. How could time feel so desperately slow whilst racing by at such a speed? Only an hour until the next phone call.

10.

The gloomy winter had long passed, and the Spring sunlight sparkled across the loch. Still, there was a coldness in the air that only tugged more at Rosie's mood. It was a short drive to the offshoot village where Brian and his wife, Gaby lived. Still, the steep edges round Loch Achray terrified Rosie. Particularly when she was in the driver's seat and felt like she had no control at all. Detective Wallace was an erratic driver; cutting corners too close, indicating too late and almost doubling the speed limit when he was sure there was no-one watching.

'Hard day, huh?'

In all her years as a detective, she'd seen some sights. She'd even witnessed one of her partner's gunned down in the street in a drug bust. Never had she seen anything happen to a friend in the same league as what had been done to Brian Houston. 'The worst.'

'I wonder if she's heard anything. This is a small place. News will travel fast.'

Rosie didn't reply but she sensed that he might be right. News really did travel fast round here. She recalled her own arrival six months earlier. She'd barely unpacked the first box when she'd already had a phone call from the local post office offering to assist with mail re-direction. They didn't do it like the big cities round here, the postmaster had announced. They liked to keep it local. They also did a grocery delivery service on tap. Would she like some food delivered now, they'd wondered? Some bread and milk maybe. She'd refused politely, having already had her fill of coffee and roadside sandwiches that day. She'd chuckled after coming off the phone. It had taken her a few sentences to adjust to the strength of the Scottish accent. Twenty minutes after hanging up, a fish supper had arrived compliments of the local fish bar. She'd accepted the gift, despite not being particularly hungry and was rather impressed at just how tasty the fish was. It didn't taste like that in Solihull.

The Houston cottage appeared in her eyeline and she felt her breath stall. There were moments in this job where she wished she'd gone with her second choice and became a dogwalker. There was still time. She turned her face to the glare of the sunlight, wiped a silent tear from just inside the indent of her shallow crow's feet.

The cottage looked smaller than it really was. Rosie remembered just how surprised she'd been when she first visited. They could comfortably fit another two children in there. Which only made it sadder because Brian and Gaby would only ever parent one child together; little Eva.

As she pushed open the car door, Rosie drew her eyes along the four other cottages in her sight. It occurred to her that a killer might dwell in one of those houses. His neighbours were next on the list of door-to-door enquiries. Not that she really expected to find much from them. Most were elderly, had grown up here when these houses were all that existed.

She watched the front door of the cottage in front of her open. Gaby Houston appeared, holding Eva on her hip.

Rosie walked slowly forward, glad that Detective Wallace had opted to stay in the car. There was no need for him, brute strength and stiff upper lip to attend this one. She could handle it. She had gotten to know Gaby's Irish feistiness and forked tongue humour very quickly, but she also sensed the great vulnerability that made her such a perfect match with Brian's quiet strength. The kindness between them could have made Rosie envious had she ever wished to be one of those people who wanted the diamond ring and football team of children.

Gaby's eyes widened.

What must she be thinking, wondered Rosie? Did she have any inkling that her world was about to be destroyed? The answer very quickly unfolded. As Rosie walked slowly down the path, she could already see the tears stick to Gaby's greying face.

'No,' the young woman whimpered, slowly falling to her knees but never letting go of the child on her side.

Rosie lunged forward to grab for her, but it was too late.

Wallace was exiting the car now.

Rosie suspected something of the truth had already reached Gaby and she had just been waiting on their arrival for devastating confirmation. Suddenly, her wails were filling the stillness and there was nothing left of the serenity that had existed just a few moments before.

*

Dave had been gripping the steering wheel so long the palms of his hands felt as if someone had gone over them with sandpaper. He'd lost track of how long he'd been here now and dared not touch the phone just in case the battery died before he got the next phone call. Maybe the kidnapper had fell down a shaft somewhere and died. That was too much to hope for.

In the time he'd been sitting here, he thought of everything that had happened in the past year. He'd always felt like they'd been destined for each other. Not even the strength of their marriage could fully survive a miscarriage intact. There was a tiny place of rage within Dave. Rage that he and his wife hadn't been able to fulfil that dream. Rage initially that nobody could understand why he would feel grief. Was it so unthinkable that a man could mourn an unborn child simply because he'd never had any physical contact with it? Then, a sprinkle of rage had been reserved for what his wife had endured. The grief they could live with. The expectation that they simply move on and try again was what really punched him hard in the gut. Their little person had been taken from them before they even had a chance to know him or her. Yet, it was quickly treated like the loss of a car. Or worse; no loss at all.

He buried those thoughts because they never served any purpose but to lull him into a deep sense of grieving. There was no time for that now. He had to fight to save both his and his wife's life. Life couldn't be over yet. He'd hardly begun to live it. They still had a lifetime together ahead of them. Their children hadn't even been born yet. For the first time since the miscarriage, he envisioned himself and Lizzie with tiny feet running around them. The thought filled him with an ache for this to be over and for them to be happy again.

The phone sparked to life. He could see now the battery was literally flashing that it had one percent. Probably not even enough to receive a full phone call. He quickly answered it.

'I'm here.'

'I know,' said the queer voice. 'Just because you can't see me doesn't mean I can't see you.'

Dave looked up. It had gotten slightly darker

since he'd arrived. He didn't know why he did what he did next but, looking round in search of the kidnapper, he locked the doors from inside.

'Locking your doors won't stop me.'

'What do you want me to do now?' He realised he was drenched in his own sweat. Catching a glimpse of his soaked face in the mirror, he waited for the kidnapper to reply.

'I want you to drive to the loch. Follow the road until you get to a house made of glass. There's a trail into the woods there. Dump your car at the entrance to the trail.'

'Okay,' he interjected.

'Follow the path behind the houses for approximately half a mile. You will eventually get to a cottage that will instantly stand out. It looks nothing like the new houses there. Cove Cottage. Make sure you are not followed and that no-one see's you. Go to the back door, it'll be open. Go inside and your wife will be waiting.'

It sounded too easy. Dave wasn't sure he believed it would be so easy to be re-united with Lizzie. He wanted to ask if she'd been hurt. Perhaps when the kidnapper said she'd be waiting... Well, he didn't even want to think about that. He didn't ask anything because right now, he feared the answer. If his wife was dead or hurt, at least he had the next few minutes to live in this world where his wife was alive and well. He didn't want to imagine the alternative.

'One more thing, Dave.'

Dave waited while looking at the deserted roads around him. How far was it to the loch? Not far, he hoped. 'Uh-huh.'

'The phone should be almost out of battery. Keep me on the line until the phone dies. I don't want you getting any funny ideas.'

Dave removed the phone from his ear. The battery was flashing now, suggesting it was about to die any minute. He had to think quickly. He needed to get the name of the house to Jason but how would he do it if the kidnapper was watching him. Or maybe that had been a bluff. Maybe the kidnapper was at the cottage waiting for him. How had he known that Dave had locked the doors though? Had the click been that audible?

He decided the only thing to do was take the risk. Holding his finger over the red button, Dave looked round himself, saw the last of dusk befall him and then turned his eyes back to the phone. He hit the button which disconnected him from the kidnapper, quickly pulled the sim card out before there was any opportunity for the kidnapper to call again and inserted his own. The battery signal was flashing wildly when he turned the phone back on. He was almost out of time. He watched in terror as he waited for his own sim card to register. Finally, he was able to open at Jason's number and quickly type a text message. He simply wrote the address the kidnapper had sent him and then hit the send button.

Dave held his breath and watched as the phone died. There hadn't been any confirmation that the message had gone. He threw the phone onto the floor on the passenger's side and grabbed the steering wheel in frustration. Right now, he had to do what the kidnapper said. There wasn't time to wait for anyone else to come. So, he turned the key in the ignition and began to follow the last of the kidnapper's instructions.

Only now did Dave wish that he had kept better contact with his family. Perhaps if he and Lizzie hadn't formed their own little bubble and existed solely for the two of them, it might have been noticed quickly they were missing. His wife didn't go to work because she preferred the freedom of her artistry and being home alone all day allowed that. Everything was hinged on Jason Barr, who Dave barely knew. As he drove into the tree lined back water that led to the village of Achray, Dave felt the last flicker of hope die.

11.

'You know, at your age, I shouldn't have to tell you to eat your vegetables.'

Adam sat across the table from his parents, absently pushing the broccoli round the plate. 'I'm not really that hungry, mum.' He didn't lift his eyelids because he didn't want to give her any more reason to engage with him. She fussed enough without encouraging her to make more of a nuisance of herself.

Gracie continued to play with her own food whilst humming a song about daisy chains.

'You have to regain your appetite. I'm sure Debra wouldn't starve herself if the shoe was on the other foot,' said his mother, scraping the last of the gravy from her plate.

Adam narrowed his eyes and snarled. 'I know you didn't like my wife but could you do me the kindness of remembering my daughter is sitting here.'

'That's not fair,' hissed his father, a man usually reluctant to put himself at the centre of any animosity.

Adam turned his gaze onto his father and thought how old he looked now. A once towering man now reduced to a curvature in the spine and a mop of unkempt grey hair that started with his eyebrows and worked up to the crown.

'Sorry,' he whispered and scraped his fork across the dish. Fatigue had long set in weeks ago but now he felt as if someone would have to prise his eyes open with a set of matchsticks. Sleep came often but rarely lasted. There was also the newfound guilt since learning that the weeks of angry feelings for his wife had been largely unfounded. Why had he been so quick to accept Debra's disloyalty? He looked at his mother, hearing in his mind an assortment of her greatest barbs over the past weeks.

Gracie got up from the table and asked in a small meek voice, 'Can I be excused, Gran?'

Delia smiled and tickled the edge of Gracie's nose. 'Of course, love. Do you want to go and play in your room?'

A wide smile passed across Gracie's face as she squealed and disappeared up the stairs.

'That's the happiest she's been in weeks,' said Adam, cautious to conceal his growing envy.

'There's something else,' his mother said, sharply. She took a deep breath and pushed her plate towards the centre of the marble dining table.

'What?'

'I can read you like a book, Adam. You think a mother doesn't know when there's something on her son's mind? You've never been able to lie to me.'

Adam shrugged and threw his hands to his head. If only he could have eight hours sleep. If only he could forget about the suggested infidelity. Maybe he could finally see his wife as the victim it seemed she was. He swithered on telling his mother the whole sordid truth. Perhaps she might become a little gentler on his late wife. He knew she was right though. He'd never been able to lie to either of his parents. Why start now?

Delia and Terry both leaned in, as if tightening the huddle would keep what they were about to discuss away from Gracie's ears.

'The police came to see me this morning. Debra wasn't having an affair.'

'What rubbish,' his mother hissed, her face barely concealing her outrage. 'How dare they add to your anguish in this way. Don't they know you've been upset enough?'

Terry hushed her with his hand. 'Let the boy speak.'

'They weren't sure at first. Seemingly, it's part of this bigger investigation so they had to keep some of the details quiet. Grey and Debra weren't having an affair. He raped her.'

His mother looked incredulous, as if someone had just told her a ship had fallen out of the sky at that very moment. She tightened her lip, burying whatever slur she wanted to spit out next.

'Surely, you don't believe that,' his father said, mirroring Delia's disbelief more subtly.

'Why is it more believable to you that Debra would be having an affair than the knowledge that she was raped? Did you really hate her so much?'

His father lifted his hand in defiance. 'I did not hate the girl. I just don't believe she'd have been secretly meeting him at that hotel if she weren't having an affair. If a pig looks like a pig, it means it's a pig.'

Adam sniffed. 'She was working on something for the opening of Grey's hotel. You know how much she wanted to get her business off the ground. I think he was trying to throw some work her way.'

Terry's face changed. 'You know Grey Carter doesn't work like that. Since you were boys, the only person he ever looked out for was himself. How many times did we get him out of scrapes? If we hadn't taken that boy in after his parents died, who knows where he might have ended up.' His father paused. 'Whether it was an affair, or sexual assault, that young man owed you much more than this.'

Adam looked down. The mention of Grey's

parents had always filled him with guilt. There were things he could never tell his father. Thing's that had happened in that house that they would never believe. 'It wasn't him who told me. He's hardly going to admit rape. The police have confirmed her injuries prior to the crash were consistent with sexual assault.'

His mother stormed to the sink. 'Even now, she's controlling what we're allowed to think.'

Adam slammed his fist on the table and followed his mother to the corner of the kitchen. 'Nobody has ever controlled your thinking, mother. That's exactly the problem. You say what you like with no regard for anybody else's feelings. You wonder why we rarely came over. You were so quick to blame Debra.' His voice was rising, and he could feel his cheeks burn as if angry tears would fall down his face any moment. 'It was me who reduced contact because I didn't want my daughter growing up in an atmosphere that's as toxic as this one. Even in death, you can't find a simple kind word to say about a young woman who has died.'

'I'm not a hypocrite,' she whispered, turning on the tap.

'There's worse things than being that. Being the source of unhappiness to other people is much, much worse.' Adam pulled away and leaned towards Terry. 'Dad, I need you to look after Gracie for a few days. Will you do that for me?'

'What are you going to do, son?'

Adam sighed. He didn't even know what he was going to do. There was no plan. All he knew was that he needed some air from the world and that he couldn't do that if Gracie was constantly chirping in his ear. 'I'm not going to do anything. I just need some space. Can you take care of her?'

His mother chimed in then, turning to face him. Under the blinding light, she revealed her tear stained face. 'Of course, we'll take care of her. You don't even need to ask.'

Adam knew that was the case. Whilst they had nothing but contempt for Debra, his parents adored Gracie. He imagined she'd always be safe in their home. Which was just as well, because whatever he did next, he wasn't sure he'd be able to come back from it. 'That includes not berating Debra, mum. Do you think you can do that?'

She looked slightly disappointed but finally nodded her head in agreement. 'Don't do anything silly,' she said, her voice quivering.

Adam gave her a quick kiss on the wet cheek, an apology of sorts, an admission of remorse. Then, he ran towards the door, determined that he couldn't face a lengthy tearful goodbye with Gracie right now. He didn't want to worsen the situation. He simply waved behind him and slammed the door shut.

*

Despite her original misgivings at sinking such a large chunk of her savings into Crystal Ridge, it had been worth it. Rosie had enjoyed serenity in a way she had never known in London. For her, the move had taken her career back ten steps but for her mental health, it had been worth every penny. Of course, she hadn't prepared herself that her past would eventually tap her on the shoulder.

She brought her knee up to her chin, sat on a wooden ledge and brushed her head against a tall pane of glass. She dared not to think of her life back in London too often because it came with a tsunami of self-loathing that she had never quite managed to escape. It was unlikely she'd ever be able to fully face the things that had driven her away. She took a deep gulp from the steaming mug and tasted the warm chocolate on the roof of her mouth.

There was almost something spiritual about the blossoming of Spring, the first one she would spend surrounded by growing leaves on naked trees. The winter had been more treacherous than she had prepared herself for and the lack of frequent footfall had made it a battle to endure in this rural little wonderland.

Rosie drank the last of her hot chocolate and rose from the ledge. Until now there had been nothing to match the adrenalin rush that she had experienced in London police life. She had even found herself wishing for the occasional murder or two. A lesson to be careful what you wish for, as a twinge of guilt twisted in her gut.

All she wanted to do was wash away everything of today. Climbing the stairs and entering the bathroom, Rosie placed her phone on the edge of the sink. She pulled back the smoked glass door and stepped into the wet room. The square chrome head gushed to life and brought down enough hot water to wash away some of the horrors of the day. There were some things she would never unsee. Maybe she would try and think of something else. The envelope. A practical joke perhaps? She couldn't think of those last months at Scotland Yard, nor the events that drove her to the decision to sell up both her own flat and the family home she'd inherited from her mother. All traces of London were physically gone but left in tiny scars in the unseen wounds of her mind. She ran her fingers through her curls and reminded herself she must make an appointment at the local salon soon.

The heat of the shower was almost blistering. It

didn't matter. Rosie needed to feel something other than the ache of regret or the want to purge herself of this new wave of grief. Tears must have fallen because she could feel herself begin to shake; snot carried off by the fall of thin strides of hot water. When it was finally over, Rosie composed herself.

Drying herself off, she moved through to her bedroom. She had chosen the back bedroom, despite it being smaller because the back of the house was good old bricks and mortar. The front bedrooms were larger, more modern but the front shell of the house was all glass. Once she had time to measure for blinds, she would treat herself to one of those rooms. For now, she would enjoy the stillness of a house that looked onto an endless forest. Pulling a pair of pyjamas over her warm skin, Rosie grabbed for a book she had started a few months ago. A chapter a day kept the demons at bay.

She was preparing herself for an early night, setting the alarm for five a.m. and drawing the curtains. Only as she caught a glimpse of the outside world through a crack between the curtains did she see something shift. A shadow. Rosie quickly pulled back one of the curtains and watched as a figure darted away. She might have mistaken it for a deer, or some other wildlife had it not been so tall. She grabbed for her phone, tackling the torch function so long that it was too late by the time she aimed it past the back fence. Still, there had been no doubt in her mind. Someone had been out there, lurking in the dark and watching her. Two eyes had leered at her. She drew the curtains quickly this time, then fled downstairs to quickly ensure the doors and windows were all locked. Between the delivery of those pictures and the death of her close colleague, Rosie wasn't taking any chances.

12.

Something burred in the eaves. A cricket, or a bat, or something completely other worldly. In this predicament, it didn't take much to corrupt the imagination. Once she woke, she checked for some indication of how long she'd been sleeping. How silly of her to let her guard down. She should have stayed on her guard.

Lizzie had dreamt of happier times. She dreamt of being home safe with Dave, the two of them enjoying a barbeque in the back garden, him flipping burgers as she threw her hair back into the chlorine infused water of the hot tub. It had been a perfect summer day last year. Long before business had become non-existent. Half a year before the devastation of losing the baby. A lifetime before someone had entered the safety of her house and lorded the threat of murder over her if she didn't comply.

Lizzie had done what her instincts had built her to do. She fought gamely. It hadn't been the fight of her life. He hadn't allowed for that. He had snatched her and bound her hands so quickly that she was quickly rendered defenceless. Still, she felt a little more comfortable now that the pain had eased off in her shoulders. Then when he approached her, she'd done something completely out of character for her. She'd spat in his face. He may be taking her against her will, but he wasn't coming off completely clean. That's when he'd smacked her in the face. She could still feel the redness on her cheek.

The loft was damp and acrid. She couldn't place the scent because it was like nothing she had experienced before. Little light pervaded but there was enough for her to see it wasn't completely dark. She had no idea how long she'd been sleeping but she was guessing it hadn't been that long because she'd heard her kidnapper talking loudly only a short while ago. She hadn't caught one of their names, but the other one was called Larry.

Lizzie pulled on the chain, as if sleeping might have loosened the lock. Maybe a hard tug would pull it from the wall. Or maybe she would use it to strangle her captor. She found herself aghast because she'd never even considered the idea of harming someone, let alone killing them. She'd heard people say that every person could be capable of murder in the right circumstances. Was that true?

Listening hard, she could still hear someone pacing the floor in the rooms below. The house she'd been brought to looked so old and dilapidated that every creak and whisper could be heard throughout. She also wondered how it was still standing. She'd been able to see out the corner of the van window as the kidnapper had driven her here. The other houses looked modern. This one looked like it could be carried away on a gust of wind.

Her thoughts were disrupted by the sound of her captor speaking. More like an angry whisper just outside the loft door. Then, it rose a little. Was he on the phone? Maybe he was speaking to Dave again. She found herself hopeful that her husband would arrive soon. Then she found herself frightened because she realised that Dave was no match in stature for the man who had taken her. Especially now she suspected there were two of them.

He was coming now. Lizzie could hear him thumping up the stairs.

'I've brought you some food,' he said, throwing

a pre-packed sandwich onto the bed. 'Do you want a drink?'

Lizzie was desperate for a drink. Her lips were getting dryer by the minute. She would ask him for nothing.

'If you don't eat, you'll die of hunger.' His voice was a mere growl. Not his real voice, she suspected. A voice created in anger and the will to deceive. His eyes flickered in rage behind the balaclava.

When he finally left, without saying another work, she snatched up the sandwich. She hadn't had a thing to eat since a croissant in the early hours of the day. She wouldn't thank him for this, but she would devour the sandwich in. his absence. It wasn't particularly tasty, and she suspected it wasn't particularly fresh. Right now, she didn't care. She closed her eyes and pretended Dave was sitting across the table from her. He was twirling his fork round a bowl of Italian spaghetti. For a moment she could smell the garlic. The look on his face, as if he had just tasted heaven in a bowl when really, she knew she wasn't a very good cook.

When Lizzie opened her eyes again, the stark reality rushed against her like a battering storm. What did the kidnapper have in store for them? She could only hope her husband had defied the order not to contact the police. Otherwise, she feared there was no hope of them escaping alive.

*

As instructed, Dave had abandoned his car in the overgrown shrubs of a desolate pathway that barely seemed safe to walk through. He'd spent the entire drive over eyeing for a public phone box and realised they barely existed anymore. There was no safety on the streets now. Everything was mobile and when that died, it left no way of contacting the outside world. Still, there was the hope that the message had reached Jason. Why hadn't he gone to him in the first place? He felt stupid! He was hedging all his bets on the hope that one man would have received a message from a dying phone.

He skulked past the glasshouse on the ridge and remembered seeing this house up for sale. It had been part of the massive re-development of this little non-existent place that had once been the campers dream. It was spectacular in the dusk. He turned and saw the reflection of this new village shimmer in the Loch, its light rapids like glitter on thick glass. A road snaked round its perimeter and crafted a treacle divide between narrow rocks and the train of new houses that hadn't quite fully grown into their setting yet. In the distance, a church towered over everything, its commanding presence a reminder that it was the holy grail of everything that existed here.

He had moved to the back of the glasshouse and saw that it's face had been latched onto a more traditional black block that stood three floors high. Only when he saw the woman throw open the partially closed curtains did he realise he was staring. He was about to try and get her attention when he realised the fear that he might put in a woman who was undressing in her bedroom only to find a strange man staring in.

Besides, when he turned, he could now see the abandoned shack that was almost concealed by rows of sky-high trees. His nerves wanted to shatter. He didn't know how far along he'd have to walk; it was as far in the distance as his view would allow. Nor did he know how bad the terrain behind the houses would be. He could see the towering trees stretched as far as the horizon allowed. Dave feared the wildlife, he feared the nettles, he mostly feared that at any moment he would be pounced upon by whoever had lured him here. He wondered if his wife was safe. Was she waiting for him in the shack that he had been ordered to go to? Was it possible she really was only half a mile away?

His face was flustered now. Fear mastered him, but there was also an adrenalin rising as he wondered if the kidnapper would be watching him arrive. The seconds turned to minutes; the trail surprisingly unfurnished by danger. Finally, he was climbing through a break in the fence, trudging in overgrown weeds and moving slowly towards a door that looked slightly ajar.

The house itself looked in complete darkness. He slowed his movements, careful not to alert the kidnapper of his arrival. Perhaps he could retain some element of surprise. Slip in when he wasn't expected. There was nothing left to do but make his move, so he trod through the gap in the door, found himself in a rutted hallway thick with dust. He felt his heartrate quicken. He was already halfway into the house when he felt the heat of someone's breath hit his face. Suddenly, he was grabbed and thrown so violently that he felt as if his skull was being crushed. It happened so quickly he didn't have time to think of retaliating or defending himself.

The kidnapper's voice, now without the gadgetry of the disguise sounded much younger. It echoed angrily through the pits of his mind. He couldn't really see because the hallway was even darker than it was outside. All he knew was that a moment later, the lurking figure was leaning over him and pressing something pungent against his mouth.

13.

Nobody would have slept in the village of Achray. News of the killing had spread exactly as Detective Wallace had suspected. Doors had been double bolted, night air forced outside by locked windows and a constant twitching of blinds and curtains. Those with hunting rifles had called each other and suggested they look out their licences. They weren't planning to use them, of course but if the event called for it, well, they would be on hand in any case.

Detective Wallace was coming along the pathway carrying a coffee doubler and a bag that hopefully contained breakfast.

Rosie could see him blocking out the harsh sunlight before she'd even opened the door. She blinked, her morning eyes adjusting to the new day.

'I would ask how you slept but the answer is probably obvious.'

She snorted. 'Charming, you don't look so bad yourself.'

'Today won't be any easier than yesterday,' he pointed out, whilst walking into her large open lounge. 'First order of business is to take Gaby to identify her husband's body. I'm not looking forward to that.'

'I don't know why they couldn't just accept my identification,' she said, quietly. She knew the process. It just didn't make her any happier with the situation. She had made a solemn promise to Brian in the night, during one of many wakeups that she would take care of Gaby and Eva. It's nothing less than any of them deserved.

Detective Wallace continued to look curiously round the lounge. 'You landed on your feet here.

Look at that view.'

Rosie didn't feel much like enjoying the view this morning. In fact, if she could brick the house up from back to front, she would. She wasn't sure whether to bring to his attention that she thought she was being watched last night. Perceptive eyes of a detective, or paranoid delusion of a grieving friend.

She donned her black stripe jacket and grabbed the coffee. 'We can drink this in your car. That ok?'

Detective Wallace, eternally laid back, simply shrugged his large powerful shoulders.

When she climbed into the passenger's seat, Rosie wanted to tell him to take it slow. She didn't feel much like swinging round the loch as if she were hanging from the top of a rollercoaster. Nor was she in any rush to get to Gaby. Not yet anyway. She still felt guilty. She knew there was no reason to feel that way, but Rosie knew all too well that it was par for the course when a colleague was taken.

Before she felt she had time to blink, Rosie could see the small house appear in the distance. The stillness had not been disturbed and it was strange to think that in these houses, someone would be in the deep underbelly of grief.

'Who did you allocate door to door?'

Rosie was still trying to remember the names. 'The two young fella's who were on the site first. You know, the ones everybody has been referring to as Dick and Dom.'

'Cruel,' chuckled Wallace, evidently trying to break the tension.

'I thought that too. Until I met them. I would say they were being too kind.'

Gaby was waiting at the door when they arrived. She wore a large pair of sunglasses that almost covered the top half of her face whilst her chin was tucked into the top of a long red coat. As she approached the car, it was evident her face was still puffy from crying.

Rosie suspected she hadn't stopped all night. She opened the door for Gaby and brushed her arm as she dropped into the back sound without saying a word.

'Morning, Mrs Houston,' said Wallace, gently. 'I'm going to drive us to the mortuary for identification this morning. Just remember we're both there with you and any time you need to stop, we can.'

Gaby simply nodded.

Rosie, unsure whether to join her in the back or not, returned to the front passenger's seat and tightened her eyes. Even seeing Gaby brought a new sense of anguish to the surface. 'How's Eva?'

Gaby turned to her and tried to smile. 'She can tell something's not right. I haven't been able to settle her.' There was a hanging loom of guilt in her voice. 'Do you both mind if we don't speak. I'm not sure I can hold things together,' she said, as her voice began to crack. 'If I sit here and look out the window, and I don't hear the sympathy in anyone's voice, at least I can pretend for another half an hour that my husband isn't dead.'

*

He'd spent most of the night alone in the room with the screen. Watching the wife try to attract her sleeping husband's attention had amused him at first. Then, as she became more desperate, he found himself beginning to grate of her. Hadn't she realised yet that he'd be watching her every move. The husband would surely know.

He looked at the many sheets of paper on the

table and remembered that today would be another busy day. He had all their work rosters mapped out for the whole week. The perfect roster married with the perfect plan. At least in his eyes.

He'd gotten up early because he wanted to see the detective. He'd become rather fascinated by her. Yesterday, he'd watched her intensely, waiting for a response that hadn't been forthcoming. It had been days since the envelope would have been delivered to her. It would soon be time to put that vehicle in motion. For now, he just wanted to see her, taunt her a little and hope she'd be aware enough to be afraid of him.

He'd left the house behind and took the half mile walk to her house. When he got there, he hid in the cavern of bushes to the side of her house and listened to the scurry of rats feet. It would make sense in this kind of damp undergrowth that they'd congregate and mate here. He liked rats. He liked all wildlife and could rather imagine having them crawl up his skin before snapping their necks and biting into their flesh.

'Are you fantasising again?'

He heard his brother's voice, just off to the side. 'You followed me here?'

'You're hardly subtle. I'm surprised you haven't gotten caught.'

The killer turned in preparation of his departure. He drew back his lips and leered at his brother. 'When this is all over, I don't care about getting caught. In fact, I look forward to everybody knowing what they did. Isn't that why we did all of this in the first place?' With that, he left Larry standing by the bushes, and disappeared into the woods.

14.

Dave woke up to the sound of his wife's voice calling his name. For a brief second, the world was normal again. Until he realised, he was chained to the wall on the other side of the loft. He groaned, fighting against the tiredness of whatever drug had been used on him. His head pounded and he had the slightest recollection of arriving in the dark. For a moment, his heart appeared to double up in panic.

Lizzie was pulling at the wall chain as she continued to call his name.

He tried to speak to her, but his mouth was so dry that the words died in his throat.

'I've been trying to get out of this all night,' she said, pulling hard at her ankle.

He suddenly realised he was in the same room as his wife. She was alive. 'Oh my god,' he said, bolting upright and pulling himself off the bed. 'I was so worried about you.'

There was no grand reunion. They couldn't reach each other, and Lizzie looked as pissed as hell. 'Do you want to tell me exactly what you've gotten us into.'

He smacked his tongue against the roof of his mouth and tried to navigate a small amount of saliva. 'I swear to you, I don't know what this is about. The first time I knew anything about it, I was being called at work to tell me you were in trouble. Until I got home, I honestly believed it was a hoax.'

'It's no hoax,' she whispered, her face twisted in bitterness.

'I've gone over everything. I've tried to think of everyone I've spoken to recently. Perhaps it's something to do with work. The number he called from has been used once before.'

Lizzie looked up, her eyes sharpening. 'Did you find out why?'

'I've passed the information on to my boss. I've told him, Lizzie. He knows that something has happened to you and he's going to be looking for us. He used to be a police officer himself so I think he'll know people who can help us without the kidnappers finding out.'

'He knows we're here?'

Silence fell for a moment as Dave dropped his gaze to the wooden floorboards. 'Not here, exactly. But he knows we're in this village. It won't take long for them to work out what has happened. The car is about half a mile along the road. Someone will notice that it's been abandoned there. I left a note, Lizzie. A piece of paper asking for help.'

She didn't look convinced. 'I'm so hungry. I had a sandwich last night. I think I would have preferred to stay hungry.'

'I could eat something myself,' he replied.

'There's two of them. The one in the balaclava is the one who I've seen the most. I don't know his name. I heard him speaking to the other one though. His name is Larry. Do you know someone called Larry?'

Dave shook his head quickly. Just then, he heard the slamming of a door downstairs. The kidnapper was back. He wanted the world to stop. He wanted off. He, and Lizzie had endured enough this past year. The only thing that mattered to him now was protecting her. He would do anything to stop her from getting hurt. He buried his own anguish and waited patiently to speak to their kidnapper face to face.

*

Gaby had been sleeping for most of the way back. She must have needed it. So, neither Rosie nor Wallace attempted to wake her. She looked like she was in a happy dream. Like the last twenty-four hours had been wiped out by closing her eyes.

The identification of Brian's body had not been the traumatic experience Rosie had expected. Even though he'd had the most traumatic death and didn't look like himself, he'd looked more peaceful than any of them had expected. It had been small comfort to Gaby, who had commented that he looked just like he was sleeping.

Rosie had heard that many times in her career. The wishful thinking of young wives, distraught mothers and distressed siblings cheated out of loved ones in a way they could never have foreseen. She never corrected it, but she'd often thought that many victims looked too pained to just be sleeping. That wasn't the case with Brian. Maybe when death came for him, he hadn't fought it too hard, in turn allowing him to slip off easily. It didn't make Rosie feel any better. If it helped Gaby, that was all that mattered.

'Have you got any leads?'

'You're awake,' said Rosie, as she spun her head to find Gaby staring up from the back seat.

'I've been awake for a while. Just laying here thinking.'

Rosie had nothing. That was the truth. They'd found some things at the crime scene but nothing substantial and nothing that made them think they had any strong leads. 'What were you thinking about?'

They were pulling up to Brian and Gaby's house now. She was rising from her position of slumber and closing the red coat over her chest as if warding off the unkind wonders of the world. 'There's things I need to tell you about. I said Brian should tell you himself, but he refused. I think he might have been worried about what you would think.'

'About what I would think?' Rosie shifted uneasily in her seat and waited for Gaby to continue.

'I'm not talking about it here. Not now. Can you come by later?' She darted a look at Wallace and then moved her eyes back to Rosie. 'Alone.' She didn't wait for an answer. She must have known Rosie well enough to know she would come. There had been something in her expression that wasn't grief. There was something else ailing Gaby Houston as she slammed the car door and stopped at the side of Rosie's window. Then, she moved towards her empty house.

'What the hell was that about?' Wallace waited until Gaby was almost in the house before he spoke.

'I don't know,' replied Rosie, trying not to work through all the potential scenarios. 'Whatever it is though, I don't think I'm going to like it.'

15.

Adam stared out the window. The day had passed in bare flashes of clarity. Only a sliver or sunlight shone through the sudden silver downpour. He had fished out the invitation that had come in the post a few days ago and now held it in his hand. It was the last insult. What had possessed Grey to send it? Was he really that arrogant? Had he no concept of what he'd done?

Most of the day had been spent reminiscing. If there had been one good thing that had come from the recent revelations it had been that he was able to properly grieve for Debra. He could now hear her speaking in her normal soft voice, rather than the gritty argumentative tone that had become his only memory of her. He was able to remember his mother's disgust and his disdain for it, rather than joining the choir of voices that had berated Debra so much. Finally, he could imagine her smile and the way she stroked Gracie's face whenever she became tearful. Maybe not the perfect mother, but someone as close as he had ever known.

Adam had gone through every drawer in the house. He'd not been fully convinced at first. There was something of a niggling doubt in his mind. Maybe it was the way Grey barely made eye contact with Debra when he came to their house. Or how she went to such ends to display her unending dislike of Grey. A shock then that they had decided to work together on the refurbishment of his recent pet project.

There was nothing. No letters, photographs or any other memorabilia that might suggest an affair. So, the policeman had been right. The only answer was that Debra had been the innocent victim of his friend's predatory grip. It wouldn't be the first time, thought Adam, remembering that Grey had been accused of sexual assault before. Of course, Grey had denied it then. Just as he would now, no doubt. How could someone be as blind as he had been for such a long time?

Adam moved towards the fireplace, the crackling embers floating up from a well-lit flame. He threw the invitation straight into the heart of the fire and grabbed the decanter of whisky from the sideboard. He'd never been a big drinker, but the situation had driven it to him. It was either that or the pills that doctor had given to him. He wasn't going down that route.

He only knew he was crying when he felt the gurgle in his throat. There was no containing it anymore. Adam looked at the wedding picture on the wall, four smiling faces, a smiling assassin to the right of his shoulder. Or the devil himself. Adam didn't know. He poured another drink, his shaking hand now sending a mild ache up his arm. A step forward, and he was touching Debra's face. She looked beautiful in white. She had never wanted a ghastly meringue dress. What she got married in was stunning and understated. She was the perfect bride.

As he stared into the frame of conflict, Adam gritted his teeth and allowed the anger within to surge to his core. Then he fired the glass across the room and watched it shatter into enough pieces that it now resembled his life. He didn't know how he would put either back together. All he knew was that for once in his life, he had to defend himself. He raced to the basement, two steps at a time and grabbed for the leather box on the top shelf.

It had been a gift. Not a particularly wanted one.

Grey had given him it shortly after the wedding. It had been a joke aimed squarely at the notion he had that Adam and Debra had been forced into their marriage by the impending arrival of Grace. The card inside was simple. It simply said;

'To Adam, just in case you get tired of your shotgun bride, your brother-in-arms, Grey.'

Adam had smiled then. Debra hadn't seen the funny side and ordered him to throw the gift in the bin. How would she ever know that one day, Adam would be standing here alone, in the tornado of grief and looking for some way to defend her honour. Even if it was now too late to save her. He pushed the Beretta 9000 pistol against the palm of his hand and suddenly felt a surge of power.

He had never used it. In fact, he hadn't ever fired a gun. Adam's mind returned to the invitation, now smouldering in the flames. He realised he had the perfect opportunity. First, though, he had to learn how to shoot. Who would be able to show him how to use the gun in the space of 48 hours? He certainly couldn't ask Grey, though the thought of it presented a nice irony. He returned to his lounge, gun in tow and began to search for nearby shooting ranges who would be willing to show him how to fire a pistol.

*

Rosie kept the light dim in the evidence room. She done her best work when she was alone. If no-one knew she was still here, there was little chance of her being disturbed. She was hungry now. Hadn't eaten a thing most of the day and was starting to feel a little wane. Perhaps she would grab a sandwich from Benny's Café across the street. It wasn't top notch cuisine, but it would fill a hole until she got her act together and went shopping.

The picture of Brian in life haunted her. The slightly knowing arch of his eyebrow leant a certain amusement to his expression and she imagined he'd probably laughed like a drain when he'd been forced to have his mugshot taken. It was certainly preferable to the other picture, which she still struggled to look at.

There were photographs of some items, most of which had already been discarded from the investigation. The only thing of any real interest at this point was the rope fibres found amongst the stones just underneath where Brian had been hanged. There was something very strange about the method of killing as well. That had bothered her. Why hang someone and then savagely attack them with a knife or whatever sharp instrument had been used? The whole thing spoke a measured attack that had then become frenzied. There was no indication that Brian had even put up a fight; no skin in his fingernails, no bruises to the fist, not even a single spill of blood that didn't appear to be his.

There was nothing she could do right now. There was no murder weapon, no witnesses, and no motive. Despite the mess left with blood spill, the murder had been surprisingly shrewd. She followed the sound of rain, now lashing it down outside and decided she would grab her sandwich and then make the short drive to Brian and Gaby's cottage. Gaby had something to tell her. She wasn't sure how related to the case it was. If it was, why hadn't she just told Rosie in front of Detective Wallace.

She crossed the road in a daze, little facts clouding her mind just enough that she could forget about what she'd seen on that board. In the café, she could see Benny animatedly entertain the few patrons who were drinking coffee. Larger than life, twice as camp and an anecdote for every occasion, Benny had become another of Rosie's small group of friends since arrival. Right now, she didn't feel in the mood for his camaraderie.

'On the house,' he whispered, as she grabbed a sandwich from the fridge and placed it on the counter.

She looked up and saw that he was eyeing her sadly. 'No, you can't keep giving away food. You're hardly run off your feet.'

'True. But I fear that if I don't give you free food, you won't eat. You look like a hag.'

'Thanks for that,' she said, chortling.

'My Lucas would die if he saw those roots. Let me get him over to you when you're off. He'll take five inches and twenty years off that bonce of yours.'

'Funny you should say that, Benny. I was actually going to make an appointment at Moira's Salon tomorrow.'

He screeched, throwing an outraged hand up. 'My friend went to her when Lucas was too busy. She came out with half the strands of her hair in a frenzy and the other half leaving in terror. She's not a hairdresser, darling. She's a butcher. Write down your day off and I'll make sure he gets over.'

Rosie, already resenting how much perkier he'd made her feel, scribbled down her days off the following week. 'How's Cammie working out for you. I heard he was doing a few shifts here?'

Benny clicked his chubby fingers, shook his bald head in dismay and leaned forward. 'Always late, permanently moping and only still here because he's easy on the eye.'

'I have to go,' she whispered, snatching the sandwich. 'We'll catch up soon. I've got a bottle of

Cabernet chilling that's got our name written on it.
I'll see you later.'

16.

Why did it always look so easy in the films, wondered Adam. He'd been here an hour at Sammy's firing range and all he'd managed to do was scream out and then go flying to the ground. It hadn't been so much that the gun was powerful but that his body seemed to react to the startling sound. He wasn't sure shooting was really his forte.

A seasoned pro who introduced himself as Gordon approached. 'First time?'

Adam shrugged. 'That obvious?'

'You're here for only two reasons. You've either discovered a love of veal, or the Missus has been a naughty girl.'

Adam felt the contents of his stomach hurl just a little. 'My wife died recently. I'm alone in the house with my daughter. I just want to make sure I am able to protect us.'

Gordon looked amused. 'Take advice from an old man. Buy a baseball bat. If you use a gun in self-defence in this country, you've not got a hope in hell of getting off. Straight off the starting line, they'll say you shouldn't have it in the first place. I'm guessing the gun you have at home is illegal. Christ, son, we're not in Texas here.'

Adam stared him down, at first resistant and then defiant.

Finally, Gordon blew the falling strand of his thinning hair away from his face and took the gun from Adam's hand. 'Here, let me show you. If you're hellbent on ignoring me, at least I can help you not shoot yourself in the face.' He held the gun up, narrowed his eyes and stood upright. His face reddened slightly and then he took a deep breath.

Adam was impressed. The man had barely flinched when the bullet hurtled towards the target. 'You make it look so easy.'

Gordon shook his head. 'It's not. I enjoy shooting at inanimate objects. I'm not interested in killing wildlife, or people. Though, I find shooting a good way of releasing tension. That way I don't have any urge to kill members of my family.' He laughed heartily. 'Listen, the secret is to remember it's only a gun. The natural response to firing it is that your body goes into defence mode. Your adrenalin goes up, your blood pressure shoots through the roof and you experience a naturally resistant reaction. Just remember it's coming, and the rest is just a matter of getting used to it.'

Adam couldn't think of anything he'd done recently that hadn't made him feel useless. He hadn't even considered himself a good father to Gracie. He'd almost been absent half the time; staring out the window in blind rage, rushing her off to his parents' house so he could be alone and forgetting to read her favourite stories at bedtime. How could a grown man be so thoughtless of a frightened child's feelings.

The gun was back in his hand now. He could sense Gordon's stare at the side of his shoulder. Then, the nudge of his hand on Adam's elbow as he fixed his position.

'Remember, it's natural for your body to be full of apprehension. Just take a deep breath, fire the gun and make sure it knows that you're controlling it. It's not controlling you.'

Adam closed his eyes for a second, tightened the grip of his finger on the trigger and finally pulled on it. The release shot through his body, but he was determined he wouldn't jump. Instead, he stood his ground against the gun and watched as the bullet wildly missed the mark. He laughed then. It wasn't exactly bullseye, but it was an improvement on his first few attempts.

Gordon patted him on the back. 'You'll get the hang of it. If you really want to.'

Adam smiled. He had quickly discovered firing a gun wasn't the undoable and frightening task that he'd came here expecting. 'Thank you,' he said, watching Gordon turn and walk away.

'Sorry about your wife, kiddo,' the older man said. 'I've lost two and it does get better. You're a young man. Don't let yourself wallow for too long.' He winked then, returning to his own range.

Adam decided he would have one more go, this time hopefully getting it a little closer to the target. Straightening up his back, he held the gun up and prepared to fire. This time, alone again, he envisioned Grey's face on the target board and pulled the trigger. This time, the bullet fired straight into the middle of the board and suddenly, Adam felt ready to face his wife's attacker.

*

There was something amusing about watching his little rats fight against the metal. He could hear the sickly exchanges of support, him declaring his love for a woman who seemed constantly surly and unwilling to return his declarations.

Funny, he'd taken a liking to the girl. There was something that ailed her that made him wonder about her. It wasn't her beauty. Not the porcelain skin, blonde curls or wide blue eyes that did it. For him, that was ordinary. He had never been drawn to traditionally beautiful women. There was something else that lay just beneath the surface.

He wondered if they knew they were being watched. Had either of them noticed the tiny red light in the far corner of the loft. How long before they knew that every breath they took was being recorded and monitored. He had the camera wired up to all his devices so he could access them either from the room below or when he was out and about.

He rubbed his sweaty hands together, leather gloves protecting one from the other. He checked the rota, just to ensure he hadn't made a mistake. It was time to make his move.

Outside, the rain was settling. It didn't matter to him. The quicker the rain came down, the less likely he was to leave any trace of evidence. It would wash away quicker than they were able to find it. He stared wide-eyed, unblinkingly at the screen and hit the same number three times.

Then, in a flat voice, he simply said, 'Hello, I need an ambulance please.'

17.

The room was in complete darkness when Rosie arrived. She found herself wondering if Gaby had fallen asleep and forgot she was coming.

'I'm sorry. Did I wake you?' She followed Gaby through into the kitchen where only a candle flickered.

'The darker it is, the better I can see.'

Rosie dropped into a seat at a small dining table and found herself staring. Had she been staring too long?

'My husband died yesterday. I've not gone mad, if that's what you think.'

'No,' said Rosie, feeling slightly bewildered. 'I didn't think you had.' The kitchen was much quainter than the rest of the house and Rosie had often wondered if they would get around to modernising it in the same way as the rest of the cottage. She then noticed the empty vodka bottle beside the hob. When she turned back to Gaby, it was evident she had been drinking. Was it any wonder? It's probably the only thing that would get her an uninterrupted sleep tonight.

'You're wondering how drunk I am,' slurred Gaby. 'Blind drunk and I'm not even halfway through the drinks cupboard yet.'

'Have you got Eva settled for the night?'

Gaby twisted her lower lip. 'My mum has her at the hotel. She flew over earlier to help me get through this difficult time.' She laughed. 'To allow me to grieve properly. Apparently, it only took her three days to get over my dad's death.' She took a sharp slug from the crystal glass.

'I'm sure that's not what she meant.'

'You've met my mother, have you?' Gaby was hovering over the table and waving the glass with her hand. She looked over with an apologetic smile.

'Gaby, what's going on?' Rosie was feeling increasingly awkward. She knew people dealt with grief in strange and formidable ways, but Gaby was behaving completely out of character. She never let that little girl out of her sight, usually drank sensibly and was never anything but congenial. Suddenly, she was three sheets to the wind, scowling and had farmed the baby off to her mother, who she didn't seem to like very much at the best of times. Even for the bereaved, she seemed completely at odds with herself.

Panic suddenly fell upon Gaby's expression. 'I don't feel safe,' she whispered,

'Why? You don't think someone is coming after you and Eva, do you?'

'Someone was threatening Brian. He didn't tell me at first. When I found out, he said it was probably somebody disgruntled with a charge.' She was looking round herself now, as if searching the dark corners for some waiting danger.

'Threatening him. In what way?' Rosie tried to think if there was anything about Brian's behaviour that had struck her odd in those last days. There had been nothing glaring.

'Did Brian tell you about his brother?' Gaby leaned in towards her glass. Her eyes were flickering against the orange light of the candle.

Brian had purposefully avoided the subject of his brother but that didn't mean people didn't talk. Rosie knew that all too well. 'I know he's in prison for attempted murder.'

'Four years. They say you can never really escape your past. I didn't believe that before. Now, I'm not so sure.'

'Tell me what happened.'

Gaby grabbed for the bottle behind her and clanked it against the empty glass. 'Care to join me?'

Rosie shook her head and smiled. 'I have to drive home. It wouldn't do to set a bad example.'

'I don't know when it started. I just noticed he wasn't himself. About four weeks ago. Did you notice?'

Rosie shook her head again. 'Nothing. Not a thing.'

'An envelope came with pictures of him and his brother. Some of the pictures showed his brother using drugs. Then the phone calls started. The only reason I found out is because I answered and whoever it was asked if I knew that Brian had been smuggling drugs to his brother.'

Rosie suddenly felt alarmed. An envelope? She wanted to delve more into that, but she didn't want to alarm Gaby when she was obviously already on the cusp of paranoia. 'It's not true, of course,' she simply surmised.

'You and I know that. Brian's fear was that no-one else would believe him. He comes from a family who've been in and out of trouble for years. It took him every ounce of blood and sweat to prove he was different. To everyone else, and himself.'

'Gaby, did Brian receive one of those calls on the night of his death?'

She shrugged. 'I don't know. I've not got any of his things back. It was usually a withheld number anyway, so you'd need to probably pull the phone records from his service provider.'

'We've already requested that,' said Rosie, absently.

'I believe they threatened his brother as well. Brian still couldn't tell me what it was they wanted. Only that the person said if Brian didn't do what he was asked when the time came, his brother would be stabbed to death in the yard.'

'You don't know what they were asking?'

'Not a clue,' answered Gaby, swirling the last of the vodka in her glass.

It was something else that jumped out at Rosie though. 'You said the initial contact was made a few weeks ago?'

'Yes. I don't know when exactly. All I know is that they sent that envelope with the photographs.'

'Do you know how long before the phone calls started?'

'A week or two, I think.' She rose from the chair and threw open a cupboard door, retrieved a second bottle of vodka and slammed it on the table.

Rosie knew better than to judge. She'd had her own demons to battle and sometimes the bottom of a bottle was the only place a woman could feel truly on top of things. It wasn't a boast. In fact, Rosie sometimes felt ashamed of how she'd handled things in her past. She wasn't going to patronise anyone else. 'Do you have the picture that was sent?'

Gaby rose from the table, searched the ends of the kitchen to ensure it was safe and disappeared for a few seconds. When she returned, she dropped a brown envelope onto the table.

Rosie didn't need to open the envelope or scrutinise the photos. The envelope told her everything she needed to know. She recognised the colour of it and the scribbled name across the centre.

It was the same as the one that had been sent to her. She gasped and threw her head back. If only she and Brian had confided in each other, the outcome might have been very different. She wondered when her phone calls would start. Soon, she imagined. The realisation that her own photos weren't the prank of a former colleagues but sought out information by a vicious killer made her want to pack up and run. Though, she knew she couldn't run. Promises had been made; both verbally to her colleagues and silently in the night to Brian. She wasn't about to let any of them down now. With that, a chill rested upon the back of her neck.

*

The ambulance arrived an hour later. He nursed the first of the nooses with a gloved hand and watched murky water wash over rocks of moss. Rage burned! A rage that he'd always known but had managed to temper long enough that he'd never killed before. Until two nights ago!

The air was damp, the skies a worn washed blue that looked as if they would drop another torrent at any moment. Even under the cavern of trees, he wasn't immune to the cold, wet whip that lashed against the back of his neck.

He could hear the paramedics searching for the injured party. One was tiptoeing along the edge of the water whilst the other ventured into rougher terrain just in case the victim had managed to crawl into slightly dryer ground.

The weariness prowled, creeping into him like some sort of force that would push him into the realms of carelessness. He couldn't let that happen. One day, he wouldn't care about the detection of evidence. It was too early to give himself up. There was still more to do. More of them to atone for what they'd done to him.

He felt the grief then. A substitute to his ever-endless rage. He didn't have the patience that Larry or his father had shown. He needed blood. It was a thirst in him that went far beyond the need for revenge. It had been woken long ago; a force of nature that spurred on every breath.

He stared coldly at the Trossachs Church, tinged yellow in Spring dusk with a shimmering reflection on the golden water. New-born leaves rose over it and formed a yellow archway that merged with the church's ever rising sharp spires. It seemed odd to think that if there was a god, it would be watching him now. It didn't matter. The first kill had happened. There was no going back now.

What happened next was so quick that even he found himself reaching for a tree bark to stable himself. The younger of the two was returning to the ambulance, oblivious to the danger that lay in wait.

The other one, slightly older looking, continued to step carefully onto pebbles until he was far enough from the ambulance that he wouldn't be heard. There was no more time to waste.

Suddenly, the killer was lunging at the unsuspecting paramedic. He smashed him on the side of the head with a rock he had found nearby before locking the noose round his neck and dragging him into a concealed undergrowth.

That paramedic was limp now.

The killer watched him, somewhat amused but not as exhilarated as he had expected.

The man was coming to. His eyes widened and his hands flew up to grab for the rope. He was dangling, kicking his feet desperately and trying to shout a warning to his colleague.

It was too late.

The younger paramedic was now calling for him.

The man dangled more frantically, perhaps hoping that if he fought gallantly enough, he would simply fall out of the air. Only when he managed a glance to the side and saw another rope dangling from a nearby tree did he stop fighting. Perhaps he might have realised that neither of them would be returning home tonight. Or maybe his thinking in those last minutes of life were that if he didn't draw the other young man in, he might escape.

The younger paramedic looked equally shocked. He put up slightly more fight but only enough to further boil the killer's rage.

He pulled the second paramedic into the noose with much less effort than the first and leaned over for his large blade. It glinted in the fading light. He could hear the grunts of the first paramedic, whose name had escaped him. The second one, Scott was pleading now. He was wriggling wildly, probably unaware that he was constricting his breathing even more.

The killer would have laughed but the second kill hadn't brought the euphoria of the first. Were the highs really this quick to wear off. He turned away, disinterested in his hanging victims and threw the bloody rock at his feet as far into the water as it would go.

Walking away, he stared blankly at Crystal Ridge. Wouldn't it be a nice touch if she was at the window? He'd be caught. Yet, he would rather enjoy the perverseness of it. Still, she'd have her turn soon enough. Of all the people involved, she was the one who deserved his death fell the most.

18.

Rosie had been unable to put Gaby out of her mind since leaving her. There had been something strange about her. Something cold and unfamiliar. Like grief had stripped away the ordinarily congenial Gaby she'd come to know. Now she had learned something of Brian that made her think she didn't know the couple at all.

'Why didn't he tell any of you? I mean, if he had nothing to hide why not come to someone for help?'

Rosie knew Detective Wallace was only mirroring her thoughts, but she didn't appreciate it one bit. She wanted someone to give her a good slap, tell her she was being ridiculous, and that Brian was one of the most solid, honest policemen she had ever met. Delivering drugs to a convicted criminal was not the act of the man she had come to know as her partner and friend.

He waited for an answer until it became clear she wasn't going to give one.

'Are you going to this?'

Detective Wallace leaned over and grimaced at it. 'What is it?'

'An invitation to the event of the year. Grey Carter's hotel opening. It was delivered here for me today.'

He chuckled. 'This close to the event. I don't know much about event etiquette but if you're only receiving it a day or two before, you're usually on the reserve list.'

Rosie agreed. There was also something about Grey she didn't trust. His smile was just a little too confident, his swagger a little too cocky. 'I'm surprised it's going ahead.'

He shrugged and delivered a scathing tusk. 'I'm not. He made it very clear when he spoke to us yesterday that he wanted us off his land as soon as humanly possible. I don't think he understands that those grounds are now in our hands until further notice.'

'He gets it,' she said. 'He just doesn't care.'

'If I'm being honest,' he said cautiously, 'he's top of my suspect list.'

'I'm not sure,' she replied. 'I don't trust him, but I don't see what he'd have to gain by killing Brian. Especially on his own land where it was only going to draw negative attention to him right before the opening. Nobody wants to stay in a hotel where a murder just happened.'

Detective Wallace looked at her and spoke sharply. 'Are you kidding? There's a world of ghoulish people out there who live for the macabre. Amateur sleuths, horror buffs, people obsessed with the current slew of real-life murder documentaries. This would bring them out in their droves. If you follow that logic, Grey has a lot to gain by having a murder happen at his hotel on the eve of his opening. I really think we should be looking at his alibi a little more closely.'

She looked at him pensively. 'Okay, let's have another chat with him. I'll call down to Glasgow and see if they can check out his alibi. If we're doing all that, we might as well investigate his finances as well. I'm curious to know where he got the money to buy the hotel and put it through such an expensive overhaul.'

He paused for a second as if he were weighing all of that up. 'I think you are suspicious of him. I just think you were waiting for someone else to plant the seed.'

'I can't look at him objectively. There's part of me disgusted that a young woman died because she was involved with him. Another part of me is curious as to what ails him.'

'Don't get dragged there. He's a chancer who got lucky. A thug who thinks he's infallible and that every woman is going to throw herself at his feet. I saw how he flirted with you yesterday. Don't think of him as someone deep who needs to be discovered. Think of him as the man who disgusts you after causing a young woman to die.'

Rosie checked herself because she knew all too well men had been her downfall. How often her heart had been broken when she was a young woman. How many times since she'd allowed her hard heart to soften at mere flirtations. It was true, she had noticed how attractive Grey was recently. She also knew he was one of the most untrustworthy men she'd ever came upon. She wasn't going there again.

'So, are you going to go?'

She held the invitation in her hand and flicked it with her thumb. 'I might. It would be interesting to see who will be there. I believe Brian's killer is a showman. The way he killed Brian was for effect. There was no need for the brutality of it. He wants to be seen. Where better to be seen than at the apparent event of the year.' She eyed the envelope at the corner of her desk. 'I need to get this over to the lab and dusted for prints. I doubt we'll find anything of interest but no harm in trying.' She still hadn't told him of her own envelope or the degrading contents. She hoped she'd never have to.

Detective Wallace began to chew on a stick of carrot. The beginning of a diet that Rosie noticed only lasted until halfway through the day.

A ringing phone at the next desk shattered the silence. She leaned across and pulled the handset from the cradle. 'Detective Inspector Cooper.'

Wallace tapped on his keyboard, seemingly unaware that something was unfolding a few yards away.

She replaced the handset and nursed her chest slowly. Horror had drained the colour from her face.

'Rosie, what's happened?'

She spun round in the chair, balanced herself against the desk and took deep breaths. 'They've found another two bodies. Down in the woods by the Loch.'

'Same as Brian?' There was a croak in his voice, a reluctance to say the words as he lowered her back onto the seat.

'Two paramedics. Someone saw their ambulance abandoned nearby and went to see if there was something wrong.' She shuddered as she spoke. 'They were hanging from trees, their throats cut and slashes across their faces.'

'You look like a ghost. Are you sure you're up to this?'

'I'm fine,' she insisted, lifting her shoulders up. She turned at the last moment and tucked a strand of hair behind her ear. 'Well? Are you coming or not?'

*

Grey suspected he must be the only person smiling in the whole of the village. He'd been down to the village centre a short while ago and noticed that everyone seemed on edge. There was nothing on their tongues but that of the policeman's death. It was eerie and disconcerting, yet reassuring that, for him it would be business as usual.

Detective Cooper and her entourage were gone for the night. No doubt, they would return with a hundred more boring questions. He would continue to give the same stock answers he'd drilled into himself. He didn't know anything about the murder. He hadn't been here at the time. He only had the misfortune of finding the body in the morning. All lies, of course. All rather unpleasant, but Grey was used to unpleasant things and his priority was self-preservation.

He swung in the chair in his office and thought of how far everything had come. When Debra had been here, there was much to be done. She had such an eye for tasteful decor that Grey didn't think he could have managed to get the place together so quickly. He wished she were here now. She was the one person he had fully opened himself up to. Now she was gone, he had no desire to repeat the experience.

The painting on the wall was stunning. The Mercury Drop, he'd heard it was called. He suspected not even an expert would notice it was a forgery without proper scrutiny. It was the same across the entire hotel. Every painting, carbon copies of their originals framed at a quarter of the price and smuggled in by a dealer from the south of France.

Grey, taking a sip of champagne from a cut glass flute, removed the painting from the wall. It was a nice irony that the money that should have paid for the original was sitting in the safe behind it. He punched in his father's date of birth and watched the digital safe unlock. Inside, piles of money that should have been spent on the refurbishment but that would now line his personal account. He had to move it. There was no way he was risking it being discovered on the night of the opening.

Taking the stash of money from inside the safe, he loaded it into a satchel and hid it under his desk. The hotel was locked up for the night. It would be safe for now. First thing in the morning, he was getting it out of here and taking it to a place that only he would have access to.

The telephone rang, interrupting his good mood. He already suspected it would be his investor. Either that, or the police to ask him more inane questions.

'Hello?'

'Everything prepared?'

Grey vocalised a grunt of affirmation. 'You got everything prepared at your end? Is the guestlist sorted?'

'I have hired you two waitresses. The food will be done outside. We don't want a mess when your guests arrive. Some of the people who I've invited are big business, if you know what I mean. They're looking for a spot away from big city eyes. You need to be on your game if you want their business.'

Grey already knew the kind of shady deals that would take place. He wasn't under the illusion his investor was whiter than white. Neither was he, though. If those cash registers were ringing, he didn't care who was filling them. 'How many people can we expect?'

'Enough,' answered his investor before disconnecting the call.

Grey checked the clock. In less than forty-eight hours he would be entertaining upward of a hundred guests. At least he hoped it would be that many. He'd spent most of his adult life working for other people. Finally, he had the means to work for himself. Locking up his office, he took to the roof of the hotel so he could stare across the skyline. Lighting a cigarette, and inhaling deeply, he scrunched his eyes and focused his glare on the sparkling loch. Life couldn't get any better and nothing was going to spoil that now.

19.

'Is there anything found at the scene that is linked to Brian's death?'

'Nothing obvious yet. We're still working on the fibres that you sent over from that crime scene and will hopefully have something for you tomorrow.'

Rosie was relieved to find the bodies had already been taken down and were now hidden by two adjacent tents. It was bad enough she would have the image of their young dead bodies in her mind when she slept tonight. She didn't need that made any worse.

'Are you okay?' Detective Wallace was standing at her side, caressing her shoulder gently.

'Strangely, yes,' she replied. It was true, she didn't feel this one was as personal to her, though she still felt an unfathomable amount of anger about the death of two young men who were simply carrying out their duties. She had no doubt their death was connected to Brian's. Her mind was already frontloaded with questions. What was their connection to Brian? What did they have in common? Had they also received envelopes with revealing photos about their past? It made her wonder again about the difference in items both she and Brian had received. What did the photos of her having sexual intercourse with her boss have to do with Brian apparently delivering drugs to his brother?

She stepped carefully over the barrier tape, trying not to kick any of the small tagged numbers now placed strategically at every inanimate object that seemed out of place.

'Who was first responder?'

A young female uniformed officer stepped

forward, almost delighted to place herself in front of Rosie. 'Police Constable Kimberly Holmes,' she said, with too much glee for the occasion.

'Do we have anything to go on?' She quickly forced down her instant irritation.

'Two paramedics were called to the scene of an accident. When they got here, they couldn't find anything so one of them called back on the radio. They were then found approximately forty minutes later when a Mrs. Barker was walking her dog.'

'I know Mrs Barker. She lives a few houses away from me,' said Rosie, turning to stare at her own house. If she had been home, these murders would have taken place right in front of her window. Would the killer have known she wouldn't be home? Was he watching her? She waved her hand in front of her face, as if silently waving away another bout of paranoia.

'Have we got names?'

The young woman consulted her notepad once more. 'Ricky Wilton and Kyle Bird.'

'You know, there's something very specific about the deaths. A killer who seeks them out and draws them to their death. He isn't just grabbing some random stranger. He deliberately calls upon them. I wonder how he knew Ricky and Kyle would be on rota tonight.'

Wallace shook his head, the last sprinkling of light spreading across his puzzled face. 'Maybe he's playing roulette. Perhaps it didn't matter which two paramedics he got.'

'Or perhaps the person has inside information.' she said, clenching her jaw and fists at the same time. Again, the notion returned to her this wasn't random. 'Is this your first murder case?' She turned to PC

Holmes, who only appeared to have two facial expressions; exceptionally excited or grave and thoughtful.

PC Holmes nodded enthusiastically. 'It's not what I thought it would be. They don't really prepare you at base for how mundane it is. I've been freezing my backside off for the last hour. There doesn't appear to be any real leads or evidence.'

Rosie sniffed. 'That's real police work for you. We stand for hours digging through mounds of grain hoping that there's the tiniest clue. Quite often we search for weeks, hitting dead ends before something very simple and obvious lands on our laps. Then, we switch on the televisions and murder cases are wrapped up in forty-five-minute episodes. Imagine if everything was that simple.' She knew she sounded bitter. She felt it right now. Three deaths in as many days. Her own life literally hanging in the balance and she didn't have a clue why.

Detective Wallace was returning now. He looked perplexed.

'What is it?'

'The team leader at the SAS centre ran a check. They couldn't find the call.'

'How can they not find the call? Did you tell them who you were?' She was raising her voice now, unperturbed by the fact that everyone else could seemingly hear her.

'Of course, I told him who I was. They were already aware of what's happened and said they'll do anything they can to co-operate. They can see on the system that Kyle and Ricky were given an emergency to attend this location for someone who was injured. There's no identity for the injured man, nor is there any recorded call in relation to the emergency.'

She paused and took a moment to assess her surroundings. 'I don't understand how that works. How can there be an emergency if no-one called it in? Someone must have created the record in order to send them here. Who did that?'

'That's the strange thing of all. There's no call taker identity either. The SAS manager said there didn't appear to be any person linked. No injured person's name, no caller's name and no call taker's name. It's as if all trace of anyone involved has simply been erased.'

Rosie became immersed in the flurry of activity around her. The lights suddenly seemed too bright, the melee of noise too deafening and she wondered if she were about to faint. She turned to look at her house and thought of how much safer she would feel in there. Especially knowing she might be next. She contemplated telling Kevin Wallace then about the photos that had been sent to her. The thought of them going into evidence disturbed her more than she could even contemplate. Suddenly, Rosie felt quite alone. There was nobody here who could protect her but herself. When the time came, she would have to be prepared to fight back. It wouldn't be an easy feat considering she hadn't a clue who she was dealing with.

20.

Back at the station, Rosie was still shaking from what she'd just witnessed. Kyle couldn't be more than twenty-five years old. Someone had taken his life and he'd barely even began to live it. She was angry now. Fear and suspicion had subsided, and she wondered how many more people would die before she caught a lead.

The evidence board was getting busier, the trail getting thicker. How were the three victims even linked? Was the killer just jagging a pin into a map and picking from a lottery of potential victims? Rosie knew that probably wasn't true, but she couldn't tell anyone how she knew that. She couldn't face the scrutiny of her past life once the reason she'd left it became public knowledge. Her new start seemed to exist on shockingly thin ground now.

When it was evident that staring at the board wasn't going to offer any answers, she moved to her desk and decided it was time to get some more intel on Grey Carter. He may not be the killer, but she suspected he could possibly offer something of a lead. Maybe he knew the killer. He was a man who had secrets. Could murder be one more of them?

His role call of petty crimes in his early twenties made for astounding reading. He hadn't been as clever as he thought because he'd been caught for quite a lot of things. What else lay in his past? It also begged the question that if he'd resorted to petty crime, how had he come into enough money to buy the hotel. Perhaps someone was bankrolling him. A killer perhaps?

She found his Glasgow address and typed it into a search engine. The image of the building flashed up;

a rather impressive six story corner block in the city centre. Nobody afforded a flat like that on minimum wage and the odd drug deal. She found herself scrolling down. There were several flats in the block for sale. Oddly, she found Grey's flat for sale quite near the bottom of the first set of search results.

'Kevin, come and have a look at this.'

He was jumping up from his seat, abandoning his mug of coffee with slight annoyance. 'What?'

She was clicking on the link now. 'Grey's selling his Glasgow flat.'

'So?'

'Don't you think it odd that he's bought the hotel, has forty odd rooms empty but is travelling back and forth to a flat that he's selling.' She was clicking through the images now.

'It's impressive. I'd buy it myself if I wasn't on a policeman's salary.'

She laughed at that. It was true that many people thought detectives were on a fortune. Whilst they earned a decent pay, it was hardly compensation for what they had to endure. She thought of poor Brian again. The ultimate price to pay for a job that he'd loved. Maybe death was the occupational hazard.

'Look at this,' she muttered, pointing to the screen. 'It says it's sold.'

Wallace was pulling a seat over. 'It does, indeed. I wonder when he sold it.'

She sighed. 'Maybe it only sold today. Maybe a week ago. Whenever it sold, I can tell you that Mr Carter isn't telling us the truth. There's no way he was sleeping at that house two nights ago when it's already marked as sold.'

'I think we better have a word with our illustrious Mr Carter.'

Rosie shook her head and held up her hand, as if physically holding him back. 'Not yet. He's oily. If we go in there throwing accusations, he'll only deny it. I want to catch him in the lie.' She printed off the page at the nearest printer and then closed that page. She was staring at his younger face again.

'What are you thinking?'

She was staring now. In that image, Grey Carter's eyes looked cold dead. It wasn't the face of the charming man who thought he was getting the better of them. It was his real face, the one he'd obviously remastered into something more cunning and deceitful. 'I'm thinking that he just became a very real suspect in this murder case. Perhaps he loved Debra Mullen more than we thought. Maybe this is payback for the death of the only woman he truly loved.'

*

It was stupid but he'd raced to Glasgow at 90mph. Speeding out of the village, adrenalin finally pumping through his raging body. His muscles, toned and athletic and so tense he felt that his veins and arteries might rip out of his body at any moment.

Sauchiehall Street was busier than he had expected. Midweek and still there were throngs of revellers moving from bar to bar, various degrees of drunk and just the kind of flesh baring that really turned him on.

He stood in the doorway of Driftwood and watched a young woman who was vaguely familiar to him. He'd been here before. It was a little warren at the start of the long road, a place with light neon colours, made almost solely of its namesake and the epicentre of student life.

She was the barmaid. Not dressed revealingly

like the other women in his eyeline. It made for pleasing thoughts. She was quite stunning. Untouched dark curls fell onto her pure pink shoulders, a face so pure in youth that she'd barely marked it with makeup. Her clothing was tight but covered most of the body and the legs. Yet, she was perfect for him.

He'd often dreamt of what he would do when he found the right one. There had been many before her. They'd never been quite right; too old, too young, too promiscuous, too pure. There had been lots that had turned him off to them. Not her, though. He could envision with clarity the moment he'd take her home, run his hands down her flesh before rendering her unconscious and peeling the skin from her.

His fantasy was shaken by the realisation he was being watched. In the not too far distance, on a bridge that hovered directly above the main motorway through the city, a figure stood watching him. They weren't close enough to exchange words, but the look of disdain was so evident that he could almost taste it.

He was walking towards the man now. A ninety second walk and he was facing the other half of himself.

Larry was bending over the fence with his arms outspread. 'How easy it would be just to float downwards and end it all.'

That was his problem with Larry. Everything was so romanticised. Even death sounded like some heavenly experience that he couldn't relate to.

'Can you come back from there?'

Larry was smiling. 'So, you do care, little brother.'

He said nothing. Simply scowled and felt a little pang of rage for Larry's presence. 'Why are you always following me. Can't I do anything by myself?'

Larry drew his lips back, revealed his teeth as he sometimes did when they quarrelled. 'I'm the other half of you. Where you go, I go. That's the beauty of being a twin. Whatever you feel, I feel. I don't have to follow you. I can find you anywhere.'

He resented it. He always had. Even as a child, he'd want to experience things as one person. Instead, Larry had always been there, like a reflection and the voice upon his shoulder.

'You've found her, haven't you?' Larry delivered the question with such relish that silence fell between them for a moment.

He simply stood and waited.

Larry chuckled. 'You've found the one. I can feel it.' He took his brother's hand and pressed it to his chest. 'In here. You've found the girl of all your fantasies. Now it's only a matter of time.'

The traffic continued to race under them, the honk of an HGV truck pulling them out of the face-off they now found themselves in.

Larry's shoulders were thrusting up and down in silent laughter. 'So, how will you do it? Wine and dine her and then take her somewhere secluded. Maybe you'll sedate her or drug her, so it won't be so unpleasant.' He was leaning in now, his voice a mere whisper in the wind. 'Or maybe you'll skip the romance, just like you did to those poor men and snuff out her life without so much as a kiss or goodbye.' With that, Larry turned and walked away.

21.

'When do you think he'll make his move?'

Dave's back was killing him. His shoulders felt sore from being stuck in the same position for hours but there weren't many positions a person could get comfortable in with their leg chained to a wall. He was now at the stage where he was silently willing the kidnapper to make his move, but he couldn't say anything to Lizzie. For her, he wanted to retain hope.

'You must have some clue why he's doing this. Do you recognise his voice?' Lizzie had asked him several times but seemed in disbelief when he replied that he didn't have a clue.

'Lizzie, I have no answers for you.' He felt exasperated. There was nothing he could add to fill in the blanks for her. 'All I know was that the call came through at work. I don't know who he is. I have no idea why we're here in this shit hole of a village. Honestly, babe. If I knew anything, I would tell you. I'm dumbfounded. There's no other word for it.'

She scraped back her hair and looked as if she were about to scream. 'There must be something we can do. I don't think he's here now. If we could get out of these fucking chains.' She snatched them up and threw them back onto the mattress.

'Short of cutting off our foot, I don't know how we'd do it.'

'Whatever it takes. Better to have no foot than to be killed.'

'Well that thought is insane. I'm not cutting off my foot. There'll come a time when he has to approach us, and we just have to be ready to fight. Both of us.'

She placed her free foot on the floor, leaned

forward and screamed, 'What the fuck else are we supposed to do?'

Dave didn't recognise his wife. He'd never heard her scream before. Not even after the miscarriage of their baby. It was the most alien sight and he thought he might laugh at how ridiculous and other-worldly it seemed. 'Okay, baby. I'm sorry. I don't know what we're going to do but we have to try and stay calm.' At that very moment he turned and caught sight of the vaguest red light.

Lizzie was staring at him now as she settled back onto the bed.

'What's that?'

She followed his gaze. 'What?'

'That light up there. Look, it's a tiny red dot. Can you see it?'

'I see it,' she finally said, after what seemed like a lifetime of focusing.

'He's watching us,' said Dave. 'That's one of those infrared cameras that will even see us in the dark. He knows everything we've talked about in here. Every whisper. He'll be one step ahead of us because we can't even make a sound without him knowing.'

Lizzie fell back onto the bed. 'We're not getting out of here alive, are we? And he probably won't even tell us why.' Suddenly she began to weep.

Dave felt helpless. Every tear his wife had cried since the day they'd met; he'd been able to wipe them away. Not this time. This time he'd unknowingly put her in peril, and he couldn't even comfort her when the time came. 'I'm sorry,' he muttered, biting back his own tears.

Lizzie fell into a deep silence.

There seemed little point in talking now because

they couldn't plot their escape, they couldn't comfort each other and there was nothing left to say that would make either of them feel any better.

Dave suspected she was right. Someone out there had the answers as to why they had been targeted but he suspected he was never going to learn of them. He had also lost hope in the message he'd attempted to send to Jason Barr. It had obviously not gotten to him. Maybe Jason would have put out the call by now but with no location to speak of, Dave had to concede that he and Lizzie were alone, and nobody was coming for them. They wouldn't be found until after they were dead. If they were found at all.

22.

Grey had wanted to call Adam for several weeks. He hadn't seen him since the funeral. At that point he wasn't sure Adam knew of what had been going on. It was obvious from the two months of radio silence that the police must have informed him. He felt more love for Adam than he did for his own parents yet, when temptation had approached him, he hadn't sent it marching.

It wasn't the first time they'd fallen out. Grey suspected Adam wasn't comfortable with some of his choices and seemed out of his comfortable space whenever he'd been invited to parties with Grey. Suddenly, the differences between them had pulled them worlds apart. It didn't stop Grey from feeling a certain measure of guilt. Still, he hoped that Adam would come to forgive him. After all, who else did they have but each other. Friends for life; that's what they had sworn to.

No point on dwelling on it. Debra was gone. She was never coming back. Adam would come to terms with it soon enough, he suspected. Anyway, he must have known what kind of temptress he'd married. It wasn't really Grey's fault. If only he had the chance to explain. He really felt that Adam would understand.

He headed to the rooftop. He loved to be up there by night. There was nothing quite like the solitude of watching the world in the witching hour. Full moon beam would cross the land; the loch turning to black crystal, the eerie silence shattered only by light winds and the knowledge that whatever was going on out there, he would be safe from it. Nobody could touch him.

He lit the cigarette with his right hand and listened to the clinking of the ice in his glass. He enjoyed a glass of red wine often but never allowed himself to get intoxicated. He wanted to be in control of his faculties. He certainly wasn't going to let anything spoil his big day. He'd waited too long for this.

He suddenly noticed the flash of blue lights down near the loch. Was something going on down there? Hadn't the village seen enough drama this week? At least it was far enough from the hotel that he didn't need to be involved.

Grey leaned over the edge of the rooftop and stared at the beams. Two nights before a man had been hanging there. The memory brought a sudden surge of guilt. He hadn't known Detective Houston very well. He'd only had a couple of conversations with him in the aftermath of Debra Mullen's death. In the past few days, he'd learned that Houston had a wife and a new baby, and it had stirred up a reaction he hadn't expected.

The truth was Grey didn't like to get involved in other people's bullshit. He'd learned long ago that playing the hero was a thankless task. It was bad enough the murder had happened in the backyard of his hotel. He didn't want to be cited as a witness. Besides, he hadn't seen the killer. By the time he'd really been aware of what was happening, Detective Houston would probably already have been dead.

He shuddered at thought of it. Grey didn't have a weak stomach and he could handle a brawl with the best of men, but he was certain the sight of that man hanging there would haunt him for quite a while yet.

He remembered the moment he thought the killer had seen him. The face had been concealed by darkness. The eyes, though. There was no concealing them. The act itself had been unspeakably evil, but those eyes had terrified even him. He'd moved back into the darkness just in time to evade discovery. In that moment, Grey had already made his decision. He wouldn't be telling anyone that he'd witnessed the murder.

23.

'I've managed to speak to the prison governor at Barlinnie. We can see James Houston later this morning. Though he's had to be taken to the prison hospital after finding about out about Brian.'

Rosie held the lapels of her coat and closed her eyes. If only she had the ability to connect with the afterlife. What would Brian say to her if she could communicate with him? She'd always found it useful to try and re-live their final moments. Right now, it was too early to function, morning light not quite finding its way through the night clouds.

'What are you looking for?'

She felt a quick pang of irritation. 'If I knew what I was looking for, I wouldn't be standing here in the early hours like a moron.'

'Ouch,' he mouthed, retreating into silence so he didn't fall on the sharp side of her tongue again.

Her heart sped up a little as she worked her way step by step from the place of Brian's death to the nearby gardens that split the hotel grounds from the rest of the land. The maze was an obvious place for someone to hide. She stood there and looked in the direction of the hotel. 'Do you think this is where he would have been waiting? You can see every corner of the hotel here. You can also see any cars coming from the village. The killer would have been watching for Brian coming.'

'What do you think they've missed?'

Rosie had been irritable since she'd woken up. She knew it but she couldn't help it. The more the days went on, the more watched she felt. Watched by a killer. Watched by her colleagues. Everybody was waiting for her to succeed or fail. Including the person who wanted to take her life. 'Something. You don't kill someone that frantically and not leave a trace. God, when is the lab going to get back to us? Surely, they must know how urgent this is.'

Detective Wallace was looking into the maze now.

Rosie looked around herself, noticed a nearby door latched open. She'd seen Grey leave as they arrived, told him they were there just to look around and seemed not to care when he gave an expression of protest. He was long gone. Was there someone else in there?

'Kev, can you come and look for a second?'

He was moving closer to her now, pulling at his shirt and following her gaze to a window on the third floor.

'Didn't Grey say he'd be away most of the morning?'

'Yes,' he replied, following her stare.

'Grey didn't come back, did he?' There was someone up there. They must have known she could see them, but they made no effort to move.

'I think he said something about driving to Glasgow. I doubt he'd be back yet.'

'I wonder if he's driving to the flat that he no longer owns,' she said, caustically. 'Look, we're being watched. There's someone in there that shouldn't be. I'd be interested in speaking to him.' As she entered, Rosie descended the dark stairs of a wine cellar. She flicked the light on and saw wooden boxes discarded along with a host of paintings.

'Tomorrow's the big opening event. Maybe some of the staff have already arrived.'

Rosie wasn't convinced. 'Why would the staff be here almost two days before?'

She was heading towards reception when she heard lift doors opening in the nearby hallway. 'Quick,' she ordered. 'If someone else is staying here that Grey hasn't told us about, then maybe they might know something.'

Wallace looked at her sceptically.

A door slammed nearby.

She, and Detective Wallace both spun at the same time.

Footsteps thundered along the marble floor of the hotel. By the time Rosie and Detective Wallace turned the corner, they barely caught sight of someone disappearing through a door.

Rosie picked up speed, the sound of her feet slapping against the marble causing a clap in her ear. Finally, she reached the open door and slipped in. As she did, an exit into the car park was being slammed shut. The only thing she caught sight of was a hand as it pulled away and turned a key in the lock. 'He's locked us in,' she bellowed, searching for a window that might give her a sight of the escapee.

He laughed. 'We don't know that the person is even involved with what happened to Brian.'

A quick turn of the head. 'Then, why are they running?'

'We better get out of here. If we're found in this place without a warrant, I reckon Grey Carter will have a field day. He'll be slapping a harassment and trespassing complaint on us.'

'Not a chance,' she said. She felt a jolt of fear but, in keeping with that protective wall she'd put up in London, she didn't allow him to see it. She simply turned from the empty room and headed back to the corridor. She was still giving chase in the hope that maybe the person had fallen in the car park and broken a limb. That would be one way of getting answers. A thought that was too good to be true. A moment later she heard a car speed off. By the time they reached the window, the departing vehicle was already well hidden in the trees.

Wallace was sidling up to her now. 'You would think he'd have spent a few quid on the trimmings.'

'I wonder what the bedrooms look like,' she said. 'It all seems to be very superficial.'

'Typical, eh? Flash Harry on the surface. Peel away the layers and there's nothing underneath.'

'Exactly.' She had a tissue on her hand that she used to blow her nose as she made her way back to the wine cellar.

Wallace tusked. 'Trust us to find the only way in and out of here is through the booze. Let's hope that door's still open.'

'Don't worry,' she whispered, good humouredly. 'If we get locked in, I'll make sure I do the drinking. You can just keep me propped up.'

They were descending the stairs, the early morning sunshine breaking through some old frosted windows. Fortunately, the door that exited the cellar onto the grounds remained ajar.

'Look at this?'

Rosie was already dashing to the exit, glad to see she could still get back out. She turned and saw Wallace thumbing the prints. 'What are they?'

'Paintings. About two dozen of them. I wonder if they're new or if they're the ones he's taking down.'

She clasped her hands in frustration. 'Maybe you can discuss his love of art with him tomorrow night if you want to join me. Right now, we need to get out of here before someone finds us in here.'

'Look at this,' he said, seeming not to notice her

desperation to leave.

Rosie sighed, mentally warning herself not to engage with him. However, she couldn't help herself, so she moved away from the back door and moved to his side. 'What am I looking at?'

He lifted one of the canvas prints. 'You don't recognise it?'

'Of course, I recognise it,' she snapped. 'It's the Mona Lisa.'

'It's not though, is it? The Mona Lisa is probably holed up in a vault at the Louvre or somewhere like that. It's hardly going to be stashed in the damp cellar of a backwater hotel in Scotland.'

'So, it's a fake. We can't arrest him for collecting cheap replicas of famous paintings.'

'I believe it's illegal actually. Da Vinci's work is copyrighted. You can take a photo of it, but I don't think you can re-create it or sell it.'

Rosie smirked. 'I'm not getting involved in this. If we arrested everyone who had a fake painting, or fake jeans, or an album they downloaded online, we'd never get any real police work done. Do you really want the hassle of completing the paperwork for this crap?' She flicked a finger at the paintings. 'In any case, how would we say we came across them? We're not meant to be in here, remember?'

Wallace stood for a while longer, either admiring the replicas, or considering his position on whether they should exist or not.

Meanwhile, Rosie climbed the two steps back to the exit and silently willed him to hurry up.

He was at her side now, following her back to the gardens.

Rosie began to chuckle, a release she needed to abate her morning gloom.

He slammed the door behind them.

'What?' She could see him thinking hard as he ran his glare across the entire horizon.

He shrugged. 'I was just wondering if Mr Carter would have noticed if I'd taken one of those reprints for my lounge. It doesn't look like he's planning to use them.'

She sniffed. 'They're tat. Once this is all over, I'll fly you to London and show you some real art.'

With that, they turned back towards Rosie's car, unaware that on a hill nearby, a killer stood in wait, patiently watching her through a pair of binoculars, knowing that in less than 48 hours, that smile would be wiped from her face.

24.

Grey arrived at Clydeport Vaults an hour after setting off. He'd been dubious about leaving those officers to rake around on his property without him being there. The upshot was he knew he couldn't really stop them when such a heinous crime had taken place on his doorstep. Neither could he be bothered with the hassle of them returning with a warrant. He just wanted them to find what they needed to find and get off his property once and for all.

He'd chosen this vault for his belongings because he knew it wasn't strictly legit. The security was second-to-none and he'd known people who swore by them. No questions, no lies. After going through security, he was escorted to a small white chamber where he keyed in his six-digit code, went through a retinal check and waited for his security box to travel through the vault.

He took the envelope from inside the bag, fingered the wad of notes and prepared to add it to his amassing fortune. Finally, the box was lowered by an electronic arm onto the table. He pulled the latch back and forth three times with one hand, placing his fingerprint on the front of the box with his other. It clicked open, his gut juddering at the excitement of it all. He'd gotten by before on shady deals that brought in enough money to pay off his flat in Glasgow and afford nice cars. Only when news came through of his parents' small trust fund for him, was he able to really escalate himself.

He took out the passport from inside the box. An insurance policy. Once the money from the trust fund came through, he'd tied it all up in buying the hotel. It wasn't enough for what he really wanted to do. That's where the opportunity of investors became apparent. Grey hadn't needed more than one though. His investor had quickly stepped forward with the complete payday. The man had been so enthusiastic about Grey's ideas, was almost willing to write him a blank cheque that Grey had almost felt guilty taking his money. The pride before the fall.

He pushed the passport to the side, grabbed for the black fabric bag and poured the new cash into the existing pile. There was no time now to count it but, from memory Grey imagined there was more than three quarters of a million pound in there. Last thing in the box was a deed for the original Mercury Drop painting. The fake was hanging in his office, so close to the source that the only person who would know the difference would be an art curator. Or, so he believed.

The final sale of his flat in Glasgow was also due to go through. He'd had it on the market for almost three months and saw all initial interest wane very quickly. Then, suddenly, last week an offer for the asking price came through. Grey felt excited to know that everything he'd worked towards was now coming into play. The deep-rooted sadness wouldn't allow him to completely celebrate.

Once he'd completed the stash away, Grey pushed a red button at the side of the table and watched as the box locked itself, the metallic arm took it and swiped it away out of reach. His nest egg was safe for now. He felt giddy at the thought of it growing and one day retiring to somewhere warm. There would be nobody to share it with. Not now that his dreams with Debra had quite literally died. He wouldn't put himself through that again.

Grey put his sunglasses on, re-joined the security

man and began his ascent back to the main entrance of the vault. Once upon a time, he might have felt intimidated in such a place but, today he simply felt liberated. As he returned to his car, Grey once more had a flash of that body hanging a few nights before. He rarely felt affected by death, except for Debra's death a few months before. That had really stuck with him though. He knew he had to put it out of his mind. He turned the engine over and prepared the hour-long drive back to Achray.

*

The sky had finally turned blue at the tip of the morning. Dave could only just make it out from the inside of the broken hatch window. He wondered where the kidnapper was. He'd been given half a sandwich and a glass of water the night before but so far, nothing was forthcoming that morning. He was sure he'd heard the kidnapper leave early doors.

'If he doesn't come soon and feed us, I think I'll start to eat my fingers and work my way up,' said Lizzie, rolling her eyes as she tossed back her hair.

Dave wasn't in so much pain now. He felt as comfortable as he would expect to feel but the knot in his stomach was relentless. He'd been laying in silence, thinking of the family that he and Lizzie might never have now. There was already a little girl absent from their lives. Now there would be nobody to tell about their big sister who was in the arms of the angels. The thought both sickened and devastated him in equal measures. He quietly wept but, just as had been the case all those months before, turned away so Lizzie wouldn't know.

'Do you think it'll happen today?'

With that, they heard the loft door open and the kidnapper clamoured up the stairs, two at a time with a tray in hand.

Dave wasn't sure if he'd spoken out loud or had managed to keep the thought to himself, but he was almost grateful for the arrival of the food.

The kidnapper dropped a plate of soggy toast on both beds and pulled at the balaclava. 'Must be scary wondering if this is your last meal,' said the young man.

Lizzie simply scowled and picked up a slice of the toast.

On the other side of the loft, Dave was in no mood for small talk. Nor was he ready to antagonise his captor. It was clear to him, just from looking at the young man's red angry eyes that he could turn at any moment. He wanted a fighting chance of surviving.

Lizzie finished the first piece of toast and flipped her head. 'Who's Larry?'

Dave flashed her a grimace, but she wasn't looking at him. She was looking defiantly at their kidnapper, willing him to answer, or react.

The kidnapper's eyes narrowed into fierce slits, his shoulders rising until he looked like he might grab her from the bed and throw smash her into the wall.

Dave shifted into a rigid sitting position.

As Lizzie licked her lips, almost smirking, the kidnapper hunched towards her. 'I can tell you all the details, but I don't think you'd sleep for a month. If you live that long.'

Lizzie bowed her head momentarily. Then, she began to laugh. It was the first time Dave had seen her laugh properly in months, heartily shaking with merriment that completely shifted the axis on the atmosphere in the loft.

'What are you laughing at?' His voice was an

angry whisper, rising only as he finished his question.

'I'm laughing at you and how pathetic you are. You really want us to believe you're going to kill us? If you were, you'd already have done it by now.'

Dave felt the urgency race to his chest. He suspected the kidnapper might turn on Lizzie now that she had tested his patience. There was nothing Dave could do. He was too far across the loft to be able to pull the kidnapper back if he did launch at Lizzie. He felt helpless.

Suddenly, the kidnapper grabbed the plate from the bed, smashed it against the wall over Lizzie's head and watched her scream as the fragments fell on top of her. Then, without giving her a second to compose herself, he grabbed her by the back of the hair, pulled her to him and pressed the last broken quarter of the plate to her throat. 'You think I couldn't kill you right here? I've shown a lot of patience with you two. Other's haven't been so lucky.'

Lizzie was shaking ferociously.

He threw her onto the bed and pulled out his phone. 'If you think this as bad as it gets, you might want to consider yourself lucky you're not one of these guys.'

Dave watched as the kidnapper scrolled through photos on his screen, though Dave couldn't tell what he was showing Lizzie.

Lizzie's face twisted, horror filling her eyes and her lip beginning to quiver. She brought her hand to her mouth and bit down on the side of her fist. She was sobbing quietly.

'What is it? What are you showing her?'

The kidnapper simply snickered.

Dave became more frantic as he saw his wife

meltdown before his eyes. 'What is it?' He was kneeling now, the metal cutting into his ankle. 'What the fuck are you doing?'

The kidnapped kicked the remaining pieces of toast on the floor to his side and then began his departure. 'Just remember, the only reason you two aren't dead is because someone wants you alive. That doesn't mean I can't be pushed.'

When he was gone, Dave turned to Lizzie, still weeping on the corner of the steel bed. 'What did he show you?'

She looked up, desperately trying to compose herself and shook her head. 'We've got to find a way out of here. He's a psychopath and if we don't get ourselves out, you don't want to know what he'll do to us.'

25.

The drive to Barlinnie Prison took them slightly longer than expected. Rosie was in the passenger's seat, thankful when they'd finally left behind the country roads and moved onto the motorway. If ever there was a driver who should never come off the motorway, it was Kevin Wallace. She wasn't sure when she finally relaxed but it must have been noticeable to him because he stuck on the CD and started tapping along with the music on his steering wheel.

'Springsteen? I know we're getting on a bit, but this is proper old school.'

'Are you joking,' he said, mocking offence. 'The guy's a legend. You mean you don't love Born to Run?'

She stared at the road ahead, sun flap down just enough to allow her to see straight. 'I'm more of a Mancunian indie girl. I loved all the Britpop stuff through the nineties. I don't mind Bruce Springsteen, but I don't know if he's one I'd be throwing my knickers at.'

He laughed. 'I never say never.'

The prison was less imposing than she expected. On a bright day, the front looked more like the entry into a football stadium. 'Hard to believe some of our worst criminals are housed here.'

Detective Wallace crinkled his nose. 'It's not really. The façade of the building really is that. Once you're inside, it's every bit as bad as you would imagine. They're actually moving many of the more serious crimes to Greenock now.'

'I'm not looking forward to this. I wonder if he's like Brian in any way.'

'I doubt it,' said Wallace. 'Still, he's lost his brother. Losing your parents is bad enough but I think losing a sibling sort of makes you aware of your own mortality.'

Rosie turned to him and saw the shadow of sadness pass his face. She could only imagine what other painful things he had endured in his life. Who was this man who, at first looked like a pampered rugby player but transpired to be a hulking shell of compassion and empathy?

Once parked, they both departed the car and Rosie prepared herself for her first visit into a Scottish prison. She wasn't sure why she'd expect them to be any different. A prison was a prison, after all. Yet, there was something about Barlinnie that forged a reputation that couldn't be ignored.

She took a deep lungful of air. Just in case. Perhaps the air would be so oppressive in there that it might be a while before she would intake clean fresh air again. Stupid thought, she muttered to herself and began the short walk into the reception area.

*

James Houston's eyes looked empty, like the life had been drained from them. He wasn't at all what Rosie or Kevin had expected. In fact, he was much older looking than Brian, despite being only two years older. His grey hair was cropped and receding, his skin freckled with lines that rather implied he must have had a hard life of drugs and alcohol.

He had Brian's eyes. Or moreover, Brian had the same eyes as him, though James' face was more pinched looking. He looked like the sort of man who might instigate a fierce bar brawl and then disappear to the toilet as everyone ripped into each other. Even before he sat down, Rosie had already taken a dislike to him. She scolded herself for being so quick to judge.

'I'm sorry about Brian. We were all very fond of him,' she offered, hoping that he would want to co-operate.

His voice, when it finally escaped, was more of a drone than she would have expected. It was clear Brian was the bright one in the family. Was it cruel of her to wonder if the wrong brother had been killed? Words she would never outwardly voice.

'I don't know what you think I can tell you,' he said, the nasal quality of his voice already setting Rosie's teeth on edge.

'You'd be amazed,' she replied, placing a Dictaphone on the table. 'The governor has given me permission to record the interview today. Are you okay with that, James?'

'Jim,' he said, absently.

Rosie took the correction as an affirmation that she was fine to go ahead. 'When did you last speak to Brian?'

He pursed his thin lips. 'Couple of months ago.'

'Were you close?'

'Sometimes. Sometimes not.'

Detective Wallace rubbed his hands together. 'Did he often visit?'

Jim shook his head. 'We were never THAT close.'

'How often would you say he came to see you then?'

Another shrug.

Rosie looked round the room and saw triangular set ups of orange tables and blue fabric seats. It was the most pleasant she could have expected for a prison visitor room. They'd been given full access to it until such times as other visitors arrived. 'What did he think of what you did?'

'What do you think? He was a pig. Not going to open the champers, is he?'

She startled at the sudden expression in his voice, though it only further sounded like he was closing his nostrils.

'Jim, I'm going to be blunt because your brother isn't the only victim we're now looking into the death of.' Detective Wallace was leaning forward, waving his hand in persuasion. 'Did your brother bring you drugs?'

'What?'

Rosie could see the expression in Jim's face. His eyes, grey and watery now, suddenly came to life in amusement.

'Brian was as square as a dice. I don't think he has ever smoked a joint. You're barking up the wrong tree, pal.' He paused, biting back whatever emotion might be ready to flood. 'Did you even meet my brother? You wouldn't even need to ask that if you knew him.' He was glaring now.

Rosie quickly stepped in. 'The reason we're asking is we think Brian was being blackmailed by whoever may have killed him. I can imagine you'd want to get justice for him.'

Jim's face softened. 'Too bloody right. You better not hope they put the fucker in here though. Police killers usually get a standing ovation. Not this time. The best he can hope for is that you lot shoot him dead in the street. It'll be nothing to what I'll do to him when I get my hands on him.'

Rosie surmised that Jim had been watching too many police shows on TV. His grip on reality, considering the length of his charge sheet, seemed a little skewered.

'Honest to god,' he said, spitting on his hand and raising it to the side of his head. 'He never brought me a thing. I had a fight even asking him to bring me chocolate.'

Moving in a different direction, Rosie began to play nervously with her fingers. 'Do you know anyone who would want to hurt Brian?'

'Not on your life. He was the most popular kid in our school. Mum always said if he fell out the window, he'd float up the way. A total hit with the girls, even though he was a bit goofy looking.' There was an urge to laugh in there, as if he were reliving a moment with both Brian and his late mother. It was gone and replaced with haunting regret.

'I can imagine that,' she said, softly.

'You knew him?'

Rosie smiled, the offer of comfort to a man she already disliked. 'Very well, actually. He and Gaby have really looked after me since I moved up from London. You don't find many people like them.'

A flash of guilt spread across Jim's face. 'Gaby. What about her? Is she coping?'

She wasn't sure how much she could say. It was obvious there was no love loss there on Gaby's side. 'Muddling on,' she said, as honestly as she could.

When the interview was terminated, Jim stood and finally showed a flicker of real emotion. 'He was the best wee brother a guy could ask for. Didn't matter how many times I punched him in the face, or stole his pocket money, or his bird, he'd always stick up for me.' He turned quickly, moving his face out of their eyeline. He wiped his nose with the edge of his sleeve and finally turned back. 'I meant what I said. You better not send his killer here. I'll spend the rest of my life in here for murdering the bastard.'

Strangely, Rosie could understand. There was a tiny piece of her who would happily lock herself in a room with the killer. She wasn't sure he would come out of that set up alive either. Still, that wasn't the real thought on her mind as she waved goodbye to Jim Houston, hopefully for the first and last time. There was still the question of her own fate. Not to mention the niggling doubt that she didn't know Brian and Gaby as well as she thought.

'What did you think?'

'I think he's telling the truth.'

'Is that because it's what you want to believe?'

She glanced across at him and wondered if he would forgive her for punching him in the face. 'It's because I knew Brian. He was a man of honour. Unlike his obnoxious brother.' She pointed a thumb at Jim, who was almost out of sight. They both began the walk back to the car in silence.

There was something Rosie was missing though. Why was Brian being blackmailed if he didn't commit the act he was accused of? She had received a similar threat, though it was still unclear what they wanted, and she knew her photos were genuine and of something that had really taken place. It didn't make sense. And if Brian hadn't done what the killer had said, why did he go to meet them? Wouldn't he just have handed the envelope over to the police in the first place? She didn't know James Houston, but she knew people well enough to detect a liar. He had nothing to gain by lying. So, why was her friend meeting a killer in the middle of the night at a remote hotel? It was something she feared she might never know.

26.

Adam stared out the window of the bar. No matter the time of day, Argyle Street was always the hub of movement. From the street buskers to the beggars, from the throngs of shoppers to the officer workers, from the drinkers to the diners; there was never a shortage of introverted movement. He threw back the last of a pint of Guinness, reassuring himself it was never too early in the day for a widower to start. He ordered another, tried not to go into that place where everything became about Debra. After all, there was still Gracie to think about.

The party was tomorrow. He'd thought long and hard, weighed up the pros and cons of going. He had never been a match for Grey. That's why he'd always been so keen to keep him in his corner. Keep your friends closer, your enemies closer, or something like that. It was a friendship born of pity, though it wasn't clear now who was to be pitied more.

Grey had come from a loveless family. His parents were moderately wealthy, fanning their friends with their apparent wealth whilst crediting everything to plastic. Still, they'd left some money for Grey in a trust fund that he got when he was thirty. Prior to that, most of what he had was ill-gotten gains; drug running, beating debts out of people, teetering on the narrow tightrope between what was legal and what wasn't. He had no-one but Adam and he appeared to like it that way.

Adam, on the other hand came from a stable family. The worst thing he could say about his upbringing was that his mother was overbearing. She ruled the roost with an iron fist. His father was the provider, whilst his mother managed just about every other elements of their lives. She had ensured to be popular through playgroups, youth groups, the boys brigade and seemed aggrieved when her boys grew up and deprived her of her social gatherings. Still, she'd been a loving mother who'd wanted the best for her boys.

Taking another gulp of his drink, Adam could feel it start to hit his head. It only made him ponder everything more. The years of endurance at the hands of bullies that Grey had eventually saved him from. The friendship that could have dragged him down a darker path if Grey hadn't wanted to keep Adam as that one constant light in his life. Now, this latest revelation that Grey had violated his wife. He wasn't sure anymore though. Only two people were there. It was so confusing, and Adam didn't know what to believe now. Why had the police still been investigating Debra's death ten weeks later? Why was the female detective who was originally dealing with it removed? His head was becoming fogged, though he never lost sight of the weapon hidden deep in his pocket. Could anyone see its shape, he wondered?

The drunker he became, the more he muttered to himself.

'I think you've had enough, mate,' said the barman, quietly when he tried to order another one.

'I'm not even halfway drunk,' he roared, drawing attention to himself as he slapped his hands on the bar. 'Give me another.'

The barman refused, eyeing the clock that said it was just after two p.m.

Adam turned and realised several disapproving faces were staring at him. An elderly couple eating a steak in one corner shook their heads and then retreated into their interrupted conversation. A young male couple seemed desperate to show they were minding their own business as Adam continued to mutter to himself and stagger away from the bar. Finally, it was a middle-aged woman the same height as him who slipped her arm into his.

'Come on, sweetheart. Let's see if we can get you into a taxi.'

Adam threw his head back and felt it turn. 'She was the most beautiful girl I'd ever seen,' he cried!

She was taking him through the double doors onto the street now. 'We all want some handsome fellow to say that about us. I'm sure she'll come around, sweetheart. Come on, I'll try and get one of the drivers to take you.'

'You're beautiful,' he whispered.

She laughed, a throaty forty-a-day cackle. 'Aye, twenty-five years ago. Your mother's probably younger than me. Anyway, I thought you had a beautiful girl.'

He pulled away from her and slumped onto a stone step a few yards out of the Helium's Umbrella. 'Had,' he whimpered, pushing his head against a terracotta wall. 'Had, had, had,' he sang, conducting with his index finger.

'You really are in a bad way, aren't you? Listen, we've all been through it.'

He looked up and smiled through his tears. 'Everybody? Your wife was murdered by a rapist?'

The woman's shock was evident even to him, despite how intoxicated he was. She was joining him on the step now. 'You poor thing,' she whispered, her face now distorted by her over-eager attempt at sympathy.

The anguish that had been bubbling in him suddenly felt fit to explode. He'd been so angry at

Debra all these weeks, his rage far outweighing any grief he'd felt for her. Now, there was nothing but the energy-sapping urge to lay down and die. He began to shake uncontrollably, sobs escaping him in bursts as his face became immersed in his sadness.

The woman stroked his hair. 'Have you family who are helping you?'

He was unable to speak now. He was completely choked up by the grief for Debra. He wiped away snot and nodded his head.

'Good,' she said, slapping him on the leg. 'Let's get you in that taxi. You get home to your family, have a good proper sober cry, love. That's the only thing that will get you through it.'

Adam attempted to pull himself together. He saw the woman move aside to let him leave. He would have thanked her properly, but he suddenly felt rather stupid. Instead, he simply gave her an awkward salute with his hand and began towards the taxi rank. He needed to pull himself together or he'd be forced to walk home.

As he sat in the back of the cab and watched the centre of Glasgow disappear, the river Clyde snake up through the outskirts and the tower blocks of the southside appear, he felt a little more composed. He'd had his cry. Now, he had to see his daughter. Just in case it was the last time.

27.

'So, this is Glasgow city centre?'

Rosie and Kevin were sitting on the balcony in Princess Square, chewing down on a club sandwich and sipping coffee.

'The one and only. I can't believe you've been in Scotland for more than six months and you've never driven down to Glasgow.'

She blew into her mug and then took a sip. 'I've been in Glasgow when I had to speak to Debra Mullen's husband. I've just not seen any of the sights or been to the city centre. Although, I'm from London. It's difficult to be impressed by a city that's this much smaller.'

'Ah, but you'll not get to enjoy the Glaswegian humour in London,' he said, emphatically.

'Or this amazing view. Is it all shops?'

'Some eateries as well,' he replied. 'Sometimes at night, they have a piano player down there. It's awfully classy, you know.'

She chortled and took a bite of her sandwich.

'Do you know, I'm completely stumped with this case. We have no motive, no evidence, no weapon and no witnesses. There isn't even anything to suggest that Brian knew the paramedics.'

Rosie had still been thinking about her own envelope, wondering whether to tell Kevin or her superiors. She thought about the moment she would be exposed. She'd go through all that again, the cataclysm of distress, humiliation and emotional abuse that she'd endured. Maybe they'd be different here. Wallace seemed decent. On the other hand, maybe they'd be just like every other man who thought she'd asked for it, called her a slut just out of ear shot, or giggled like a schoolboy when the photos were discovered all over the walls of the male toilets.

'You okay?'

She looked up and realised she must have been idling.

'You looked a million miles away.'

'I was just thinking,' she confessed. 'So, Jim Houston doesn't know anything about drugs or his brother smuggling them into him. However, the killer had something on Brian that allowed him to feel threatened enough to go meet them.'

'The slashing wasn't part of the plan,' offered Wallace.

'I've been thinking that all along.'

'You saw how frenzied it was. That's the act of someone who has worked themselves into a rage. The hanging was planned. You don't ask to meet someone to talk and turn up with a rope in your hand to hang them with.'

'So, we know that he died as a result of the hanging. The knife attack was merely to inflict as much pain as possible. A cruel afterthought probably. It didn't look as frenzied on Kyle or Ricky. You'll notice how similar there's was. Almost like it was part of a method. I think the killer must have enjoyed that part of it so much that he made it his MO.'

'What about the rash on all of their eyelids?'

'The pathologist said that's a response to the hanging. Essentially they're being strangled of breath when hanging so it'll cause that sort of redness on the lids of their eyes.'

Wallace was scribbling on his notepad now. 'Was there any sign of a struggle? Brian, at the very least would have known some self-defence. We're taught that at the academy.'

'Mike said there are signs of trauma but that's obvious from what they would have endured.' She still couldn't equate Brian's death, or anything she was learning with the man she'd worked with and befriended over the past six months. Perhaps a lesson to be careful who you trust. 'There was nothing under the fingernails to suggest they'd fought back. I'd say they were all caught by surprise.'

'What about the ropes?'

'They're with the lab, along with some of the fibres we found at both crime scenes. At first glance, they look a lot like the ones you can buy from DIY shops. They'll sell them by the dozen so actually getting information at point of sale might be very difficult. Once we catch the killer, and we're able to get transaction details from them, we might be able to get that into evidence.'

Wallace was staring past her.

As she continued, Rosie finished the last bite of her sandwich and washed it down with the last of her coffee. 'I think we should be focusing on whatever linked Brian, myself and the two paramedics.'

He turned to her sharply. 'Why you?'

Rosie realised what she'd said. Her stupid mouth had run away with itself. 'Did I say me? I just meant because I worked with Brian and now, I'm just worried that the link may include me.

Wallace seemed satisfied with her answer and shifted his focus away from her.

Rosie's eyes followed. 'What are you staring at?'

'That man over there. Is he taking pictures of us?'

A few days ago, Rosie might have laughed. However, she was still convinced she was being watched and that suspicion had unsettled her so much that she almost instinctively jumped out of her seat. 'Pay the bill and let's go.'

He eyeballed her. 'It's probably nothing. He might just be photographing the architecture of the building.'

'No,' she said, quietly. 'I think you might have been right the first time.' When she turned back though, the photographer was gone. She scolded herself very quickly for allowing panic to overcome her.

Kevin was throwing a twenty-pound note on to the table as the waitress approached.

'Everything okay for you both?'

Wallace smiled. 'Absolutely. Keep the change.' He trailed Rosie out towards the escalator.

She was staring at the descending lift where the photographer now travelled. 'I think he's following me. I know him from somewhere.'

'What?'

Did it sound as ridiculous to him as it did to her, she wondered? Maybe it was time the truth came out. There was only so long she could keep it to herself. Finally, standing beside him on the escalator, she turned to meet him face to face. 'I think I'm being watched. Not just today, but for the last few weeks. I know I sound paranoid, and everything that's going on probably makes me feel that way but I'm certain of it. I'm certain I saw someone at my back fence the other night. Just staring in. I was about to get undressed for bed. As I was closing the curtains, he was right there.'

'Shit, why didn't you phone for help?'

She snorted at how ridiculous she felt. If it had been any other female, anyone else in fact, she would have been reading them the riot act for not reporting it. 'I wasn't sure. It's so dark out in those woods that I simply didn't know if I was imagining it.'

'You seem like an instinctive person,' said Wallace. 'I reckon you should trust your own gut. If you think someone is following you, I don't believe you're being paranoid.'

She wanted so badly to tell him about the envelope. The words were right there in her mind, ready to float out and relieve her of the growing anxiety. Yet, she couldn't. The hooded man with the camera was gone. She'd only caught a glimpse of him. Not long enough to really recognise him or place where she thought she'd seen him before. He might have an every-man face, she mused. There were lots of people like that. Yet, nothing would settle her nerves now. There had been too many instances.

Rosie followed Kevin to the car in silence, keeping a keen eye on everyone around her. Even though the photographer was gone, she couldn't help but wonder if he wasn't just hiding in the crowd, snapping frantically and furthering his portfolio of her. The thought made her skin crawl. As soon as they reached his car, she climbed in quickly and made sure she locked the door on her side.

28.

They were on their way to Grey Carter's old flat when Gaby phoned. Rosie quickly moved into an alcove by a bar to allow herself to hear. 'Gaby, everything okay?'

'I need to tell you something that I should have told you. What they said about Brian,' she paused, as if looking for the best way to say it. 'It's true what he was accused of.'

'What?'

Gaby sniffed and it sounded like she was crying.

'Gaby, how do you know it's true? Did Brian tell you?'

'In a way. I found the drugs in his pocket. I asked him why he had them. At first he said he'd arrested someone for possession and forgot to check it into evidence.'

Rosie pushed the palm of her hand against her forehead, silently slapping it with frustration. 'Was it for his brother?'

'Sort of,' said Gaby, cryptically. 'It was to protect his brother, but Jim doesn't know anything about it.

Rosie believed her because she knew Jim wasn't one of Gaby's favourite people so she didn't expect she would lie for him. Not now that she was telling the truth.

'Please tell me you'll keep this to yourself. My husband would never break the law unless he absolutely had to. Someone was threatening Jim's life. That's why he did it.'

'Who was he smuggling it into?'

Gaby paused for a moment. 'I genuinely don't know. He never told me. Only that the person was very dangerous, and that Jim would be in real trouble if he didn't get it in.'

'Bloody hell. Didn't he realise it wouldn't have stopped there. If Brian hadn't died, this person would have had him over a barrel for as long as Jim was in that prison.'

'Please don't judge him,' pleaded Gaby.

Rosie wasn't judging him. At least one of her questions were answered now. 'Look, I have to go. I'll call you later. I'm still in Glasgow now.'

She hung up and watched Wallace walk towards her.

'That's us parked. We've got an hour to speak to the concierge at Grey's place.'

*

The concierge at the block of flats immediately greeted them and asked them who they were here to see. His face dropped when Wallace pulled his badge out and introduced himself.

'We're here about Grey Carter. I believe he's one of the residents who live here.'

'He was. Not anymore.'

Rosie went into her phone and started searching for a picture of Grey. As she scrolled through, she spoke again. 'Are you sure we're talking about the same person. He would have been here a few nights ago.'

'You don't forget a character like Grey. Handsome young fella, cropped hair, bit of a hit with the ladies. Good tipper as well.'

Rosie smirked. Were there any eyes that Grey couldn't pull the wool over? 'This is him, here. Definitely the same guy?' She held up the picture she'd found of Grey on social media.

'That's him. Definitely. Sold the flat I think about a month ago. New girl just moved in there this week.'

'And he definitely wasn't here a few nights ago?'

'As I said, his flat is sold. I doubt he'd be here unless he was sleeping on the stairs.'

Rosie realised they'd been lied to by Grey. Was there anyone who was telling her the truth anymore? She pulled on Wallace's sleeve. 'Come on, let's go. I think we're barking up the wrong tree here.' With that, she fumed out onto the street and stormed towards the car park.

Wallace struggled to keep up with her but eventually caught up to her as she approached his car.

She pushed her face down onto the bonnet of the car. 'I can't keep the facts straight in my head anymore. I'm honestly completely lost.' She bit on her lip, one last attempt to retain some composure. It wasn't working.

Wallace put his large arm round her, pulled her closer and gave her a gentle pat. 'You know what it's like when you're investigating something like this. Perhaps you should have told the chief how close you'd gotten to Brian.'

If only he knew exactly what was going through her mind. Investigating the death of a friend was enough of a mind twister. Knowing that you were possibly next played with a person's psychology in ways that she might never have imagined. Every person was a suspect to her now. Even Wallace. As stupid as she knew that was. She fastened her seatbelt, prepared for the rally race to the village and warded off his need to make her feel better with incessant chat. She didn't want to talk now. She just wanted silence.

29

Gaby phoned screaming. She was certain someone had been in her house. She was with the next-door neighbour, coddling her equally stressed baby and resisting any comfort being offered in person or over the phone.

'You need to calm down,' urged Rosie. She, and Wallace were not far from Achray now, the car speeding into the red sky of folding clouds and him throttling down on the accelerator as if he was campaigning for rally driver of the year. 'I'm just on my way back. We'll come straight to yours. Who is with you?'

'Mrs Blyth next door. I'm in her house,' she said, through panicked breaths. 'I can't go back there. What if Brian's killer is after me now? What if he hurts my baby?'

'Nobody is going to hurt you, sweetheart,' promised Rosie, soothingly. 'We didn't know Brian was in danger, or we might have been able to save him. Now that we know someone is out there and could potentially harm any one of us, we're on our guard. I'll come and stay with you tonight. Detective Wallace will come and check in with us. Everything is going to be alright.'

Gaby paused, as if she might be discussing it with herself.

'If anyone wants to hurt either of you, they'll have to go through me and Kevin. He's built like a brickhouse and I'm hurtling into the menopause. Believe me, he'd have no chance.'

Finally, Gaby sighed. 'Alright, but I'm not going back home until you get here. Is that okay, Mrs Blyth. Are you okay with me waiting here until my friend gets here?'

An inaudible muttering broke the silence at the other end, and it sounded like the neighbour had agreed.

'Okay, my neighbour said we can wait here. You won't be long, will you?' An increase in her already rapid breathing.

'I'm on my way right now. Sat nav says we're about half an hour away from the village, another five minutes until I get to yours so ask Mrs Blyth to make you a nice warm cup of black tea, sit yourself down and let her have a hold of the baby. I promise, you've got nothing to worry about.'

*

One more day. That's all he had to wait. He wasn't sure that he could wait until then when he already held the fate of two of them in his hands. Couldn't he just take the man and hang him from the roof of Detective Cooper's house. After all, it was him who had started all of this.

He was looking at the photos. They'd come through a few minutes ago. Detective Cooper had been to the prison and then she'd been for lunch with her other detective friend. Where would they be headed now? Their field trip was bound to conjure up some sort of information they could use. Or maybe they'd come back as fruitless as they'd left.

The rats in the loft had been bickering. There were tears, mostly hers as she ran through the potential recriminations. The man still swore he didn't know what he'd done. It was likely he didn't but that didn't make any difference to the outcome. His confession wasn't essential to what they had planned.

Larry entered the room at the back of his

shoulder. 'Enjoying yourself, my voyeuristic little brother?'

'Younger by an hour,' he replied angrily. 'Remember that, big brother,' he continued, emphatically.

'You're thinking about killing him, aren't you? Can't even wait one more day.'

'You really think you know my every thought. Maybe he'll watch her die first. Then, I can deal with him.'

Larry tusked. 'I don't think the plan was to murder anybody in the first place. I think you've gone off the rails and I'm just along for the ride.'

'If you don't like it, get off.'

'And leave them at the mercy of your wicked temper. No! I'll stay and make sure that everything goes according to the plan. Anyway, you need me. I know you don't think it but where would you be if I wasn't around to keep you on the straight and narrow.'

The killer rose in anger, slamming the seat into the back wall. 'You're so stupid, Larry. Do you think that when this is all over, that the kind detective will shake our hand and let us walk away? I've murdered three men. I'm going to have to kill again if I'm to keep our identities secret. You think you're here to protect me. It's me who is protecting you.'

Larry whistled, then smirked. 'It seems I've touched a nerve.' With that, he sauntered out of sight.

30.

Grey smoothed down his silk grey shirt and caught a glimpse of himself in the mirror. In the shadow of blistering sunlight, he couldn't quite see the hard edge that his face had taken in recent years. All he could see was those baby blue eyes cocooned inside the bronzed chiselled face.

He thought of his parents again. Whenever he was faced with death of any sort, they came to mind. He hadn't liked his father very much. He was a stern man, keen to assert his authority, be it with his booming voice or his leather belt. His mother, who he liked only a smidgeon more, had been a cold expressionless woman. She'd been beautiful; a trophy on his ordinary looking father's arm. Yet, his father hadn't respected her. Which is where she must have gotten her hardened streak. Grey himself had gotten his mother's looks and coldness, yet also knew he'd gotten his father's brutal cruelness. The worst of both parents. Perhaps its why he had seduced Debra despite his love for Adam. Just because he could.

The painting hung in his eyeline. Grey didn't often feel cocky in his cleverness. He'd been smart as a whip for as long as he could recall. It's how he eventually evaded his father's beatings, coped with his mother's lack of love and eventually became street smart. He never commended himself for managing through all of that. Nor did he give himself a pat on the back when he burned the family house to the ground with his parents sleeping inside. A gas explosion the investigators decided. A run of luck for traumatised little Grey; teenage heartthrob and psycho in the making.

Of course, Grey wasn't a psycho. His father was.

Grey was just a little bad, the full shilling with a score to settle. He would have saved his mother if she had been better, but she'd been so encompassed by her own self-interest that she'd barely noticed the light dying in her son's beautiful eyes. No regard for his increasingly sullen behaviour or the distance that had grown between them. She'd carried on draping herself in designer clothes and jewels that his father only approved of because it gave him a more respectable standing in the community. If only everyone had known the truth.

After their deaths, the Carters had become martyr's. Rich givers to charity who had loved their lovely son, now orphaned and wayward because he didn't have his responsible parents to guide him anymore. The doors were quickly opened to Grey, every home offering to give him a proper family. He was like a stray dog; cute and cuddly, big eager eyes begging for somewhere to be. Until he bit. And Grey liked to bite. Slowly, the doors closed in his face and he was left out in the world all alone. No house, no family and no money until everything was sorted out. It was a stipulation of his father's, no doubt that he'd have to wait for the money until a responsible age. Even in death, the old bastard was controlling him.

How the worm had turned.

Grey didn't need the hotel now. He suspected he had enough to disappear to a warm island somewhere and set up a bar. Or go live with the rich people and multiply his fortune somewhere exotic. Yet, he loved this hotel. It had given him hope in the past months and now it was finally going to open its doors to a throng of eager customers.

He blew into the cool Spring air and moved his thoughts along to Detective Houston. He wondered momentarily about the young wife and the baby. Maybe he would set up some crowdfunding site, donate a token himself and take away some of the worry of paying for a funeral. That might make him feel better about not saying anything of what he saw. Yet, he didn't want to bring attention to himself. Perhaps he should just stay out of it. He didn't need that kind of attention right now.

Grey realised he had a lot to feel guilty about recently. The main loss to him was his friendship with Adam. He knew what the police had suggested but he also knew it was nonsense. Everything with Debra had been consensual. Would Adam believe him? He wasn't sure. All he knew was that he wanted to take care of Adam and little Gracie. He was able to help them, but he dared not speak to Adam right now. Maybe one day they'd all be together again and what happened with Debra would be just a distant memory. He would wait for Adam's call for as long as it took to come.

*

Someone else was in the hotel. Grey had sensed it a few times recently. He'd gone in search but found nothing. Until the night of Brian Houston's death where he'd heard angry conversation at the back of the hotel. For months, the place had been eerily quiet, so it was almost amusing to hear someone exchange words.

He'd only been able to watch so much. The savage knife attack was hard for even him to stomach. He'd caught a glimpse of the nastiness behind the attack; the flaring eyes and angry swing. That attack was designed to kill. Grey wasn't putting himself in the firing line. That's why he'd retreated and decided to stay quiet.

Now, though, he was certain someone was here. He was certain he had heard footsteps outside his office. When he opened the door, he imagined a shadow turning a corner though he'd convinced himself since that it was only in his fertile imagination. This was a big lonely hotel. Sometimes, even Grey could feel fear. Especially after witnessing such a horrific murder.

'Hello?'

The only response for the reverb of his own voice. As he passed a set of bay windows, his own reflection lit by a golden lamp he could see the fright in his own face. Maybe he was letting his nerves get the better of him. Opening day was upon him, a murder had almost put paid to that though the police had finally given him access to that part of his grounds again.

Maybe it was time to stop seeing ghosts. If he knew how to feel guilt, he might have suspected his conscience was catching up with him. Grey wasn't a man who had that kind of remorse in him.

Finally, he reached the end of the building, admired how the fake artwork looked along the pale walls and told himself that he was being silly. Nobody was coming for him. No ghosts of the past, no vengeful killers and no mental health crisis to pay him back for all the wrongdoing they might have perceived he'd done.

He turned back, famished and in need of a drink. Soon, he would be sitting down to Salmon and a glass of red. He'd waited long enough for the life he deserved. It was happening and nobody was going to stand in his way. Not even the man who now stood a few feet behind him, murderous intent in his blazing eyes and a score to even that Grey would not see coming.

31.

All the way back Rosie continued to fret over the photos. She wanted to burn them. Build on her firepit, throw them on the coals and watch the embers of her sordid history disintegrate in flames.

The skies were still clear, blazing sun flatlining in the horizon. The promise of a healthy Spring. Yet, even in the pleasant heat, Rosie still felt the Baltic chill on her fair skin.

Brian, never far from mind, was in her thoughts again. How could she judge him now? All he'd done was try to protect his family. Wouldn't she have done the same thing? Sometimes, no matter how a person tried to escape their roots, there was always something pulling them back.

Her blues deepened as they raced towards Gaby's house. Not even the soft lilt of John Denver from the car radio could make her feel better. So, she snapped the radio off, ignored the stare from the driver's seat and snarled at the window.

Rosie would love a glass of chardonnay right now. She thought of the glass sitting on the draining board at home, the half-drunk bottle in the fridge and the comfort of her sofa as she stared into the loch. All those comforts seemed so far away now. Nothing she was doing felt natural, or remotely like living. She was on edge with every single movement she made.

The jingle from her phone rose in volume. An unidentified number. That was new. Her breath recoiled and she wondered if this was her turn to fall prey to the killer. Maybe Brian's torment had started out this way; the photos in the envelope, then the phone calls and finally, death.

'Hello?'

'Detective Cooper. Hello, this is Mike Speirs from the lab.'

She took a deep sigh. 'Mike, hi. What have you got for me?'

He paused for a second. 'We've managed to find some DNA on the rope samples that you sent me. We've also matched some fingerprints.'

Her eyes widened and she waved for Wallace's attention. 'Do you have a name?'

Mike was one of those irritating types who fancied himself a gameshow host. Everything came in bursts of drama, paused silences and the sudden announcement of the information everyone was holding their breath for.

Rosie found herself snarling some more.

'His name is Gary Turner. I don't know anything about who he is or why his fingerprints have shown up on our database. You would need to find out yourself.' He paused again. 'Something else you should know though.'

'Okay?' She grabbed a pen from her pocket.

'We found his fingerprints on items from both your murder crime scenes. But we also found his fingerprints on articles from three other crime scenes.'

'You mean three more murders?'

'No. Not exactly. Three very different crimes in fact. A robbery, a knife attack and a suspected sexual assault.'

'That's strange. Nothing like what we're dealing with here. You sure they're a match?'

His indignation was so apparent she could almost taste it. 'I'm not sure what you're used to Detective. Where we come from, things are done thoroughly. I would not have called you about this if I wasn't confident in my staff's ability.'

'I understand,' she said, feeling amused that she'd ruffled his feathers. 'Well, thank you, Mark.'

'It's Mike.'

'Sure, if you could get that over to me A-SAP, that would be amazing. Thanks again for being so prompt.'

*

'You've really chucked me under the bus. I was looking forward to spending the night on the couch watching the match.'

She looked at Gaby's house and saw the curtains were still drawn. 'Twenty-two man-boys running across a field after a ball. I think you've had a save.' With that, she threw open the door and headed towards the Houston house. 'Will you get us some food?'

Gaby was just emerging from Mrs Blyth's with Eva in her arm.

Rosie threw her arm round Gaby as she approached and walked her to the door. 'Are you alright?' She could tell from Gaby's shaking and the trembling of her lip that nothing was alright at all. She took the keys from her and unlocked the door.

Gaby looked reluctant to go inside, hovering on the porch and eyeing the dark hallway suspiciously.

'Everything's fine. There'll be nobody here, I promise you.' Rosie pointed to the car. 'Look, Detective Wallace is going to be right there. He's not going anywhere; I'm not going anywhere and you're going to be just fine.'

'Everything's not fine,' whispered Gaby, as she followed Rosie into the house. She allowed Rosie to switch on all the lights. The house looked exactly as she had left it. Nothing out of place, nothing taken, no real reason to believe someone had been in the house or watching her.

'What happened to make you think someone was after you?'

'I don't know,' replied Gaby, her eyes still darting round the room. 'After I came off the phone to you earlier, I'm sure I heard someone. We were napping upstairs. I woke up and heard a door closing. I came halfway down the stairs and I'm sure I saw someone staring but when I got to the bottom, there was no-one there.'

'That must have been scary.'

'Terrifying,' admitted Gaby.

'Look, you get yourselves settled. Detective Wallace is going to get us some takeout in a while and I'll put the kettle on. Okay?'

Rosie walked through the door to the kitchen and saw it instantly. A length of rope that had been twisted into a noose. She gasped loudly and stepped back out of the kitchen. Why would the killer choose to target Gaby? How exactly was she involved? She dialled Wallace's number. 'Forget the food. There's something here you need to see.'

32.

Adam arrived at his parents' house just as his mother served up dinner. It was the usual menu with the usual ritual and the only difference at the table was that Gracie brought a little life to it.

'You're just in time for dinner,' said his father, seemingly unfazed by Adam's appearance.

'Jesus wept on all the disciples, what the hell happened to you?'

'Thanks, mum,' he said. 'You always know how to make me feel good about myself.'

'You're as drunk as a monkey. What kind of way is that to show up, knowing your daughter is here?'

'Delia, hush,' said his father, in an uncharacteristic voice of authority.

'Well, mum, she wouldn't know I was drunk if you hadn't decided to announce it, now would she?'

Gracie looked thoughtful. 'Daddy, I didn't know monkeys got drunk.'

'They don't princess. Nana's only joking. Just eat your dinner and then you and I can go upstairs and have a chat.' He could see his father staring at him.

'It's gammon for tea. I know you like that. Do you want some potatoes?'

Adam nodded. He had already felt his hangover kick in halfway along the road after the taxi driver had thrown him out. 'I'm really not that hungry. Besides, I don't want to take anyone's dinner off them.'

Terry bellowed with laughter then. 'Your mother thinks she's feeding the Women's Institution every time she switches on the oven. What you don't eat will go into the garden for her fox friends.'

'You've got fox friends?' Adam found that

amusing considering his mother had near died of terror when he brought a stray cat home once.

'Not exactly friends,' she said, haughtily. 'More like acquaintances. I feed them the leftovers and they don't climb in the window at night and rip out my throat.'

'Exactly,' agreed Terry, when he saw Adam's incredulous expression.

'That's silly, Nana,' said Gracie, squeezing her eyes shut.

Delia looked embarrassed that everyone at the table appeared to be mocking her. So, rather than dish up for everyone else, she served herself and Gracie before slamming the ladle into the bowl. 'Help yourselves. You're both grown men.'

The rest of the meal passed without much conversation. At one point, Adam was sure the room was spinning but he couldn't be sure because when clarity came, the room was perfectly still. Finally, after playing with a small amount of food, he ran to the toilet and vomited. It had been sitting in his stomach ever since he was in the taxi, but he'd managed to keep it settled, even when the driver suspected he wouldn't. Finally, when he'd finished, he went back into the hall and gasped at the sight of a tearful Gracie standing at her bedroom door.

*

'Gracie, I need to talk to you about something,' he said, sitting her on the bed.

She nodded her head in silence, the sadness of losing her mother to heaven a permanent fixture in her eyes.

'You know that I love you, right?'

She nodded again.

'No matter what, that'll never change. So does

mummy. We would both do anything for you. You understand that we'll never leave you. Not fully. No matter where we go in the world, we'll always be here.' He pressed his hand against her heart.

'Are you going away too?' Tears filled her little green eyes, a feature given to her by Debra.

'I hope not,' he said, his own tears beginning to appear. 'But if I ever had to, you know that you'll always have nana and papa and the rest of the family. You understand that, don't you?'

'Please don't go, daddy,' she sobbed.

Adam wondered what a breaking heart felt like. Was it like this now, the ache pulsing through his entire being that he would never see this beautiful gentle child of his again?

'I need to go somewhere to fix something. Something that will make me less sad and then we can get back to the way we used to be.'

'I'll still be sad,' she said, her gaze turning to the sky outside.

'I know you will, princess. But I don't think you'll be sad forever. Mummy wouldn't want that for either of us.' He felt like a hypocrite. All these weeks he couldn't bear to discuss Debra with her. Now he was following his own selfish path, rather than following the advice he was now imposing on Gracie.

'I miss her,' she said, her little lips curling as the full flow of heartbreak began.

Adam couldn't bear to watch her now. He simply took her hand, gave it a tight squeeze and kissed her on the head. 'Don't cry, Gracie. Come on, let's go down to Nana and Papa.' He led her down the stairs, said goodbye to his parents without fuss and then left. He had one more night of sleep before he took on Grey. If he hadn't been so drunk, he might have recognised the utter fear that wormed through him. Instead, he felt a little brave, felt the gun in his inside pocket and walked the five-minute trail back to his own house. This might be the last night he would spend in his marital bed, the last time he'd feel close to Debra and if it was, he wanted to know that he'd made the choice of a man and defended his little family. How could he look his daughter in the face again if he hadn't?

33.

Gaby would be staying at Mrs. Blyth's tonight. It was the best Rosie could arrange at short notice. Gaby's mother had offered to have her stay at the hotel. She would pay for another room for Gaby and Eva. It was more than Gaby could tolerate tonight. Besides, Mrs. Blyth was a tough nut and Rosie was certain that she would do anything to keep Gaby and the baby safe. It was more than she could promise now.

After locking up the house and double checking there were no unlocked windows or doors, Rosie returned to Wallace's car.

'Are you okay? You look whiter than she does.'

Rosie nodded. She didn't feel okay. It was bad enough she was certain that she was in a killer's sights. Now, a young woman and her child might be under threat. What the hell was going on?

They made the drive back to the station in silence. It was an old gothic building that looked more like a church than a police station. It was lit only by the orange of the streetlights and looked more like an ancient psychiatric unit.

Across the road, only Benny's was still open.

'Do you want to get some food now?'

Wallace shook his head. 'That would be good. Do you want to go?'

She got out of the car, jumped at the sound of a dog barking nearby and crossed the small road. Benny was talking to Cammie by the counter, an extroverted re-telling of one of his larger-than-life stories that was wasn't evoking much of a reaction.

'Oh, here she is. The lady of them all.'

Rosie smiled half-heartedly. If only Benny knew what was going on internally; her stomach a tornado of terror, rage and intense stress.

'Are you still working? God, don't you ever take an hour off,' he bellowed.

'With everything that's going on round here, I'll be lucky if I'm not either ready to retire or dead before things calm down.'

Benny began to make her coffee, staring intently at her. 'You're doing the best you can,' he said, a rare moment of seriousness.

'It doesn't feel that way. I feel like everything's escaping me. I came here for peace. To start a new life and get away from the violent streets of London. Three dead bodies in three days and I'm no closer to finding the killer.' She suddenly looked round herself, aware that she shouldn't even be discussing the case.

Benny winked knowingly. Her secrets were safe with him. 'Are you sitting in?'

She looked round the empty tables. 'Aren't you ready to shut? You're completely empty and still open. Why?'

'Lucas isn't home until well after ten tonight. I'd be up in that house, shoving the cats off the sofa and flicking the channels for something decent to watch. I'm as well here. Anyway, young Cammie is about to finish his shift, aren't you?' He leaned forward so as only Rosie would hear him. 'Turns up almost an hour late and doesn't offer to stay back. Oh, what the hell, as you say; we're not busy anyway. So, are you?'

'Am I what?' She curled her upper lip.

'Sitting in,' he repeated, the inflection in his voice rising.

'Oh no,' she laughed. 'Just do a latte for Kev as well, will you? Oh, and I'll take two of these chocolate muffins.'

As she opened her purse, Benny gave her a wave

to close it again. 'On the house. For all you're doing for our community. If you weren't working so hard, I wouldn't feel safe in my own house.'

She thanked him, dropped the muffins into her pocket and grabbed the coffees. 'Get home safe, Benny. You too, Cammie,' and with that she was heading back across the street to the station, still unable to appease the nagging hurl in her gut.

*

Wallace was on the phone when she reached her desk. He was scribbling something down on paper.

Rosie placed the cup holder with the two coffees onto the desk and fished the muffins from her pocket. She was so busy biting into one of them that she wasn't aware of Wallace trying to get her attention.

She looked at her own pencilled notes beside the keyboard and started to read them to herself. She did that often because maybe one of these days, a penny would drop, and she would suddenly have a clue that she didn't even know was in there. 'Three dead bodies. All hanged. All assaulted with a sharp weapon, probably a machete or large knife. All worked in one capacity or another for the emergency services. Possibly met at more than one emergency but haven't had a chance to cross-reference them yet. No witnesses. Is the killer local?'

Wallace slapped on his desk a couple of times. As Rosie looked up, he was beckoning for her with his finger.

She frowned, walked towards his computer and saw he had an image of a young red headed man on his screen. Looking closer, Rosie saw that his name was Gary Turner and that Wallace had already received the results of the search on the national fingerprint database. A surge of impatience as she indicated for him to wind his call up. She wanted into his seat now, desperate to get a look at their potential killer. She wondered what this Gary Turner would have against her personally. There was nothing about him that she recognised. Didn't appear to be any crime against his name. On the surface, it looked like he'd been previously clean. So, why were his fingerprints on the database at all?

Finally, Wallace ended his phone call and pulled away from his desk to allow her a proper view.

'So, this is Gary Turner?'

'The one and only. Look like a killer to you?'

Rosie clenched her mouth. 'What do they look like?'

Wallace threw his hands up. 'Well, think of the height and body build of our three victims. They weren't my build, but they weren't weedy either. This guy looks like he weighs about nine stone?'

'Some of our most prolific serial killers look like they needed a plate of mince.'

'Well, he's not our guy,' said Wallace.

Rosie was taken aback, shocked by his certainty. 'We don't know that.'

'Yes, we do.' Wallace stood and held up his phone. 'That was the lab on the phone there. They've made one almighty cock-up.'

Rosie drew her eyes from the red head on the screen to her colleague.

'Gary Turner is as clean as a whistle. Incompetent probably, but as clean as a whistle. He's a lab technician who was put in charge of some samples yesterday. In his stupidity, he didn't follow process and has contaminated many of them.'

'Shit,' she said, infuriated that this could have happened. 'Then, can we charge him with stupidity?'

Wallace snorted. 'Unfortunately, not. That's not the worst of it. If we were to continue investigating the samples he has contaminated, Mike said we'd probably be arresting him for thirty-four crimes.'

Rosie threw her head into her hands and let out a frustrated scream. She was so certain they finally had a lead. Their lead had just gone up in flames and Rosie, for one wished she had Gary Turner in her custody when she'd learned of his screw up. 'We're back to square one,' she said, feeling completely defeated. Watching Wallace nod only made her feel worse. He couldn't possibly know just how personal this felt to her. Unable to stand it any longer, Rosie simply grabbed her purse and stormed out the door.

34.

'You're becoming quite a regular here. Business or pleasure?'

Rosie turned to greet Grey with a smile. She didn't feel much like smiling now. 'Neither. I just feel like I'm missing something.'

Grey twitched. 'Missing?'

'Yes! They've taken everything that could potentially be entered into evidence, but I've got a feeling there's something else. Something that's staring me in the face.'

He pouted mockingly. 'You know, detective, sometimes things aren't always what they seem. Most of the time they're exactly how they seem. This might be one of those times where you just have to accept you've done everything you can. Perhaps he's just too clever, even for us.'

'He?'

Grey squirmed slightly. 'The killer. Assuming it is a man. I don't think a woman could do that.'

Rosie lifted her shoulders and let out a short burst of laughter. 'You would think that was the case. Did you ever hear the story of the woman who lifted a car off her child after he became trapped underneath?'

'No!'

'Good,' she muttered. 'It's a load of crap. A fable that's been passed through the years to re-enforce that women are every bit as strong as men. You think women aren't capable of murder.'

He shook his head. 'They're probably more capable in the right circumstances.'

'Are you?'

His eyes widened. 'Me? I don't know. Probably. I haven't found the right victim yet.'

They both laughed then, a little tension breaker that allowed him just enough time to light a cigarette and her enough time to collect her thoughts.

'Remember when you told me that you were staying in your flat in Glasgow on the night that Brian Houston was murdered?'

'Yes,' he said, seemingly undisturbed by the question.

'Was that a regular occurrence? It seems pointless having to make that journey back and forth.'

'Is there a reason you're asking, Detective?'

She nodded. 'I'll get to that. I just wondered how often you stay here at the hotel.'

'You're asking me if I lied about being here, aren't you?'

She thought about the question, how she wanted to answer it and if she wasn't digging a hole for herself by questioning him off the record. 'I don't need you to answer. I already know you lied. You cleared out your flat weeks ago and sold it recently. I'm just wondering why you lied to me.'

Grey drew on the cigarette and then threw it to the ground. 'Honestly, I didn't want involved. I knew if you thought I was here that you would have me listed as your first suspect.'

'Actually, I didn't have you pegged for it until after I found out that you'd played me. Now, I'm wondering why you would opt to lie about your whereabouts on the night of a murder if you weren't involved.'

'I'm not,' he said, quickly. 'I don't know who done it. I swear that to you.'

She lifted her shoulders and moved away from him. Staring into the distance, Rosie blinked. 'I must be daft. I'm actually inclined to believe you. I still don't think you killed anyone but if I catch you in another lie, I'm having you for obstructing the course of justice. I spent most of the afternoon in Glasgow, chasing your tail. I could have been here in Achray, solving the crime.'

He smiled apologetically. 'I just want this opening to go well. I've got a lot to do. I've got some artwork still to get on the walls. I must be here for staff who will be working tomorrow. I know there was mention of one of them coming a day early to help get things prepared.'

'You're not organising this yourself?'

Grey began to walk towards the maze at the back of the grounds. 'I've left most of the organising up to my investors. They've got more contacts in the industry and they're far more qualified in party planning than I am. I didn't even bother celebrating my eighteenth.'

'Bummer. I had a huge party for my eighteenth. You know, I don't think I've seen most of the friends who were there in more than ten years. People come; people go.'

Grey stopped walking and turned towards her. 'My parents died that year. The family house burned to the ground. They were sleeping in it.' He looked as if he regretted the candid revelation almost as quickly as he'd revealed it.

'I'm sorry,' she said, genuinely feeling bad for him. 'That's a hard age to lose your parents, I'm sure.' She'd already known about his parents. He had a colourful history that began shortly after their death.

'Not any harder than losing them at any other age,' he replied bluntly, the invisible cold wall appearing to go up between them again.

Rosie felt stupid then. In those moments she had

warmed to him, even wondered what it might feel like to kiss him. Then, she reminded herself he looked nothing more than a well-groomed thug. She dropped her eyes to the ground, hoping she would suddenly discover some tiny fragment of evidence that her team had missed. There was nothing, she now realised. This case wasn't going to be wrapped up with hard work. It was now starting to appear that the only thing that would shift the balance in her direction was sheer luck.

'You fancy a drink? I'll give you the guided tour.'

She snapped her eyes up, aware this was the first time she would be in the hotel by invitation. Each time before was either due to police work or the one time she and Wallace had ventured in of their own volition. She longed to ask him about the artwork. It was evident most, if not all of it was fake. Yet, how could she approach the subject? She wasn't going to give him the nod that she had already been in there without a warrant. What if she told him someone else had been there that day that she and Wallace had been on the grounds? Maybe she'd be able to tackle him that way. Measure the element of surprise as she blurted it out. For now, she refrained. 'That would be lovely,' she finally replied and followed him, sheepishly into the hotel foyer.

*

'You know, I've been watching you, detective,' said Grey, as he handed her a steaming mug of tea. 'There's something unusual about you.'

Rosie laughed, nervously. 'Unusual. I've been called many things. Unusual isn't one of them.'

'I've had my dealings with the police over the years. I'm sure you'll already know that if you've done a check on me. Many of the female officers I've met have a huge chip on their shoulder, intimidate you with their wit as if trying to outdo all the men in the room.'

'I can't decide if that's a compliment or not.'

'It is,' he whispered, setting himself down beside her.

'I've probably been that person. I know what it's like to want to succeed in a male dominated workplace. Being a bitch doesn't really seal the deal.'

'So, you kill them with kindness?'

'Not exactly,' she replied.

He was edging closer to her and she couldn't decide whether she would let him go ahead with the kiss or if she should stop right now.

'You're beautiful.'

'Am I?' She was looking round the room now, to avoid eye contact with him. The artwork above the blazing fireplace caught her eye. 'That's a nice painting. Who's it by?'

'It's a Monet,' he answered, his tongue curling round the sound of the last syllable.

Rosie didn't know much about art. She knew who Monet was and suspected that was no more original than the paintings in the cellar. 'Is it genuine?'

He smirked, as if teasing her. 'Is anything genuine? No, I don't think so. You think we could afford to buy genuine art to furnish an entire hotel that hasn't even opened its doors yet?'

Rosie pulled from him then. 'Tell me about your childhood?'

'Are you interrogating me?'

She laughed. 'No, I'm intrigued by you.'

'My childhood has little to do with who I am

now. What would you like to know?'

'Were you happy?'

'No!'

'Did you feel loved?'

He licked his lips. 'Not really. My parents were in fierce competition to outdo each other. I felt more like a pawn than a child.'

'Is that why you seem so undisturbed by their deaths?'

'Do I. I wasn't intending to seem that way. The truth of the matter is they didn't appear to like me much, I certainly didn't like them much and when they died, I think I felt a normal amount of grief. I certainly didn't let it affect the rest of my life.'

Rosie suspected it had affected him in more ways than he would ever admit. It perhaps explained the coldness, the lack of human contact, the need to succeed that obviously drove him. 'I was devastated by my mother's death. It was only her and I when I was growing up. There's been no greater loss to me.'

'What about your father?'

Her shoulders rose. 'He's a nice man. Very kind and caring. He always provided for us, but he was a cheat and a liar. He broke my mother's heart more times than I can even imagine. Things were okay in the end though. They made their peace with each other and he even contributed to her care in the final days. I think they always loved each other but my father couldn't be faithful, and my mother couldn't live with it.'

'You're lucky,' he said, echoing her melancholy speech about her parents.

Rosie found herself wondering what really lurked under those layers. A man who had lost his parents, lost the woman he loved and lost the best friend who appeared to be his only one. She would love to get closer, but she had compromised herself too many times to do it again. Rising from the sofa, she thanked him for the tea.

'You're leaving?' He placed his hand gently on her elbow. 'I was just starting to find you interesting, detective.'

She flinched at the barb. Perhaps getting close to him would be like slithering in a nest of vipers. Rather than allowing him to manipulate her, she was already fleeing through the door. She heard him say goodbye, but she pretended she hadn't. Finally, and only when she was outside the hotel, she felt she could finally take a deep sharp breath. When she looked up at the window of the room she'd just fled, he was there staring coldly at her. His expression told her she'd had a lucky escape. Grey Carter wasn't a man she should ever allow herself to get caught up with.

35.

Grey didn't like not getting what he wanted. From the age of eight, he'd been able to get whatever he could because nobody had ever challenged him. An art learned from his mother.

She had taught him everything she knew, unwittingly about manipulation. Whilst he hadn't liked her much, he had been impressed by her.

He'd never felt remorse for their death. He'd only ridded the world of trash and would never apologise for that. Of course, he had known there would be some acting required afterwards. Who would believe such a distraught boy could have lit the match of death himself?

Life had been simple after that. He never allowed anyone to get too close, always ensured he was one step ahead and only took what he really thought he deserved. Now, he felt as though he deserved Detective Cooper. Not because he was particularly entranced by her looks but because he knew she would make it so damn difficult.

Of course, the one person who had defied all of that was Adam. Forever and more, Adam would remain the one person in the world he truly loved. Having Adam angry with him hurt more than anything else he could think of. There weren't any romantic feelings there. Grey only slept with women, but Adam was the one person he would take a bullet for.

He had never forgotten that day. The day he had decided he would burn the house down whilst his parents slept. Adam was the only person he would trust with that secret and to this day, he truly believed his friend had kept it. Perhaps it was self-preservation. Maybe he knew that if he told anyone then he would also be implicated. No, Grey didn't believe that. He truly believed that Adam was all good and would keep the secret out of loyalty. Then again, what would it do to Adam's parents if they were to learn that Adam himself had helped pour the accelerant that started the fire? Whatever had been between them, Grey was certain that Adam would come back to him. If not out of loyalty, then maybe out of fear.

*

Rosie faced ahead as she continued to drive home. She was making it an early night tonight because she was so exhausted that the fatigue was grinding her down. Her car eventually turned on to the road that circled round the loch, her house reflected in the treacle coloured water. Rosie loved the house. Yet, she still hadn't been able to shake the feeling it gave her. There had been a sense of not belonging. Maybe it was too grand for her. Maybe she didn't belong in this village.

She was trying to work Grey out. The feeling that he was flirting with her clashed with the feeling that he was preying upon her. She'd never forgotten those bruises on Debra's thighs after her death, nor the feeling she had when Grey nonchalantly announced Debra had liked it rough. That, after all, was why she wasn't having sex with her husband.

Yet, he was so cool and collected. Maybe that's what made him attractive. Without the knowledge of his past misdemeanours and the certainty that there were probably many more, she might have been tempted to lunge into bed with him. Another notch on the bedpost, another crevice for her self-loathing to rest in.

Finally, she was pulling up to her house and it was only then that she noticed the vehicle was still there. She had noticed it yesterday but assumed it was a family touring the woods. It would be an exciting place for kids to discover. Yet, that had been more than twenty-four hours ago. She wondered if they might be lost, or in trouble.

Taking the phone out of her pocket, she switched on the torch and left her own car abandoned on the roadside. Moving slowly, she could hear her boots squelch against a few dead leaves. With everything that was going on in the village in the last few days she couldn't help but get a little nervous. Nervous of what though? It's not like there was a body for her to see.

Rosie halted just as she reached the back window of the car. She moved slowly round it with her mobile phone held high. 'If there's anyone there, call out if you're in need of help.'

Silence.

'If you need help, please call out,' she said, this time more dominantly.

Finally, seeing that there was no-one in the car, she stared in the side of the driver's window. The car was pristine. There was also no sign of a struggle. She began to walk round the car, shining her phone torch on the vehicle. It was on the passenger's side that she noticed a large block of muck had been spread on the car and right in the centre, someone had scribbled two words.

Rosie stepped back, moving away from the abandoned vehicle. Another gust of wind, this time carrying the cry of an owl and she found herself terrified. Rosie ran like she hadn't ran in years. Before she had a chance to take a deep breath, she was climbing into her own car and locking the doors.

She hit re-dial on Wallace's number. Steam had covered the windows so that she couldn't really see outside now. Her breaths had deepened, almost as if they were echoing back at her. His mobile number was ringing as she pushed the handset to her ear.

She turned sharply, something shifting to the left of her eyeline. She was about to scream when she saw it. She threw her hand over her mouth as Wallace answered at the other end, realising that the thing moving in her eyeline was the torch from her own phone reflecting back from the passenger window. She'd been in such a rush she hadn't turned it off.

She laughed, felt stupid and tried to regain her composure. There were no monsters waiting in her backseat or lurking behind her to bestow an ugly cruel death. Not right now, anyway. Rosie double checked that her doors were locked and answered him when he spoke a second time. 'Kev, I need you to run this registration plate for me. I've found an abandoned car with muck spread all over the side. Someone has fingered the words HELP LOVE onto it.'

'What the hell does that mean?'

She was staring intensely at the car, almost as if she expected someone to climb out of the boot. 'I don't know but the car is immaculate. I wouldn't be surprised if it had been through the car wash in the last few days. The muck is deliberate. We just have to work out what the message is.'

*

Something rattled on the window. Gently, at first, but more prominently as Gaby rose from the sofa. She hadn't slept in a few days now and the little gift left for her hadn't exactly settled her down for the night.

She had been grabbing cat naps where the grief subsided but not long enough to relieve her of her exhaustion. Maybe that's how grief was supposed to work. Drill out every ounce of all that kept you functioning until all that was left was fear and paranoia.

An outdoor light sent shadows across the walls. Branch ends became claws. Clouds became faceless ghouls. The dead silence became the eerie reminder of all that had been taken from her already. Not even a hint of what could still be taken.

Eva was fortunate. She was too young to know what had happened to Brian. She might well feel the tension from Gaby but when it became time to sleep, she seemed to go to that still dreamless place that babies seemed to inhabit. For just one night, Gaby wished she could join her there.

Right now, her only thought was discovering whatever now rattled at the window. Was someone there? She wished now she had taken the sleeping pill offered to her by Mrs Blyth. Why would someone want to target her? She'd had nothing to do with what Brian done. In fact, she had been incandescent with anger when she'd learned what he'd gotten himself into.

She eased slowly towards the window, listening to the thudding of her own breaking heart. Was it fear, or was it grief that kept her heart beating?

Walking towards the window, she tried to focus her eyes. Splashes of rain and condensation on the inside made it difficult to see. Then, the sound of the rattling rose again. She shifted in beside the sofa, so she was now standing directly at the foot of the window.

On the other side, two eyes rose from beneath a

black hood and met her face on.

Gaby screamed. It hadn't been her grief or her paranoia. Someone was there.

He was leering at her now. Smiling, taunting her.

The baby joined her with a piercing scream that jolted her out of her terror.

The face was gone.

Mrs Blyth was rushing down the stairs now. She muttered something in a sleepy haze.

Gaby had already acted though. The figure had disappeared as she began to dial the police station. She wasn't leaving her safety in the hands of a friend, even if they were a trusted police officer. Gaby wanted proper protection. They owed her that much, at least.

36.

Background noise. Everything was becoming a collision of noise in her ear and Rosie was no longer focusing on what anyone was saying. She'd never gotten like this over a case before. She didn't recognise the fluttering in her gut, nor the occasional skip of her heartbeat and it frightened her. Perhaps it was the fact that she, herself felt threatened. Perhaps it was time to tell Wallace the truth about the envelope and how it appeared to come in the same form as the envelope sent to Brian. She couldn't believe she'd allowed herself to conceal evidence.

'Anything?'

'As far as I can tell the car is as clean as a whistle. If someone's been snatched, it doesn't appear to have been from inside the vehicle.'

Rosie was always impressed by the ability of forensic teams to put together so much information. Without them, the police departments wouldn't have solved half the modern-day crimes. Yet, she missed the old days of policing when she first started out. DNA was in its infancy then and police detectives relied very little on its outcome. The young detectives now didn't have the bloodhound nose of the older generation. Rosie was stuck somewhere in the middle; an under-developed nose for the job and an over-eager sense of reliance on forensics. If it got the job done, she didn't much care who fired the final bullet.

Wallace was walking towards her now with his notepad in hand. 'David and Elizabeth Hawthorn. They're a young couple from Glasgow. I know the estate they're living in. I looked at a house there myself.'

'Anything else on them? Criminal records? Complaints of harassment? What about any calls made to emergency services in the last few days?'

He nodded. 'He was picked up fifteen years ago for fighting in the street. Nothing since. His wife is a self-employed designer and he works at the police contact centre.'

'At Govan?'

'You know it? I thought you were a novice on Scottish geography.'

She was about to retort with some smart-arsed retort, but she'd already probably given him enough earache tonight with her performance earlier on. 'I've spoken to them a few times. I've never been there.'

'Do you think it's anything to do with the deaths?'

She turned to look at the car. 'Don't you find it strange that it's one more person who works for the emergency services.' She was staring into the distance now, trying to understand what would link people together who didn't even know each other. The water sparkled in the darkness ahead of her, a soothing moment turned chaotic by the frenzy in her mind.

'So, what are we talking about here? Something that involved Brian, the two paramedics and this Hawthorn couple.'

'And me,' she said, resolutely.

Wallace bagged the piece of paper and scowled. 'You?'

'There's something I've been too embarrassed, actually too afraid to tell anyone.'

He must have sensed her extreme discomfort because he turned her away from any eavesdropping. 'You don't have to tell me or anyone else anything if you don't want to. And you don't have to worry about being safe. If you need me to stand by, I'll be there for you.'

'I can't ask you to lie for me,' she said, her voice quivering, yet she sensed he would. She could no longer justify the secret to herself. It didn't seem as important as saving lives, especially her own. 'Come to my house. I've got something I need to show you.'

*

Once Wallace went to bed, Rosie felt the sombreness return. She had been reluctant to accept his company for the night, but she was also weary of being afraid over the last few days. She barely knew Wallace, but she was already starting to trust him in a way she didn't often trust. Not since the things that had happened with her previous colleagues. Crystal Ridge was in darkness, the air thick with her ever-increasing uncertainty. Wallace had promised he would keep her secret if they were able to. If it ever had to enter evidence, he would find a way of adding it in the most inconspicuous way.

The last forty-eight hours had been surreal at the house. Every time she looked out the window, she saw those boys hanging from the trees. Ghosts everywhere she went in the village and she didn't think she'd be able to rest them until their killer was locked up.

It was nights like this she longed for the company of a man. Friendship didn't cut it in the darkest hours but there was no-one she felt close enough to allow them into her bed. Not now.

The photographs of her naked and in the act of sexual intercourse were now tucked back in their safe place. The betrayal felt raw all over again. Someone had taken those pictures, circulated them round

Scotland Yard and called her names she didn't even feel able to repeat. Only one person had been angrier than her. She hadn't been able to speak to him at any great length since. Tonight, she needed him though.

'Dad?'

'Rosie,' he gasped. 'It's lovely to hear from you.'

She could weep for hearing his lovely soft tones, his tongue curling round the Irish lilt that he'd never lost in sixty years.

'My girl, you've no idea how it fills me with joy when you call, so you do.'

She felt the tears form, a grown woman ready to fall into her daddy's arms because, despite his flaws, no other man could compare. 'Dad, somebody sent me those pictures. You know, the one's that got plastered all over the station.'

'Pay no heed, my girl,' he said, his voice commanding and gruff.

'I didn't at first. I thought it might be some sort of prank. Maybe someone had gotten my address or something. Dad, you didn't give my address out to anyone, did you?'

He snorted. 'Me? I wouldn't give those bastards the skin off my shite.'

Rosie laughed then, glad that she'd called her dad because if ever there was a night where laughter was required, it was tonight. 'I'm sorry, dad.'

'Sorry for what? For being a grown up and thinking you can trust men. Let me tell you, girl, from experience. There's not a man fit to lick your boots and if someone set out to embarrass you, that's their problem, not yours. Give it no more thought. It'll just be someone playing a childish prank. Ignore it.'

'I can't,' she confessed. 'The same envelope with pictures of my colleague went to him and his wife.

Then, the other night he was found murdered. I think someone wants me dead dad.'

His voice deepened, took on a grave sincerity. 'Rosie, pack a case right now and come home. I'll book a flight for you. I'll get Tessa to make up the spare room with all your favourite things.'

Rosie suspected her father would do anything to get her home, whether her life was threatened or not. 'I can't do that, dad. I sold mum's house and my own flat to afford this place. I can't just turn my back on it.'

'It'll only be temporary until this person is apprehended. I'm paying no mind to you. I'm ordering a flight on the internet for you.'

'I don't want you to do that,' she said, more firmly. 'I will come and visit when this is all over. My new colleague, Kevin is built like the side of a house. Between him and I, I think I'll be safe.'

Her father sighed loudly, accepting the headstrong response of his stubborn daughter. 'Then, do me a turn, Rosie. Call me tomorrow and the next day, and every day after that. More than once if you can. I need to know you're safe. If you don't call me, I will be booking a flight. Not for you, but for me and I'll be up there within four hours.'

37.

'How long do you think we've been here?'

Lizzie felt panicked. Their captor hadn't harmed them yet, but he also hadn't gone out of his way to be hospitable. In fact, since the first day, he'd visited less and less.

Dave, every so often shifted on the springy mattress, so much so that Lizzie feared his bed might collapse and snap his ankle.

'Days, I think,' she replied, running her fingers across the dry smudged mascara under her eyes.

'I'm sorry,' he whispered.

'For what?'

He clenched his teeth and pulled his shoulders forward. 'For this, for putting us in danger.'

'You said you didn't know why we were kidnapped.'

'I don't,' he said, his eyes widening. 'But adding two and two together, I think it's fair to say that the psycho has some grudge against me. I don't know what it is. I don't know if we'll ever know but I'm sorry anyway.' He threw back his head and sighed in defeat.

'I'm hungry,' she said, feeling her stomach and hearing the growl of her hunger pangs.

'When we get out of here,' he whispered reassuringly, 'I'm going to take you for the biggest slap up meal you've ever had.'

She wanted to join him in his enthusiasm. It wouldn't come. All she felt was exhausted, hungry, emotionally drained. She thought of her life back home. Dave had made it so lovely for her. When they thought a baby was coming into their lives, he'd turned the spare bedroom into a nursery. He'd also removed it all when she'd miscarried. Which had angered her because she didn't want to forget a baby had lived inside her, albeit briefly. She wanted to hold onto that feeling forever. The anger had relieved itself though because she knew what a wonderful husband Dave was, and he would never have done anything to hurt her. She was sure he would volunteer to lay down in front of an oncoming train for her. Yet, here they were. In front of whatever train was hurtling their way and she wasn't even sure she trusted him. He might swear he knew nothing of the kidnapper's motives. Lizzie wasn't sure she trusted anyone anymore.

'I wonder if he's watching us now,' said Dave, nodding towards the tiny red light at the far corner of the loft. It was almost concealed by cobwebs but was just about clear enough that they were able to see it if they looked hard enough.

She felt her neck tighten and drew back her jaw. 'Come on then, you sadistic bastard. What is it that you want to do? Come on and show yourself, fucking scum.'

'Lizzie,' snarled Dave.

She twisted her neck in fury, her eyes blazing as she hurled insults at her husband. 'Why didn't you get help? You must have had the chance to stop and phone the police. You work for them, for Christ sake.' If she allowed herself to panic anymore, she might begin to hyperventilate.

'Calm down, Lizzie. Just take a deep breath. What's the point in turning on each other? Maybe someone will come for us.'

'Who?'

Dave appeared to follow her gaze to the camera. He was staring at it now. As if realising, someone might be listening, he turned back to Lizzie with sadness in his eyes. 'No-one, baby, he finally admitted. 'I don't think anyone's coming for us.'

*

They were started to break. That was almost as much fun as watching them squirm over their future. He was alone now and thankful for it. He felt suffocated sometimes by Larry. His parents would never understand just how comforting and distressing it was to have someone delve into your every thought and know every move.

A minute past midnight.

The day had finally arrived. He hadn't murdered the married couple because they were essential. As was the detective and the hotel owner. He didn't care for any of them. He'd have lined them all up and hanged them one by one if he'd been doing this alone. Instead, he'd lashed out at the ones who were being given a pardon. Why weren't they part of the plan? They were every bit as culpable as the rest.

It was at that moment he allowed himself to think of his mother. He didn't do that too often. It brought waves of grief and rage in equal droves and he didn't feel able to control it. She'd been taken from him too early. Her death unpunished and unmarked. Still, today she would finally have her moment. They would rue the day they'd killed her and simply got on with their sad little lives.

38.

Morning hadn't quite dawned. Not that it mattered to Rosie as the last few days had all merged into one. Now she was no longer sleeping. Crystal Ridge, once a refuge that had saved her from the past, now felt like a prison. A noose around her neck. She brought her hand to her neck and shuddered.

Across the water, the last minutes of moonlight illuminated an old Gothic church and poured its reflection onto the water. She hadn't been there but had heard many stories of its history. It would be the one lasting reminder of the loch as it once lay. Before the property developers got their hands on the surrounding area and turned it into this new money paradise. There were plans afoot to expand but for now, it was a place of tranquillity and beauty. Which is what had brought Rosie here in the first place.

She thought about Gaby, still frazzled in the early hours by the appearance of someone at Mrs Blyth's window. Could it have been the killer? Nothing would have surprised her now. She was also still trying to connect the dots on the Hawthorns' car. Where did they fit into the equation?

'Good Morning.'

Rosie spun round. 'You startled me. Do you know, I almost forgot you were here?'

Wallace smiled. 'You weren't woken by my snoring. That's a new one.'

She cracked her knuckles, suddenly feeling a little exposed in her nightwear. 'The soundproofing's good in these houses.'

'Will I do coffee? I can't function until I've had at least two cups.'

Rosie rose from the window seat. 'No, I'll do it.

It was nice of you to stay with me. I have some crumpets as well. Would you like one?'

Wallace slapped his stomach. 'I won't say no. Is it okay for me to shower here? If not, I can rush back to the hotel.'

Rosie suddenly flushed. It hadn't occurred to her to even ask about his living arrangements. He'd only been transferred up very recently. 'You're staying at a hotel? You didn't mention it.'

'Why would I? It's paid for by expenses. I don't know if the long-term plan is to offer me the permanent position up here. In which case, I'll have to decide whether I want to commute or move up here permanently.'

She found herself offering before she'd even really considered it properly. She wasn't sure if it was pity for him, or fear for herself. 'You can stay in my spare room. It's got to be more comfortable than a hotel room.'

Wallace cocked his head. 'I can't ask you to do that. We don't know how long I'll be here.'

Rosie was moving to the kitchen now. 'You didn't ask. I offered. Besides, you've already said that if the job becomes permanent here, you'll have to find a place. We don't know how long it will take to find Brian's killer. Anyway, you'd probably be doing me a favour. I'm seeing shadows in every corner just now. I think I'd feel safer if I have someone in the next room.' She felt it was important to emphasise that the wall between them would remain that way.

'I'll collect my things from the hotel later then. I really appreciate this. The hotel's fine, but it's basic and can get a bit lonely at night when we're done at the station.'

She threw the switch on the kettle and smiled. 'It

can get just as lonely here. I can't promise I'll be immense company but if I get a little tired and grouchy, remember I'm a woman of a certain age.'

His smile widened; the sort of boyish grin probably best saved for flirting with someone not as long in the tooth as Rosie was. He was departing now, an awkward silence falling between them and she was grateful when he was finally stomping along the hall.

She was buttering the crumpets and listening to the hissing of the coffee machine when she heard something fall through her letterbox and land on the floor. It was surely too early for the post. Who else would be dropping something off to her this early in the day? She looked at the clock. *6.40.a.m.* Too early for junk mail to be delivered.

Rosie moved from the marble island in the kitchen and began to shift, almost cat-like into the hallway. She was shaking, she realised. Why was this getting to her so much?

It was too dark in the hallway to see anything on the floor, so she flicked the light switch and watched everything become eye-wateringly bright. It was then that all her terror was realised, and she let out a skin crawling scream.

Wallace was already running from the bathroom and hurtling down the stairs.

Rosie was leaning against the wall, having knocked a picture from its hanging place. She followed Wallace as he approached her front door. She moved slowly as he knelt and looked at the familiar looking contraption.

Wallace was backing away. 'We'll need to get forensics over here. If that's someone's blood, we can't take any chances.'

Rosie nodded, still in shock, as she continued to

stare. Someone had threaded a noose through her letterbox, pinning it to the entry point and dousing it in blood. She had been threatened before in her career. They were almost always empty threats, or ones that came from verbally abusive drunks in the back of wagons. This was different. Whoever was doing this meant business. They were tormenting her first and she imagined it was only a matter of time before she was hanging from a similar noose and begging for her life.

*

He watched the light come up through the frosted glass and waited. Her scream excited him more than he could have imagined. She wasn't as tough as she liked to pretend. He'd been watching her for weeks. The men had been different. They were simply getting what they deserved but she was different. That's why he enjoyed toying with her so much. He wondered what it would feel like to break in when she was in the bath. He would skulk up the stairs and find her naked. He would follow her into the lounge. She wouldn't even know he was there until he was grabbing for her and pushing her face down into the naked flame of a candle. Or, perhaps he would drown her before she'd gotten out of the bath. Or maybe he'd simply fulfil his fantasy and skin her until her blood splashed up the walls in every direction. He imagined that would become his MO because it thrilled him so.

Suddenly, he realised she wasn't alone. The male detective was there. He wasn't familiar with that detective until a few days ago. It wasn't clear where he had come from, but he wasn't on the radar.

'You're here again. I don't know why you don't just hurry up and kill her.' Larry arrived then, needling him into action, a smiling assassin who

didn't want to get his own hands dirty.

'She needs to know what she's done. It'll all be over tonight.'

'You know that you're just a pawn in all of this. You think you're in the driver's seat, but you need to know that you are being manipulated. We're being manipulated.'

'We're doing it for her.'

Larry chuckled. 'Except, I haven't killed anyone. That's all on you. If you're caught, the blame falls on you.'

'They'll all be dead tonight. Who will they tell? Once this is all over, we can disappear, and nobody gets caught.'

Larry moved between him and the house. 'You really believe that, don't you?'

He dipped his eyes and then brought them back up, now watching her frantically pull at the blinds in her lounge. The male detective was evidently trying to calm her. It wasn't working. 'The more she fights, the more fun it will be,' he finally said, then began the half mile walk back to the cottage.

39.

Adam had decided to set off early. Once he was on his way, there would be no stopping him. Right now, he could almost imagine his mother turning up at the house and dissuading him from doing whatever he had planned. Thankfully, they didn't even know the gun existed, or that he planned to use it on the very man that had gifted it to him in the first place.

He pulled on his brown velvet jacket, another gift from Grey and wondered if there was any part of his life that Grey hadn't infiltrated. The odd thought that entered his mind was his own brother. He'd never been close since childhood and he knew that his brother thought he was strange and insular. Perhaps that was another part of his life that Grey had destroyed. After all, Grey was an old child. Perhaps he wanted Adam to fill that void.

He remembered the fire. It was something he had never fully been able to move away from. He hadn't realised Grey's intention for murder. He had believed Grey only wanted to scare them, put some distance between himself and their cold ways. He'd insisted his parents were out at some charity function. Now, he sensed he'd been misled even then. Maybe it would be one more thing he would confront Grey about now.

He held the gun. Felt the powerful extension of his hand. It was almost like discovering a new sense of self. Debra was dead. His parents and brother no longer recognised him. He might not see his daughter again. The one thing that fuelled him was his growing hatred of someone he once cared enormously for. He knew of Debra's reluctance for him to keep the gun. She didn't know that he'd hidden it away in a safe place but that it still lived in the house. He was glad he'd made the decision not to bag it up and discard it into the murky depths of the Clyde. He wondered if Debra would now approve. Maybe it would excite her in a way she'd never appeared to be excited during their marriage.

Adam dropped into his car, pulled the gun from inside his sleeve and hid it under the seat. For a moment he thought he heard her voice. A soft sensual whisper in his ear. It was gone, just as if it had been carried on the wind and then blown away again. He tightened his eyes, longing for it to return. When it didn't, he thought of Gracie and how she might feel when both of her parents were dead. Was it going to come to that? A quick glance in the mirror and Adam wondered why he didn't recognise himself anymore.

Quickly shaking his head, he turned the key in the ignition. No more thoughts. He wanted to just sleepwalk through today. The invitation said the event started at seven thirty p.m. It would be more than twelve hours before he'd have his moment. Could he wait that long now he was in the car? He wanted it to be over. He wanted Grey to confess everything in front of everyone. Then Adam realised he didn't want the confession. He just wanted to beat the living daylights out of Grey. Or shoot him. Anything to unleash this pain he was in. The pain; worming through his every fibre, day after day and long into the lonely nights.

Grey Carter owed him everything. So, perhaps he wouldn't settle for a confrontation. Perhaps, once he got there and saw his oldest friend, he wouldn't be able to show any mercy. Suddenly, the gun beneath his seat seemed like the best gift Grey could ever have given him. He slammed down on the clutch, put the car into gear and began the journey to the place his wife had died.

*

Rosie felt calmer since her uniformed colleagues and someone from forensics had arrived.

Detective Wallace had wrapped a blanket round her shoulders, finished making her the coffee she'd started and was now force feeding her the crumpet she'd began to butter. 'These guys won't let anything happen to you. You should know that better than anyone.'

'Really?' Rosie hadn't quite experienced the familial protection of the police family, having been thrown under the proverbial bus and exposed as the force harlot. 'That's not really my experience of my colleagues.'

'Maybe in London. I don't think that's the case here. I do think you have to go to the Chief about the photos though. If they're linked in some way to what's happening here, it could be the difference between life and death.'

She recoiled in sharp anger. 'You said you would keep it a secret.'

Wallace held his hand up to calm her. 'And I will. I don't think you should though. If anything happens to you, I'll feel terrible. Your secret isn't nearly as bad as you think it is. This isn't your shame. It's the shame of every bloody man who thought it was a weapon to beat you with.'

She wished she could believe him. A change of subject was required. 'Have they managed to get in touch with either of the Hawthorns yet?'

Wallace nodded. 'Neither are answering any of the numbers we have on file for them. Elizabeth mostly works out of her house so there's nobody to really contact. I've contacted the Govan contact centre to find out if anything happened there. Seemingly, he ran out of work a couple of days ago and didn't tell anyone where he was going or why.'

'Not even his boss?'

'Well, I think he spoke to his boss afterwards, but he's not heard anything from him since. He was considering reporting him as a missing person today, in fact.'

Rosie had been thinking about them throughout the night. Each time she found herself wondering about the message on the car, those simple two words she found herself wondering why someone wouldn't just make a call to the police instead. 'If someone has time to cake the car and write that message, however short, they have time to report it to the police. Especially when they know the process and what happens when a crime is reported.'

Wallace nodded in agreement. He looked distracted by the movement in the hallway. 'Unless they have a good reason not to report it.'

'Like what?'

'I don't know. Maybe they're in trouble with someone. Or maybe their family is being threatened. Who knows?'

'Makes sense,' she agreed.

'Are you still going to the hotel opening tonight?'

Rosie hadn't really thought about it since the day before. She didn't know if she was in the mood for socialising with the local hoi polloi. Then again, there was still a chance that she might come across some new information that would help catch the killer. 'I might as well. You should come with me,' she replied.

Wallace nodded. 'Me, in a penguin suit. I don't think so. I did that for my wedding day and won't be repeating it.'

She laughed. 'Don't wear one then. I'm sure you'll have a nice pair of trousers and a jersey that will fit perfectly.'

Unconvinced, he left the room and went back upstairs.

Rosie could still see the small bustle in her hallway, and it made her want to scream at them to get out of her house. Her only hope was that there was something in the blood or on that rope that would finally give her something to work with. For a moment, she was almost tempted to get on the flight her father had offered to pay for and disappear again. How many more times could she run away from the things that threatened her? She climbed back on to the window seat, this time focusing her eyes on the rising dawn on the dark green peaks. Surely, her luck had to change soon.

40.

The day had finally arrived for Grey's big grand opening. Suddenly, he felt out of control. He thought about all that had happened recently. A cataclysm of bedlam. Up until the night before, he'd been full of confidence. This was his new start. There was money in the bank, plenty of it. The hotel would either make or break and it wouldn't make a difference to him because he knew he could simply disappear.

It had all started with Debra. That affair. The heated passion that had tempted him away from everything he should have been focusing on. The interior décor had fallen behind. The opening had to be delayed. Grey's investor had become agitated in the weeks leading up to Debra's death. The man had ploughed most of his life savings into the hotel. His wife wasn't happy, and she wanted to see results. Not that they'd ever turned up to see the finished result.

His friendship with Adam was probably dead in the water. He wanted to reach out. Perhaps pass some of his recent good fortune Adam's way. He knew his friend better than that. Adam couldn't be bought. Neither could his silence. Yet, even in the event of all division, the anxiety that he'd suddenly get a knock on the door for the death of his parents had never transpired. Adam; as loyal as a lapdog and every bit as easy to tame.

It was the death of Detective Houston that had really pushed him to the edge. He'd told himself it was none of his business. He'd called the police in the morning when it was easy to pretend that he had only just found the body. Now that had been exposed as a lie, he felt stupid for not calling the police in the first instance. He wondered if Detective Cooper would now be gunning for him. Would he now be at the top of the list of suspects?

His phone rang. A number he didn't recognise. Perhaps it would be somebody calling to confirm for tonight. He hadn't dealt with the guest list. He'd left that to the investor, just as he'd left the catering and the staffing to him as well. He should have been excited now. The staff would be arriving soon. Instead, as the sun rose in his eyes, he simply squinted at the phone and took a deep breath.

It was him. The investor. A man he'd spoken to many times. Probably calling to update him on the running of tonight's event.

'Grey? Listen, everything's all in place for today. We're all really looking forward to it. By the way, can you check the rooms on the ground floor to make sure they're all made up. I think a few in attendance tonight are hoping to stay. You know, keep the wine flowing and before you know it, they'll be filling the beds. I'll send through a list of their names, room allocations and debit card details. I hope you don't mind but I offered twenty percent off their first night stay.'

Grey listened with growing irritation. He wasn't sure why because it sounded perfectly reasonable that they would want to fill the rooms. However, the artwork wasn't on all the walls yet. His own staff wouldn't be starting to the following Monday. He was now left with the task of hanging pictures along the ground floor. Those who said you should never work with animals and children had obviously never worked with middle aged investors, Grey mused to himself and ended the call.

He was working his way along the rooms and taking notes now. He needed to make some of the beds that were still in their delivery wrappers. There were indeed half a dozen pictures still to go on the walls. Most importantly, he hadn't filled the swish new bathrooms with the personalised toiletries provided by the hotel. He'd probably need to slump into one of the beds before the night was through.

He reached the final room in the corridor and stopped. It was the last room he and Debra had made love in before her death. Grey had never been able to enter it since. He was sure it would have been fixed up during the previous week's deep clean. Still, he felt like he was about to step into a ghost house, relive something in his past that was now too painful to remember. Would he remember her face? Hear her voice? Would it be just as he remembered it? Maybe her ghost would be hiding there and waiting to unleash her anger. If he believed in the afterlife.

Grey pushed open the door and almost threw himself back from what faced him. Slowly moving in, he grabbed for the wall and felt his heartbeat quicken. Time appeared only to slow as he moved into the centre of the display. Someone had certainly been in here since Debra's death and they wanted to remind him of it.

Across the room hung a picture display, just as someone might hang their washing on the line. A montage of different images. It started with his young face; eighteen-year-old Grey with his cheeks blackened and tear stained. Still life flames filled the next few pictures before he found himself looking into his father's deep hateful eyes and his mother's stern scowl. They were dead for so many years but, in that moment, they might as well have been standing in that room, leering at his shock. The next images were of Debra, cold and dead in the snow. Her body and head were surrounded by blackened blood, treacle coloured veins travelling off into the frost. Finally, another face. One he didn't recognise. A dead woman who lay in the snow. Grey suddenly felt confused. Who was she? It most certainly wasn't Debra. The woman was older looking, her wide grey eyes sparkling lifelessly above her blue iced lips.

Grey couldn't take his eyes off the images. He ran his glare across them one more time, still holding onto the wall and not realising until it was too late that someone was moving up behind him. If only he had turned a moment sooner, he might have warded off the angry swing of his attacker. He didn't though. He simply felt something crack the back of his head and the blackening of his vision as he hurtled forward. The last thing he saw before crashing to the ground was the glower of his parents, long dead and probably relishing that someone was taking revenge on their behalf.

*

Rosie felt like she was still being watched when she locked the bathroom door. It wasn't even just the attack of the noose being put through her letterbox but the intrusion of all those men she barely even knew. She was trying to piece together everything she now knew. Which didn't feel like very much. Three men were dead, all employees of the emergency services. A couple were missing, again one of them working for Police Scotland. She, herself had become the target of someone who had decided to play with her. There was no doubting now that the envelopes received by both her and Brian were relevant to the case. Nor did she doubt that the noose left through her door was designed to taunt her, to let her know he was still out there, and he was probably coming for her next.

The hot steaming water fell upon her skin and felt momentarily refreshing. If only the rush of clear water could eliminate everything else, she would simply remain here forever. In those early days she'd believed the envelope had been sent from London. Who else would know anything about her sordid past? Now she knew it was coming from much nearer. Who though? What did her past have to do with Brian's? Or the paramedics? Or a Glasgow couple who she'd never met? Something linked them all and she just hadn't discovered what it was yet.

She squirted more green tee tree shower gel into her hand and gave herself one last wash. Her eyes stung for a second. If only she could place everything on the floor before her, perhaps she would start to put everything together. Right now, it was a jigsaw with a hundred missing parts.

There was another hour before she was due at the office. Wallace had already left, stating that he had a few things he wanted to do before they began their day. What on earth could he possibly be doing in this nowhere village that was miles from anything? She dared not to ask and was glad that she was finally going to have an hour alone. Even if it meant locking the house tighter than Alcatraz.

The files were open on the table where she had left them. The images of two young men dead on the ground only yards from her house was disturbing enough before she even got to Brian's pictures. Even more so was the distressing idea that she might be joining the pile any day now. The waiting sent nettles up her skin.

It was Kyle's picture with his crooked tooth that caught her attention. His life picture that she'd managed to acquire from his mother. Rosie had wracked her brain to remember where she'd seem them before. Suddenly, that tiny detail brought the memory hurtling back to her. She was reaching for her phone. Wallace's errands could wait.

'It's me. I need to talk to you, Kev. I remember now where I've met Kyle and Ricky before. I also know what likely links them to myself and Brian. I'll get you at the station in fifteen.'

41.

Dave had been working on the chain for almost three days, trying to loosen it from his ankle. It had become apparent that wouldn't work. So, he'd began to dig whatever utensils he could get his hand on into the screws on the wall. It had been surprisingly easier than he first realised, thanks to the wood rot that had probably settled on a good portion of the property.

He was free, though the chains attached to his ankle clattered onto the floor.

'Quick! Cut me loose,' commanded his wife.

He could see her desperation, the days of defeat suddenly falling away. Dave raced over to her, leaned in and quickly kissed her.

Lizzie was pulling away from him. 'There'll be time for that later. You have to hurry.'

He began to dig a butter knife into the screws attaching her to the wall. It didn't appear to happen so easily.

'Just break it,' she said. 'It doesn't matter if you injure me. Better to be injured than dead.'

Dave wouldn't harm a hair on her head. He most certainly wasn't going to risk breaking a bone in her body. Her ankle was more inflamed than his. Perhaps she'd been pulling harder to try and free herself. He wanted to kiss away the pain, settle the trembling on her lips that now made her look so fragile.

Lizzie's whole body was shaking now.

As he looked up at her, Dave wanted to hug her. Hold her and keep her safe but he knew the only way to safety now was to get her out of there. He hadn't been sure why they'd been kept alive so long. Perhaps the kidnapper was only bluffing. Though, Lizzie had seen the pictures of the dead man. Had they been real? Maybe their captor had downloaded some horrible images to scare them. Maybe he had no intentions of killing them at all.

Lizzie shifted to the side as the attachment began to break away from the wall.

Dave continued to jimmy the knife in and coax it away. Still, it was screwed on much tighter than his had been.

'Oh my god,' said Lizzie. 'He's back.'

Dave had heard the door beneath them slam. It could only be the captor and the elusive Larry who hadn't made himself known to them yet. He became more frantic.

It was too late though. The loft door was creaking open. Their captor was returning and had obviously noticed that the camera lens had been shifted away. There was nothing Dave could do but wait. It's not like he could attach himself to the wall again. All he could do was fight.

'The beauty of modern technology is that I see everything. Even when I'm not here,' said the young man, glowering at Dave. The redness round his eyes looked as if they were on fire and it almost seemed like he'd been crying.

Knowing he had no more time to waste, Dave lunged forward and brought an upper cut to the captor's jawline.

The young man simply laughed. 'I hope you've got more than that. If you're going to fight me, I want it to be worth it.'

Dave put all his power behind the next punch, brought his arm swinging round and laid his fist on the side of their captor's face. Still, the young man simply laughed.

Suddenly, he had his large thick hand round

Dave's throat and was forcing him back to the wall, that had held him in place for the last few days. The chain wrapped itself round Dave's other leg and he found himself hurtling to the floor.

Lizzie was screaming and it was the only thing keeping Dave from shutting his eyes and simply giving up.

He swung at the younger man but found that he was too strong. He was trying to bring up his arm but everything he did, the captor seemed one step ahead.

Finally, he went limp. He couldn't fight anymore. He could see his wife slump on the bed, and he knew there was nothing more he could do. He took a deep sharp breath and nodded in defeat at the captor.

The young man held on to Dave's throat for just a few seconds more. Just enough that Dave wasn't sure if this was going to be the moment of his death.

Finally, he was free. He fell to the floor, took a desperate lungful of air and looked sorrowfully at Lizzie.

The captor was leaving now. He was descending the stairs and addressing someone on the floor below. The door slammed shut and a lock turned sharply.

Dave ran to Lizzie. 'At least he didn't kill me,' he said, still gasping for air.

'He doesn't need to,' said Lizzie, sadly. 'As long as he's got me, I think he knows you won't leave me.'

42.

'I don't know why I didn't remember before. I feel so stupid. I just think the shock of everything made me forget.'

Wallace threw up his arms. 'Don't give yourself a hard time. You probably see so many paramedics in our line of work that you won't remember all of them.'

'True,' admitted Rosie. She was staring past him now, as if reliving the case all over again. Not that it had really been a case. She didn't know why she'd felt so haunted by it. The fact was that Debra Mullen was her first real death since arriving in Achray. She thought she'd left the harsh reality of murder and betrayal behind in London. The sad realisation after Debra's death was that death had a way of creeping up on you no matter where you ran to and, sometimes you don't get to bring justice to those who have died.

Wallace remained still, no doubt giving her the space to dig it all up again.

'It's one of those situations you find yourself in where you know that someone died due to someone else's behaviour. Yet, nobody physically harmed Debra Mullen. An accident, they said. A young woman running from a man that they suspected had raped her. There were bruises on her thighs. We really believed Grey had assaulted her. Yet, all the evidence since suggests that she was there of her own volition and, without her testimony we can only guess what might have happened.'

He looked confused. 'So, no case?'

'Just a series of blunders. The call came in that afternoon. The call taker sent us on a wild goose chase. We went in the wrong direction. So did the ambulance service. Eventually, we got there first. Still, it was too late. Debra was already dead. Thrown ten feet from the window of her car. Who knows what might have happened if we'd got there a few minutes earlier? Maybe we could have saved her.' Rosie stopped, felt the tears smudge at the top of her cheeks.

'Or, maybe she was already dead by the time she was thrown from the car,' he offered, reassuringly. 'Why do you feel so bad about it?'

'I don't know,' answered Rosie. She pictured the little girl she'd met. Little Gracie, whose face she would forever remember for its sadness at the realisation her mummy wasn't coming home. 'Maybe it's because we haven't been able to give her husband and daughter any kind of peace. The only thing her husband learned was that his wife was a cheat and a liar. Grey Carter has come out of it smelling of roses and flirting with anything in a skirt. We failed to do our job effectively. Pick any of those reasons.'

'Do you think he loved her?'

'Grey?'

Wallace nodded silently, but his gaze remained frozen on her.

She shrugged. 'Maybe. I don't think he loves anyone but himself. You know the reason we were able to rule out rape was because her husband confirmed that she was there by her own choice. Supposedly helping with the hotel. It didn't make sense. Why would someone drive all the way from Glasgow to here to help someone who, her husband said, she didn't like? You know the husband and Grey had been best friends since childhood. Considered him like a brother. His parents gave Grey a home after his parents died in a fire. He was too wild for them, though.'

'You have done your homework on him.'

Rosie felt her stomach tighten. Maybe she'd shown just a little too much interest. She hadn't found much; a few misdemeanours, a fiery temper and a small wealth left to him by his dead parents that probably explained the ability to buy the hotel.

Wallace swung round in his chair to get closer to her. 'I think you have to let it go. Even if you got him on sexual assault, you wouldn't get him on murder. It sounds to me like a horrible accident that left a young woman dead. There's no reason sometimes. We just have to accept that these terrible things happen and that nobody's to blame.'

'Except, three men are dead who all attended the scene of her death.' A shadow passed across her just as she dipped her eyes. 'I think I need to take another look at Debra's file. The chief won't be happy that I'm accessing it again. He's already dragged me across the coals for spending my time on something that he said wasn't murder.'

'What about the husband? Did you look into him?'

'Adam Mullen?' She laughed. 'No, I don't think there's a bad bone in his body. Dull as dishwater. Why would he be going after Brian and the paramedics anyway? Or me?'

'His wife's dead. When did you last see him? A few months ago, maybe? He's probably a changed man. Angry and vengeful.'

Rosie was almost shrieking with laughter now. The very notion made her laugh. Adam Mullen, arms like matchsticks, hauntingly pale and so very stiff, murdering anyone was a ludicrous notion by any stretch of the imagination. 'That's gave me the best laugh I've had all week,' she crowed. 'Honestly, you're way off the mark on this one. You'd likely die of boredom in his company.'

'What about Grey then? The same can't be said about him. There's something dark about him. You're only in a room with him for two minutes and it's there. The air's thick with it. You said yourself he was having some sort of torrid affair with Debra.'

Rosie knew she was being just a little too protective of him. Maybe he was a cold-blooded killer, or a rapist. Why did she find it so hard to believe? Perhaps she was allowing her growing feelings for him to cloud her professional judgement. Back in that stupid box again. 'Like I said, I don't think Grey Carter loves anyone but himself. He has a possessive streak. He wants to possess things. People, even. I think he's possessive over Adam Mullen. It wasn't love for Debra that incited that affair. It was a need to encompass every part of Adam's life.'

'Why, though? You make Adam sound like the most boring man alive.'

'To you and me, maybe. There's something between them. I don't know if its friendship, a loyalty, some hidden secret. I couldn't work it out from speaking to either of them. In the end, it doesn't matter why. It was ruled an accident. I was taken out of the equation and the chief moved me on to something else.' She looked across the office. 'Basically, he told me to get out and do some real police work and stop trying to turn an accident into a crime.'

Wallace smirked. 'Then, what the chief doesn't know, won't hurt him. Come on, let's pull the file and look together. If there's something to lead us to the killer, we can't simply ignore it.'

She slapped his shoulder gently. 'I'm liking you

more and more by the hour.'

43.

The van hurtled over uneven mounds, winding towards whatever destination their captor had decided to take them to. Would this be the inevitable death they'd been warned of? Was there something else on the agenda they didn't know about?

'It feels good to have that thing off my ankle,' said Lizzie, her arm tucked into Dave's elbow. 'You must be in pain.' She rubbed his hand gently with her other free hand.

'It's okay,' he said, biting back the urge to sob. He wasn't sad for the fact that he might be meeting a grisly end any hour now. His sadness was that he couldn't save his wife and that he'd used none of his resourcefulness to get them out of the situation. Why hadn't he just fought back from the moment he received the call. He'd been so frightened that something would happen to Lizzie that it had almost choked him. He only truly felt relieved when he finally saw her again. Then he'd laid there for days without so much as an escape plan formed.

Lizzie was hanging off his shoulders now.

'I'm sorry I haven't managed to get us out of this.' He felt close to breaking. His voice crackled when he spoke. There was a judder in his gut that sent a spasm racing across his groin. He would have yelped in pain if he wasn't trying to hold it together for her.

'It's not your job to save us. It's both of our jobs to save each other and ourselves. We're in this together. Whatever happens now, we'll both be in it together. I love you. I couldn't have asked for a better husband.'

She deserved better, he told himself. It was he

who had landed on his feet. Punched above his weight, as his friends had said. 'I love you too. I'm sorry for everything.' He wasn't just talking about the kidnapping now. Everything that had happened before. From the moment their baby was gone until this moment, he began to weep for it all. Cry as he had never cried before.

Lizzie was running her hands over the side of his head now, gently soothing the angry red on his throat. She turned his face round so his sorrowful eyes met hers. 'You've nothing to be sorry for. What happened with the baby was nobody's fault. Not mine, nor yours. We can try again when this is all over.'

He felt the merest surge of happiness. He had never dared suggest another attempt because of how fragile Lizzie had been after the miscarriage. Here and now she was offering that chance without him indelicately proposing it. If only they hadn't had to go through this for her to find his way back to her. Yet, he didn't want to mention the obvious. There might not be another opportunity. Not if their kidnapper had anything to do with it.

Another sharp bump in the road and they were both almost thrown from the wooden bench.

Dave shifted to the back window and saw that Loch Achray lay behind them. From this angle, it might well be the most picturesque image he'd ever seen. It was hard to imagine something so evil lay in wait for them here.

'I wonder where he's taking us.'

'I don't know, but it doesn't look like there'll be much civilisation.'

The van turned then.

As Lizzie grabbed for Dave and leaned against him, they could suddenly see an archway of trees laid out behind them. It was almost like travelling into a tunnel.

Dave suspected it was an entrance to somewhere. Sunlight caught his face and he had to turn away from it. It had been days since he'd seen real daylight, so his eyes had become unaccustomed.

Suddenly, the van stopped. A door opened, then slammed shut.

Dave waited, perfectly still, listening for movement. Muffled voices then came into play. The kidnapper was speaking to someone else. Larry, probably.

Someone was banging on the side of the van now. There was a slightly angry exchange but neither Dave nor Lizzie were able to decipher the words.

He held his breath. Could this be the moment? The idyllic spread behind them couldn't possibly prepare them for what might happen next.

A click and the back door swung opened.

The kidnapper stood there, smiling brightly. Finally, he'd revealed his face. He was only a young man; red hair to match his fiery eyes, some light stubble that was almost invisible against his freckles and a surprisingly congenial expression that made him look far less intimidating than he had behind the balaclava.

Then, another figure was moving into the frame. They were finally going to meet the second kidnapper.

The other door opened.

The second man swung a poker at his side. He was slightly smaller than the other, much older, dark hair but there was something so similar in their eyes that there was no mistaking they were related.

'Oh my god,' muttered Dave, the shock catching

up to him. He stared speechlessly. It was the last thing he expected, but it explained why no-one had been able to save them.

Jason Barr was leaning against the edge of the door with a torturous smile. 'You got my invitation then?'

44.

Adam clutched a picture of his wife and daughter in his hands. He wasn't sure he'd done the right thing now. The gun sat on the passenger's seat, the extension of his arm now a foe rather than a friend. He'd worked himself up and then back down again. He realised how stupid the notion of shooting someone now felt. He'd walked in and out of that maze twice, muttering to himself and then laughing as he realised that if anyone saw him, they might think he'd gone deranged.

He couldn't just turn back and not say anything to Grey, though. He needed to confront him. This was the one thing he could never forgive. Even the affair might have been forgivable but not this. Assaulting Adam's wife had finally opened his eyes to the monster that Grey Carter really was. He found himself questioning everything he'd ever believed. He'd known Grey could kill his own parents, yet he'd been able to turn a blind eye. What kind of man did that make him?

The clouds shifted slowly in Achray. Just like everything else, the serenity was almost chilling. Adam had been used to the bustle of the city. He'd never particularly liked it and had often wondered what it would be like for him, Debra and Gracie to uproot their lives and move to somewhere like this. Now that he had the smallest taste of it, it didn't seem very palatable to him.

A van appeared in the distance. Maybe the caterer's for tonight's event. Or some box of fireworks that Grey had ordered to make the night go off with a bang. A bang! He turned to the gun again and pressed his hand against it.

The van was pulling into a parking space at the front of the hotel. As a tall, red-headed man in his twenties got out of the front, he was suddenly joined by a dark headed man who was much older. The older man was emerging from the hotel lobby. That wasn't what caught Adam's attention though.

He knew the older man. Recognised him instantly. He pulled the gun from the seat beside him and tucked it into his pocket. He was about to get out of the car when he noticed that both men were entering into some confrontation. Then, the red head was throwing his hands up angrily and moving away. He banged on the side of the van.

Adam opened the door of his car and slipped his feet onto the ground.

The pair were speaking to someone inside the van now. Things seemed to be getting heated. Then, suddenly, a man lunged from inside the van and landed a punch on the side of the older man's face.

Adam was standing now. He wanted to walk over, confront them but something made him uneasy about what he was witnessing.

A young woman was getting out of the van and slapping on the younger red head's chest.

Suddenly, the man who had first lunged out of the van was being beaten down by a poker.

What the hell was going on, wondered Adam. He really wanted to confront the older man. He wanted to know why he was here. Something told him that what he was witnessing was something dangerous that he didn't want to become part of. Perhaps he would be better to call the police. Wait! The older man was the police. Adam couldn't fathom it. It was the detective who had come to his house a few days ago. The one who had told him about the rape. Why was he here at

Grey's hotel on the day of the big opening? He slipped back into the car and lowered himself down. Suddenly, he realised he'd been lied to. This detective had suddenly turned up out of the blue and Adam hadn't questioned anything the man had said. Why should he? He heard what he wanted to hear about his wife. Now, he wasn't so sure that he hadn't just been dragged into another collection of lies. One thing was for sure, he was more determined than ever to speak to Grey Carter.

45.

As Rosie settled into another coffee and looked over the notes for Debra Mullen's accident, she started noting everybody who had been in attendance that day. She'd just come off the phone and had confirmation from her colleagues in Glasgow that David Hawthorn had been the one to take the call about the accident. They'd also confirmed that David had to be spoken to after the call because he'd taken the wrong location details. It had been difficult because the hotel address didn't yet come up on a postcode search and there was nothing else around for miles. David had done his best to get them as close as possible to where the accident had happened.

She took a loud slurp, much to Wallace's annoyance, and then slammed the mug on the table. 'What?'

'Has nobody ever told you that you eat and drink like a horse chewing on glass?'

She blew through her lips. 'Has nobody ever told you it's rude to comment on how a lady eats?'

'Touché!'

'I just don't get it. All of us targeted by this maniac have one thing in common. Debra Mullen. Yet, none of it makes sense. Some of the information this person has used to target us would take some digging. My photos would have had to come from London. How would Grey or Adam get their hands on the person who would provide those? What about the drugs that Brian took to the prison? How did the killer learn about that?'

'Maybe they're in it together.'

Rosie laughed again. 'Adam and Grey. I don't think so. Adam can barely speak Grey's name right now and honestly; I don't see Grey pulling this off himself. He's too pre-occupied. I agree with you that there's something underlying with him and I'm sure he's got his fingers in some dirty pies, but these murders don't fit. Anyway, he's hardly going to hang someone from his own premises if he's wanting his event to go without a hitch.'

'So, who else was there at the accident? Was there a lot of personnel?'

'Really, no,' she answered. 'It was cut and dry. Brian and I attended. We were the first responders. Discovered Debra was already dead. The paramedics followed shortly afterwards, worked on her for a few minutes but by then she'd already been dead for several minutes.'

Wallace looked at her, ruefully. 'Honestly, you could strangle that lab technician who screwed up the samples.'

'Yup,' she said, sharply.

'So, no-one else was at the accident site. Not Grey?'

'No, I don't think he'd realised it even happened until we went to the hotel and spoke to him.'

Wallace drank from his mug, deliberately emulating her slurping sound.

She decided to ignore him.

'So, who phoned in the accident then.'

Rosie looked down at her notes and then at the screen. She quickly scrolled and then pursed her lips. 'It doesn't actually say. I assumed it was probably the other couple.'

'Other couple?'

'Yes, the other couple who were involved in the accident.'

'Shit! Why didn't you mention them?'

Rosie shrugged. 'Well, we've only just made the connection. They weren't hurt. Their car skidded off to the side and they had to call for roadside assistance. They were both fine. Actually, they were visibly distressed by Debra's death.'

'Not so distressed they'd go on a killing spree, though.'

A snort as she took the last dribble of coffee. 'I wouldn't have thought so but let's dot the I's and cross the T's anyway.'

'I'll run it,' offered Wallace. 'What's their names?'

She quickly fingered her notes until she came to the two names on the page. She handed it over to him and left him to run a search. Then, she continued to scroll through the information she had on the screen. 'I think this is the most stumped I've been in years.'

'Found them, not that they're hard to find,' Wallace said, raising a championing fist. 'He's a retired police officer. Wife's a nurse. They don't actually live in Achray anymore, but it looks like they own some property here.'

'Oh?'

'You know that scabby rundown house about a mile from where you live? It's an old family house. They had to report a series of robberies there a few years ago when the rest of the shacks were being demolished. They refused to sell at the time and seemingly still own it.'

Rosie stood and rushed round the desks. She was faced with images of the couple who had been so upset that day by the death of a woman much younger than them. The lady had been very quick to point out that they hadn't seen her coming. The husband, the level-headed one had shushed her and allowed everybody to get on with their business. 'That's them. Jason and Carolyn Barr. Seemed nice enough. I certainly don't think there's any reason for them to be involved.'

Wallace didn't look so sure. 'We're running out of options. I've got an address for them here. I think we should go and have a chat.'

46.

Dave didn't recognise the images that hung across the hotel room. Was he supposed to? He'd been separated from Lizzie for several minutes. Jason and his son had forced Lizzie back into the back of the van where she'd kicked and screamed until they'd dragged him out of earshot. He'd fought back gamily, landed a few jabs on them both. The younger man was starting to look like he'd gone ten rounds with a world champion. Dave consoled himself that he'd fought back and had done everything he could to get his wife to safety.

He looked at the images again. Two different women laying in the snow. One surrounded by blood, the other perfectly still with frosted eyes wide open. Both images were as haunting as the other, but Dave didn't know what either of them had to do with him. He wanted to speak to Jason. To get answers now that he'd calmed down. All these weeks of getting to know his new manager and joking around, this is what had been planned all along.

Dave slumped onto the bed. At least it was more comfortable than being chained up in the loft or thrown around the back of a cold damp van. He couldn't get Lizzie off his mind though. Would she be able to handle both father and son, or would they finally get the better of her? He could picture her still kicking up hell as they dragged her into the hotel. What room would she be in? What pictures would she be seeing?

He lay back, placed himself at an angle so he was looking at the back of the pictures. He couldn't bear to look at those two women any longer. He wondered if Jason was related to one of them. Maybe his wife?

The younger one might be his daughter. Dave could understand the anger of someone hurting his wife. He was living it right now and there was nothing he wouldn't consider doing to save her. The thought forced him from the bed, and he was rummaging round the room now. He'd already tried the door and it was locked from the outside. No way he was getting out. Maybe he'd find something to defend himself when they came in.

*

The Barr's house was anyone's dream home. Even compared to Crystal Ridge, it was stunning. She found herself wondering if they owned all the surrounding land. There were no other houses anywhere near. A boat sat at the end of a wooden pier which led onto a vast lake. The house itself was on two levels and probably consisted of at least six bedrooms upstairs. The front door had a porch with a hanging trellis made up of a variety of coloured roses. Soft solar lights were screwed into the ledge of the roof which probably lightened the dirty white paintwork of the house.

'I wonder how many children they have.'

She was knocking on the door now. She'd only ever met them during the chaos of the accident. Now at their house, Rosie wasn't even sure she would recognise them when they opened the door. She remembered Carolyn being homely. Probably drag her inside, offer her lemonade or hot chocolate that she made herself and look horrified at what was going on in their nearby village.

There was no answer.

'Maybe we should have called.'

Rosie shook her head. 'No, I prefer the element of surprise when I'm investigating. Don't give people a chance to get their stories aligned.'

'You think they've got a story to align?'

'No,' she said, beginning to walk round the house. 'I don't even know if they can help us. You got any better ideas?'

'Maybe try the shack. It's the perfect time for retirees to hit the village and enjoy the peace. I think I could get used to it myself.'

Rosie wasn't ready yet to give up. So, she knocked on the back door, rattling the glass more robustly than she'd intended to and then found herself staring in the window. 'Come and see this.' The kitchen looked like it had been overturned. Dishes lay piled high in the sink. Bottles were overturned alongside filthy mugs on the sideboard. A dining chair was toppled over with several other items strewn across the kitchen floor.

Wallace was joining her at the window and peering in past the reflection of the sunlight.

'What a tip.'

'Do you think they've been robbed?'

'I don't think so but there's something not right,' she said, instinctively. 'You didn't meet this pair. They were immaculate. They both work in responsible jobs and have a house that would cost more than half a million pounds. They probably have a cleaner, for Christ sake.'

Silence followed.

Finally, Rosie moved away from the window. 'I think you're right. I think we should try the cottage near mine. I'll drive. Can you call headquarters and see if you can find out more about the Barrs'? I have a bad feeling about the state of that house.'

47.

Lizzie sat at the kitchen work top and watched Jason scramble eggs.

'You must be starving. My son doesn't know the inside of a microwave from the rings on a cooker.'

She wasn't interested in eating now. She just wanted to see her husband. Though the eggs did smell good. 'Why are you doing this? Dave liked you so much. What could we possibly have done to you that would make you want to do this?'

'There's a reason for it. Unfortunately, you're collateral damage. Which is why you're sitting here and not still locked up. Salt and pepper?'

Time was running out. Lizzie knew it. They'd been moved from the loft after days of being locked up there. She'd only just been given some clean clothes a few minutes ago and couldn't believe she was now in clothes that she hadn't urinated in. Dave hadn't appeared to be so lucky.

'You'll have to forgive my son. He's always been intense. He has his reasons, but I know it can seem odd to other people. You're new to his peculiarities. I've lived with them for twenty-four years.' He eyed the door as if not wanting his son to walk in on the conversation.

'You know he says he's murdered someone?'

Jason laughed awkwardly. 'He has a vivid imagination.'

It was obvious to her though that Jason wasn't comfortable.

'You know, don't you?'

Jason moved the pot from the gas heat and stepped towards her.

Lizzie flinched.

'You have to understand, he's been through a lot recently. It certainly wasn't my intention that he would kill anyone. Things got a little out of hand. I blame myself. He has a far wider list of people he blames. I just want the people responsible to know what they've done.'

She couldn't believe what she was hearing. A little out of hand was probably the understatement of the year. 'You know it's more than that. How can you be so glib? If he has murdered people and you are here, then you're an accessory. You'll never convince anyone you weren't part of it.'

His eyes widened. 'I didn't ask him to kill anyone. I asked him to keep you and your husband safe until we could have this conversation. And you don't need to quote the law to me. I'm a retired policeman.'

Lizzie scoffed. It seemed Jason was as deluded as his son was mad. 'We've seen both of your faces. You and I both know you'll never let Dave and I walk away. What is it you've come here to do anyway? What has Dave done to you that has caused you to concoct whatever this is?'

'I'm simply evening a score.'

'What score?' Her voice was rising now, frustration and panic clashing and causing her to shout.

He was pouring the pan of eggs into a bowl and moving it towards her. 'Spoon or fork?'

There was something so unnaturally calm about the whole interaction. Lizzie looked at the eggs and could think of nothing worse than eating them. She would rather starve.

'Dave didn't do you justice. He said you were

very attractive. I think beautiful would be more appropriate. He's a lucky boy.'

In anyone else's hands the compliment might have caused her to blush but from him, it merely made her want to vomit. She squirmed and picked up the fork he'd placed into the eggs. She pushed the eggs round the bowl and contemplated taking just a morsel. It had been days since she'd had anything that was more than barely edible. 'Who is Larry?'

His head snapped up, anger narrowing his face. 'Who told you about him?'

Lizzie sensed she'd touched a nerve. 'Nobody told me. I heard your son talking to him. Is it his friend?'

Jason's eyes dipped.

'His brother?'

'Nobody. Larry's nobody. He doesn't exist.'

'What do you mean?'

Silence fell between them.

Jason was turning to the door now. 'What the hell? What harm can it do? My wife was expecting twins. We were excited when we found out they were going to both be boys. We picked out everything matching for them. A month before the babies were due, Lawrence died in the womb. My wife had to deliver both babies early.'

'I'm sorry,' she said, enraged that her own recent experiences would allow her to empathise with a man who had taken her prisoner.

'We were wrong to tell him about Lawrence. We should have never mentioned it. He was so convinced that there was another half of him lurking somewhere that we thought it would help. He became obsessed. Convinced really. We had to pay to get him psychiatric treatment in his teens when it became apparent Larry wasn't just a passing phase.'

'It doesn't look like it has worked then,' she said, sarcastically.

Jason simply went silent.

'Do you own this hotel?' Lizzie wasn't really interested but the silences were unbearable.

'Some of it,' he replied. 'I'm more of a silent partner. I don't think I'll be involved in it much after this.'

'Why?'

'Took my eye off the ball, shall we say. Had a personal tragedy to take care of and didn't notice until now that the little git that owns it has been fleecing me. Buying in shoddy second rate materials and sending me faked invoices. Anyway, that's nothing to do with you. That's a side issue.'

'Is that why you've taken us? Do you think Dave was involved in that? I swear he wasn't.'

'No, I just told you that has nothing to do with you. I'm dealing with that separately. I've got a few bones to pick with Mr Carter,' he smiled, revealing a set of perfectly set veneers. 'You're not here because of the hotel. You're here because your husband let me down very badly.'

'In what way?'

The kitchen door swung open. With the open door came the unmistakable scent of petrol. The younger man entered and slammed two empty cans on the ground. 'Done.'

'What are you going to do?' Lizzie's voice was a nervous whisper now.

Jason gave her another smile and a wink. 'That's easy. I'm going to burn this place to the ground.'

48.

'Shit, I think I get it now,' said Rosie, as she stepped out of the car. 'The message wasn't HELP LOVE; it was HELP COVE. I think the Hawthorn's were trying to let us know they were here. Look, the name of the house is Cove Cottage.' Rosie hadn't appreciated just how dilapidated it was until she was standing on the moist porch. She was certain if she moved an inch to the left or right, she'd be crashing through sodden wood. She knocked on the door and waited.

No response.

'I'm going in,' she said, swiftly pushing the door wide open.

'We don't have a warrant. If we find anything in there that could lead to a conviction, it will be inadmissible in court. You realise that, don't you?'

'I'll take my chances. We could very well be saving another four people's lives here. If you want to wait on a warrant, I won't hold it against you.'

It was the magic words. She had learned enough about Detective Kevin Wallace to know he wouldn't be left on the side-line.

The inside of the house was as bad as the outside. The kitchen was an off-shoot of the living area and even more untidy than the Barrs' own kitchen. The cooker was ancient, one of those high-top grills that people had in the eighties.

'I'll have a squint downstairs if you want to have a look upstairs.'

Rosie frowned. 'Are you scared there's someone up there. Don't worry. I'll protect you.'

He raised his shoulders, emphasising his impressive width. 'I think it's me who'll be protecting you.'

She was climbing the stairs with the torch on her mobile phone giving her some illumination. She could see there were some pictures at the top of the stairs. There was also an open bedroom door with a dim light.

There was no sound, but she slowly drew her torch light into the room and found that the bed was unmade. The light inside the room came from a tiny ancient looking computer monitor which showed another room. If there had been someone there, they were gone now. Rosie searched the rest of the room and found no-one there. She had a quick fumble through some items on a messy desk but there was nothing that would have struck her as particularly odd.

Leaving the room behind, Rosie stepped into a nearby bathroom. It was every bit as filthy as the bedroom and the downstairs area. She couldn't imagine having to use the toilet here. She swallowed back her disgust and moved to the last room in the hallway. The door swung towards her to reveal another flight of stairs. It led to the loft that she'd just seen on the screen. As soon as she reached the top stair, she knew someone had been held here. Two messy beds with a set of chains on each told her exactly what she needed to know.

'I think I know why we can't get a hold of the Hawthorns,' she said, meeting Wallace on the middle landing.

'Guess who I've just ran into?' Wallace was beaming with a sense of his own worth. He'd obviously discovered something he was dying to share with her.

She waited patiently for him to get to his reveal.

'Who is this?' He lifted a framed picture that he

must have taken from a wall.

She lifted her torch and watched the light spread across the faces. 'It's Jason and Carolyn.'

'Who else?'

Rosie narrowed her eyes and let out a sharp gasp. 'Oh my god. Is that who I think it is?'

He pushed the picture towards her. 'Recognise him.'

'I recognise him alright. That's Cammie from the coffee house. He must be their son.'

49.

Cammie held his phone up to his father's face. 'She's found out about the house.'

Jason sat across the chrome worktop from Lizzie and stared at him. 'Very good. That means she's close. Have you covered every corner of this place in petrol?'

Lizzie still pushed the egg round the plate knowing it would be cold now. She had already gone through half a dozen escape scenarios, including burning them with the egg. How stupid. Everybody knew scrambled egg was literally lukewarm within a couple of minutes. The best she could hope for would be a short delay in them catching up to her when she hit them in the face with the bowl. She looked round the kitchen, a warren of dangerous equipment but she knew she couldn't move fast enough to inflict any real damaged.

Jason was walking towards his son now, reaching for his face. 'I don't want any more bloodshed from you. This was never about creating carnage. Let me deal with it.'

'It's for her I'm doing this.' For the first time, the young man looked vulnerable, the potential for a giant blubbering wreck in his father's arms.

'You're seeing him again, aren't you? Larry?'

'No,' said Cammie, turning to Lizzie just in time for her to see the fury flash in his eyes.

Jason pulled his face back round. 'Don't lie to me, boy. I know you better than you know yourself.'

A quiver of the lips. 'Yes, dad. I see him all the time. I always have.'

'Does he tell you to do these things? Is that why you defied me? Why you've killed all those people in barbaric ways?'

Lizzie couldn't believe she was hearing this. A murderer scolding a murderer. She ran her eyes along the chrome hanger above the worktop where pots and pans sat. There were hooks that homed various utensils and a plethora of knives that ranged from small to frighteningly large.

'You said we had to avenge mum. Make them pay, you said.'

Jason tusked. 'I wanted the people responsible to pay. I didn't want them to become martyrs. You know they'll always be victims now. Nobody will care about your mother's death now.'

Cammie pulled away from his father's grip. 'You think this is different. Locking them in rooms and burning the hotel to the ground around them.'

Jason raised his shoulders and let them lag in disappointment. 'I guess you'll never see the bigger picture. That was always the problem. Maybe the best place for you is a psychiatric unit. Just be prepared for when we need to go. It won't be long now.' He took the phone from Cammie's hand and walked through the swinging doors, leaving Cammie and Lizzie alone.

Cammie's head was hanging. 'He doesn't believe you're here,' he whispered.

Lizzie took the moment to move the plate closer to the edge of the worktop.

'I'll tell him it wasn't your fault,' said Cammie, staring at the empty space at the far end of the kitchen.

Lizzie followed his intense stare, curious about the other brother who he had created in his mind. Had he only created him as a justification for his bad behaviour, or was Larry's existence so integral to

Cammie that he couldn't live without him? She had the bowl at the edge of the worktop now. She could see he was still muttering to his invisible brother. It might be just enough to distract him while she acted on her escape.

Cammie threw his head back, seemingly pushed to the edge by his father's disrespect and disavowing of his other long dead son.

Finally, Lizzie acted. She pushed the plate from the edge of the worktop, watched it smash into several pieces, egg strewn everywhere and the fork clattering to the ground.

Cammie spun.

She leaned forward only slightly, reaching for the fork and seeing that he was already hurtling towards her.

He kicked the plate out of her reach and lunged to the fork, so he'd get it before she did.

Lizzie pulled back, reached up, grabbed for a knife and brought it down towards his throat.

Cammie couldn't act quickly enough. He'd only just managed to pick up the fork from the ground and was still bent over when his angry eyes met hers.

The plunge didn't feel how she imagined it would. It wasn't like carving a pumpkin or slicing a finger. The knife went straight in, ripping through an artery in his neck and causing blood to spurt everywhere. Lizzie felt her breath catch in her chest. She wasn't breathing. She was standing perfectly still, waiting for time to start again.

Cammie was spinning to the ground now, gasping for air and trying to scream out. He had one hand on the knife trying to pull it from his neck, the other one battling with the pouring blood. Then, a few seconds later, he fell to the ground and seized. He reached out to her as his body convulsed.

Lizzie had her bloody hand over her mouth in horror. She knew if she hadn't done something, she was waiting for her and her husband to die.

The young man who had been fitting just a moment before suddenly went still and took one last effortless breath. Then, his eyes slowly glazed over as the life disappear from his body.

*

Rosie took the call as she was leaving the battered house. She was glad to be back in the open air, having realised the worst thing about that house was how oppressive it was.

'Hello, I'm calling from Glasgow division here. I understand you were waiting on some information. Firstly, we've been unable to contact the Hawthorns. Maybe they've went on a holiday somewhere. The other thing you phoned in earlier about was the Barrs'. You were quite right; they were involved in the car accident back in January. They were both fine at the time. However, unfortunately for Carolyn Barr, she died of a blood clot a week later. Her husband found her in the garden and rushed her to hospital. She was unresponsive when he found her, and they were unable to resuscitate on arrival.'

'Jesus Christ,' she muttered. 'Why weren't we informed of this as part of the investigation. I knew nothing about this lady's death. I assumed they were both off living their lives as normal whilst we were delivering the bad news to Debra Mullen's family.'

'It's marked down here as an accident.'

'Yes,' she snapped.

'Then, it probably wouldn't have been considered essential to include that information in the findings. It wasn't relative to the outcome of Debra

Mullen's death. It also wasn't conclusive from the post-mortem that the accident even caused the clot. It could have been any number of factors.'

'Fine. Do you have any idea how we get in touch with Mr Barr? I know his son works at the local coffee shop here in Achray.'

'I'm not sure, but it's funny you should mention that. We've had two calls come in for incidents in the Achray area; one of them is in Benny's coffee shop, the other being at the Milton Carter Hotel. Do you know them?'

'What kind of incidents?'

'A fight broke out in the coffee house. The owner is nearly keeling over with rage. Not sure about the incident at the hotel. All I've been told is that there's some event there tonight and a member of staff has been sacked. They're refusing to leave without payment. Don't know if it has broken into a fight. You want to check one of them out?'

Rosie ended the call and got into the car. 'Drop me at my house and I'll take my own car. You want the coffee shop or the hotel?'

Wallace nodded his head. 'They both sound like crap but you'll be wanting to do your nosy over tonight's event. I'll let you take the hotel.'

Rosie felt a little giddy. She was looking forward to getting into her frock. Only a few hours until the event started. Would Grey find her attractive away from the staid business suits she often wore? She wondered why she'd even been invited at all. Staring out onto the loch, she thanked god that nobody, but Wallace had learned of her disgrace. She wasn't sure she would be able to take that exposure a second time.

50.

Lizzie could hear Jason on the phone as she fled towards the entrance of the hotel. If she had not been brought here against her will, she might have taken a moment to enjoy the serene surroundings and some of the artwork that adored the marble partitions of the walls. Instead, she was running away from the direction where Jason's voice travelled. The hallway curved like a crescent, twenty or more doors with outward brass locks to support the electronic additions that would probably have been made recently.

She had dumped her shoes. They weren't particularly noisy, but her feet would be even less of a giveaway as they pressed against the cold floors. She tried every door handle along the way and found that she couldn't access any of the rooms. There were no keys in the old-fashioned locks, so it's not like that would be a giveaway as to what room her husband was being held in.

At the end of the curve, she found a lift. Maybe her husband had been taken upstairs. From what she could remember there was only one floor above. Probably another thirty rooms. Right now, it might as well have been a maze. Maybe once she was off the ground floor, she could call his name. Would it be sensible at the risk of being found? One thing she knew was that she had just halved their kidnappers' chances against them. The thought made her feel hopeful. She finally found a door to the stairs beside the lift and pushed it open. She threw her shoes under the stairs and slowly closed the door.

*

Jason didn't know what happy was. Not anymore.

Since the death of Carolyn, there was barely a day that he hadn't been fuelled by anger and resentment. Initially, he knew it was normal for that level of grief. Something had happened though. Something that tipped him over the edge. He suddenly found himself needing to face all the people who had failed his wife. The detectives on site that day had barely broke breath to her. The paramedics had failed to do a proper assessment. It was a week before Jason himself even knew that his wife had been in pain since the accident. Then there were the others. Grey Carter, he had learned had been playing the field with the young woman that died. The call taker, Dave had reduced anyone's chance of survival by giving the wrong location. Two women dead because people had failed to do their jobs properly.

He had begun the plan by inserting himself back into the work force. It wasn't hard to get the job at the Govan centre. He had been stationed there for many years and only had to make a few calls to find out if they were hiring. He would have taken a job as a call taker but a few of his old buddies had managed to secure him in a Team Manager job. What a stroke of luck that he'd managed to get Dave in his team.

Jason liked Dave. He was the kind of man he would have befriended back in his force days. Maybe played some five-asides with him. Went for a few beers. Maybe he would tell Lizzie that to make her feel better before they were consumed by flames. He wouldn't allow himself to become distracted though He needed them all to know what they'd done. How their incompetence had cost him the love of his life.

Then, there was Cameron. His beautiful son. He'd almost had two boys. It was heart-breaking that only one lived. There was something different about

Cammie. He wasn't like other boys. He'd always been sensitive. However, there was also a destructive cunning side to him that had been evidence from young. Carolyn had defended it. Of course, she had, it was her only surviving child. She had resented Jason's push for them to have him evaluated. Even threatened to leave him once. Until she realised that there was something dark lurking in Cammie's mind.

The death of Carolyn had pushed Cammie over the edge once more. When Jason saw on the news that the police officer had been murdered, he couldn't believe it at first. His initial plan had never included anyone getting killed. Even tonight would have ended up in a blaze but he would have made sure after confronting everyone, that he got them to safety. That didn't seem to be an option anymore. His son had murdered three people. He was about to be exposed. Jason had to do something to protect him.

He was walking slowly back from the reception area now. He'd made all the right noises on the phone and didn't think Detective Cooper would be suspicious. Once he got her here, locked her in the room with her past, there would only be one other thing to take care of.

Jason had planted the seed with Adam Mullen. Told him what he wanted to hear, just enough to fuel his rage. The invitation would get him here. He'd be coming for a confrontation with his oldest friend. What he would find is that he would be going to prison for the murder of three emergency services workers, his best friend and the people he blamed for the death of his wife. It was perfect. Nobody would even link Jason's wife's death to the whole sorry affair. He, and his son would have avenged Carolyn and would be able to move on with their lives. He felt bad for Adam. He, and Lizzie were collateral damage. Jason had to protect what was left of his family. So, the maths added up to this.

He was back at the kitchen door now. He'd barely even stepped in when he found his son dead on the floor. Jason howled. It was the final thing that would push him to become a killer as well. He ran towards Cammie, snatched some tea-towels from the side and pressed them into the man's bleeding neck. It was too late though. He could tell from the faded colour of his eyes, the blueness to his lips and the way the blood was lessening that his son was dead. It could only have been Lizzie. He stood and let a powerful rage surge through him until he was clenching every muscle in his being. Then, he turned and went in search of the little bitch who had done this to his boy.

51.

Adam hadn't seen anyone coming or going from the hotel in quite a while. What the hell was going on in there? Two people had been practically dragged in at the forceful hands of the policeman and the younger man who appeared to be helping. Where was Grey? Surely, he'd have been out and about, or walking the grounds to make sure everything was ready to go ahead.

He was walking towards the entrance now. A gust of air passed him as he climbed the few deep stairs into the reception area. It was deathly silent, not what he expected from a hotel that was about to open its doors to several guests. What the hell was going on?

He was climbing the stairs now, his brown jacket flowing behind him as he saw the top landing come into view. One last turn as he got to the top of the stairs. His wife had died near here. He found himself wondering where. It had been difficult to see the entire landscape because of the trees and the new growth of leaves that hung heavily from the branches. In all the time Debra had been dead, he'd never found himself feeling closer to her than he had in the last few days. Now, he suspected he'd been duped in some way. Should it make a difference? Couldn't he just forgive Debra for whatever had taken place? She was still his wife and if he'd learned anything in the last few days, it was that he would do anything to protect his family.

There was no-one in view, so he quickly returned to the reception area and found envelopes with several names on the desk. Nobody was here to attend to the arrivals but perhaps that would happen later.

Adam found his own name, for Adam and guest, one last stab in the heart from his oldest friend to remind him he'd be coming without the love of his life.

There was an unpleasant smell in the foyer. He could almost swear it was petrol but surmised it was probably some cleaning fluid they'd decided to use that would be buffed up until the place was of sterling quality. Right now, he wanted to get out of sight. For some reason, the room key addressed to Adam and guest had really wound him up. Any misgivings he might have had about coming here and confronting Grey suddenly dissolved and he found himself feeling for the gun in his pocket once again. It was going to happen. Nobody would die but he wanted Grey to believe in the very real possibility.

Adam's room was on the ground floor. He crumpled his envelope as he searched for room twelve. There were two types of keys in the envelope. A key card that he'd seen many times in different hotels but there was also an old silver key that would simply turn a standard mortice lock. It was a strange choice, he mused. Still, there was no-one stranger than Grey, so nothing surprised him.

He found the room, slipped the key card into the lock and tried to turn the handle. It didn't work. So, he took it out, and used the standard key instead. It appeared to unlock the door, but it still wouldn't open. Perhaps he needed to use both. Adam slipped the key card in again and watched as the door slipped open. He was heading inside now, aiming to be hidden until the event began later.

Before he'd even entered the room, there was something amiss. He had to push his glasses up and switch on the light to see the washing line of photos in their entirety. His hand tightened in horror as he saw the images of his wife's dead body. He'd never seen them before. It was one thing he'd chosen not to live through. Yet, there they were for his perusal. It had to be a cruel joke at Grey's hands.

It wasn't only those pictures that disturbed him though. There were also images of another dead woman who he had never seen before. She looked as if she'd died in similar circumstances to Debra, except with less blood. There was also images of Grey's parents and their burning house which only served to make Adam think that this was a display of the damage Grey had brought to people's lives.

Adam was going to vomit. Before he did, he turned to make his way to the en-suite toilet. However, he was met with another image, this one much larger and even more disturbing. It was his friend, Grey, hanging from a noose. He saw the terror in Grey's eyes and in that moment, Adam realised, he had been duped and all of this hadn't been the work of Grey at all. Something far more sinister had taken place here.

52.

Rosie took the dirt road to the hotel at almost sixty miles per hour. She couldn't believe the day she'd had. She still couldn't believe that a second person had died in that accident and she hadn't known about it. Her belief that nothing stayed secret in small villages had suddenly been turned on its head. In fact, she was starting to believe that there were more secrets and lies in this village than she had ever encountered in the large city of London.

As the days had gone on, she had come to accept that perhaps Brian Houston hadn't been the person she thought she knew. He had committed an illegal act that she couldn't equate with him. At first, she had wanted to believe in his innocence. His brother had been compelling enough to allow her to live in that lie. However, now she knew there had been no lies in this investigation. Only ugly, twisted truths.

The hotel came into view. She didn't want to be going here on any more official business. Not today. Didn't Grey Carter deserve his moment? He wasn't the kindest person she'd ever met. However, she now believed him when he said he'd had nothing to do with the deaths. She wanted to go there tonight with a clean slate. That wasn't going to be possible now. She was going to be turning up in her capacity as officer of the law, laying it down as if she were its gatekeeper.

There weren't as many vehicles in the car park as she had expected. A van sat parked near the entrance of the hotel. A couple of cars parked round the side. Hardly the bustle she might have expected in event of the so-called furore. In fact, there was anything but a furore. The foyer and reception area were anything but busy. With the shadow of gathering clouds blocking a portion of daylight, it was rather sinister.

Rosie found her own name on the desk. She was just one of forty names. She didn't recognise any of the other names on the desk either. None of the folk from the village appeared to be invited. Which made her question again why she had made the list.

Picking up the key, Rosie let her curiosity get the better of her. She would seek out someone to speak to about the disturbance. However, she also wanted to have a sneaky peek at the bedroom that had been allocated to her. It seemed strange that she'd be given a room. It hadn't mentioned that on the invitation. Nor had Grey ever mentioned the suggestion that she'd be staying over after the event. Not that he'd mentioned the event at all. Considering the starting time was only a few hours away, Rosie found it strange that the whole place seemed so deathly quiet.

She walked towards room four, passing the dimly lit kitchen and large dining room. There wasn't a single person in sight. Finally, she arrived at the door, feeling somewhat apprehensive about the whole thing now. Why had she allowed herself to get carried away? What was she even doing here?

After some fidgeting with the locks for thirty seconds or more, she finally managed to push open the door.

Walking into the room, her mind raced. She couldn't believe what had been laid out for her. She gasped and reached forward. Who would have done this? She caught a glimpse of the look on her face in the nearby mirror. There was also a note on the bed. She picked it up, still reeling from what had been set out for her.

She dropped the note and picked up the silver

cocktail dress from the bed. Spinning round towards the mirror, she held it to her breast and pulled at the skirt. Had Grey done this? Had she completely misread him? The moment caught up with her and she found herself staring at the matching heels, the diamantes that had been attached to every strap. Suddenly, a panic stirred, clotting the excitement in her stomach. She couldn't shake the deep sense that something strange was happening here. It didn't seem like the work of Grey, yet who else would it have been.

The door behind her suddenly slammed shut. As Rosie dropped the dress back onto the bed and ran towards the bedroom door, she heard the lock click. Stupidly, she had left the key on the outside. She banged on the door. 'Who's there?'

Nothing.

Another bang on the door and Rosie found herself pressing her ear against it. It was then she realised she had smelt the petrol on the way in. She had assumed at first that it was from the van sitting right at the front door. However, it hadn't wavered. Someone had locked her in this room, and she was certain they hadn't done it to allow her time to get dressed.

Rosie dialled Wallace's number. 'Hi, are you finished at Benny's?'

He blew into the phone. 'I never got started. The only thing that's got Benny on the ceiling is that Cammie hasn't turned up for work again. Benny didn't know anything about Cammie's mother dying either. Don't you think it's strange that he wouldn't have mentioned that?'

'I think from everything we've seen today, it's safe to say that Cammie's our guy. But listen, that's not why I'm phoning you. I need you to get to the hotel. I'm locked in room four with a creepy dress and sandals that have been left here for me. I can also smell petrol. I think whatever is planned for me is going to happen soon. If you don't get me out of here, I'm probably going to be burnt to death.'

53.

Lizzie felt as if a hammer was thumping at her stomach. She thought she'd experienced fear in that loft. It was nothing to what she felt now. She was a murderer. Even with all the justification in the world, she didn't know if she could ever learn to live with that.

Along the corridor on the first floor, she had tried just about every door. The only door that was unlocked was a cleaning cupboard at the far end of the corridor. She had knocked gently on the doors but been unable to cry out loud enough for her husband to properly hear her. Or perhaps he was already dead. She didn't know.

The thought stiffened her. She had already stabbed one killer to death. She was now being hunted by another. What if her husband was locked up on the ground floor? Would Jason Barr take it out on him? Maybe Dave would already have paid the price for what she did. They'd been brought here in innocence, her belief that Dave might be guilty of some untold act. If they left here alive, it would be her who would be leaving the guilty one.

A door crept open at the end of the corridor. It was far enough round the curve that she couldn't see who it was. She could hear the footsteps though. He was coming for her. The terror that bubbled was almost crippling her, but she couldn't stand here waiting for him to catch up to her. Suddenly, his black shadow appeared on the cusp of the corridor's turn.

Lizzie couldn't wait any longer. She had to hide. Throwing open the cleaning cupboard door, she slipped inside and pulled the door closed behind her.

Would he try all the doors? Would he even assume she was still in the hotel? Perhaps he might be torn between searching the hotel for her or burning it down in the event that she might have escaped and called for the police. How she prayed he would believe that. She could escape the flames. She wasn't sure she could escape a second potential killer.

'Lizzie?'

She took a deep sharp breath and listened to the footsteps edge closer.

'You might as well come out. I will find you. The longer you make me look, the more painful I'll make your husband's death.'

She could almost have cried out in joy. Her Dave was still alive. For now.

It didn't make her want to show herself. It was dark and smelly in the cupboard. It wasn't the scent of cleaning products, but rather of a smelly old mop that had been left in dirty water too long. There must have been something else in there that might have helped her.

He was at the door now.

Lizzie could almost hear him breathing. She could certainly see the tiny block against the strip of light under the doorway. Had he found her, she wondered? Perhaps he knew it was the only unlocked door on this floor. She slowly ran her hand down the wall and finally found something that felt solid. Then she waited, still only breathing lightly enough to keep herself alive.

He was turning the knob on the door. He'd found her. 'Come out, Lizzie. It'll be better for you. Better for me. Certainly, better for Dave.'

She was holding onto the smooth round cannister as if her life depended on it. It really did.

The door was suddenly opening.

Lizzie held her breath, allowed the light to flood the cupboard and looked at his leering face. It was a contrast to the pleasant mild-mannered face she'd seen in the kitchen before she'd killed his son. Now she understood he was every bit as insane as his son and would never let her live.

Jason was reaching for her now, preparing to grab for her hair and drag her out of the cupboard screaming.

She had to act. Suddenly she brought up the fire extinguisher in her hand and smashed him squarely in the face.

He yelped and fell back with a startle.

She turned towards him, carrying the heavy contraption with her and brought it down on his face.

Jason was covering his head with his arms now.

Lizzie didn't stop though. She brought it up one more time and let out a scream. She stared fiercely at him. 'What have you done with my husband?'

Blood covered his face. It only added to the ferocity of his glower. 'This place will be in flames before you ever find him.'

Suddenly she noticed the keys hanging from his pocket. She had to stop him. There were too many there for her to risk guessing. So, before grabbing the sets of keys from him, she brought up the extinguisher one more time and brought it down with a ferocious thud. Then, she snatched the keys and ran for her life.

54.

'Dave?'

Adam could hear the woman screaming in the hallway. She sounded frantic. What the hell was going on, he wondered? He'd came here to face off with someone who was both his best friend and his worst enemy. All those weeks ago, Detective Cooper had contacted him to tell him the case was closed and that his wife's accident had been just that. Then, three days ago a different detective turned up and told him what he wanted to hear. That his wife had died the victim of a rape.

He had always been gullible. It was his mother's fiercest criticism of him. She said he would have brought home a stray snake and still insisted on keeping it even if it had bitten him. She meant Grey. He knew that. His father had no trust in Grey from day one. He'd always wondered what had gelled them so tightly together. Why couldn't Adam have that relationship with his own brother, their parents had always asked?

Truth was, Grey was the only person who hadn't treated Adam like he was incapable. His parents were overbearing, his brother judgemental and in the end, only Grey had made Adam feel like he had a place in the world. Grey had needed him. Nobody else before Gracie had ever looked at him with such dependency. Now, he had brought a gun with the intention of harming his oldest friend. He was all mixed up. One thing he was sure of was that the detective who had visited him wasn't really a detective at all. The rape had been a lie. Debra really had been sleeping with Grey. He didn't have the energy to fight any more. Everything had become so contrived that his mind was struggling to compute what was real and what wasn't.

He looked at the picture of Grey hanging and suddenly felt that he needed to get to him. He needed to try and save him. Could Adam really leave his friend to die after all they'd gone through together? Even now, when he was so fuelled by his hatred of their betrayal.

Adam heard the woman's voice again. She was closer now. He ran to the door and began to bang on it. He'd already tried to unlock it from the inside but there was a key jammed in it, stopping him from threading his through.

'Hello?'

The lock was turning now from the other side. He ran and pulled at the door.

A woman appeared, cautiously peering in. She was small in stature but looked like she as on a mission to kill from the expression on her face.

'Who are you?'

'Lizzie. I'm looking for my husband. He's locked in one of these rooms.' She held up the two keys she'd fished from Jason's pocket. 'Who are you?' She stepped into the room; mouth agape when she saw the collection of photos that had been left hanging.

'It's a long story. My friend owns this hotel. I came here to speak to him and found myself being locked in here with these photos.'

'I was kidnapped by my husband's boss and his psychotic son. I think I've killed them, but we've got to get out of here.'

'Okay,' said Adam, suddenly realising just the extent of danger he might be in. He ensured he had the gun that he had so badly wanted to discard earlier and felt glad he hadn't acted too hastily.

They were both fleeing into the hallway now, the scent of petrol now burning up Adam's nostrils.

Lizzie fumbled frantically with the keys, each of them with their own individual numbers on the keyrings. They'd evidently been the older locks from before this new refurbishment had taken place. She ran towards room four, called for her husband in desperation and began to shake the key into its lock.

'It won't make a difference. Flames will rip through this place before you find him,' snarled a voice from behind. Jason appeared at the start of the curved hallway, blood dripping from his battered face onto his shirt.

Adam was standing between them now. 'Does someone want to tell me what the hell is going on? Where's Grey? And why did you pretend to me you were a police officer?'

'I was as police officer,' he hissed. 'Not now. Now I'm just a man who has lost his wife and both his children. All of you. Every last one of you have made sure I have nothing left. So, today I'm going to make sure that not one of you get out of here alive.'

'What are you talking about?' Adam was perplexed. He was here because of his dead wife, not because of anyone else's.

'Your wife died in the car accident on 11th January. Yes? Well mine died of her injuries one week later. Nobody gave a damn about her. At least someone fought for justice for your slag of a wife. Mine is rotting in a cemetery and nobody has even come to ask me about it.'

Adam snatched the gun from his side pocket. 'Don't call my wife that.'

'Why not? It's what she was. A slut who cheated on her husband. I could have sympathised with you but when I met you and realised what a snivelling little prat you were, it's no wonder she jumped into bed with someone else.'

Adam was walking towards him with the gun shaking in his hand.

'I hope you know how to use that thing. If I'm not dead with the first bullet, you'd better run.'

He heard Lizzie turn the key and open the door. Then, he heard a voice that was more familiar to him.

'Adam, put that gun down.'

He edged to the side, so he was able to see Detective Cooper from the corner of his eye but without losing his glare on his target. 'Hello, Detective. Nice to see you again. Pity it's not under nicer circumstances. Have you seen Grey?'

'No,' she whimpered, pushing Lizzie gently out of the way. 'You don't need to do this though. This man,' she pointed toward Jason, 'is going to prison for a long time. Him and his son.'

'My son? It's too late for my son. He's already dead.' His raging eyes focused suddenly on Lizzie. 'Ask her,' he roared.

In that moment, Adam knew he'd had enough. Whatever the woman at his side had done, she must have been pushed to it. He briefly thought of Grey, possibly dead somewhere and knew he had to do something before this maniac killed them all.

He aimed the gun sharply, steadied his hand and finally found his voice again. 'Then you'll be glad not to have to share a cell with him.' Adam pulled the trigger and watched as the man hurtled backwards.

Jason was on the ground now, groaning in pain. It wasn't enough to fully deter him though.

Adam rushed to Detective Cooper. 'This young lady is looking for her husband. We need to help her find him.'

'Are you Elizabeth Hawthorn?'

She quivered. 'Lizzie.'

'Your husband David is here, too?'

Lizzie handed her the last key and watched as she made her way to unlucky room thirteen.

Adam could hear the calamity of Dave banging on the door now. He must have been disturbed by the gun shot because he was shouting his name's wife with the same tenacity she had when calling for him. It could almost have made Dave envious.

Suddenly, a flame shot up the wall.

In their rush to get Dave to safety, they hadn't noticed Jason getting up and dropping a lighter to the ground. He was making a dash round the curved hallway now and leaving them behind. The flames were spreading as if carried by a wild wind, fanning up the walls and ripping through the hotel corridor at a ferocious speed.

'Quick, get her out of here.'

Adam was grabbing for Lizzie, but she didn't seem to want to move.

'Not without my husband. Get him out of there. Please.'

Rosie's hands were shaking uncontrollably. She was only inches from the flames now. Pushing the key into the lock, she twisted it quickly and felt the door being pulled open.

Dave Hawthorn leapt out and grabbed his wife by the hand and pulled her to him.

The fire spread so quickly that it now appeared to be engulfing the entire ground floor. Cammie and Jason had ensured that the reception area was the most flammable because there was no way any of them were going out the front door.

'Dave, how are we going to get out of here?' Lizzie was clutching at him in terror, pulling at his shirt and keeping her gaze away from the fire.

Rosie then spoke. 'Don't worry. I think I know a way out. My colleague, Detective Wallace is on his way here. Even if we don't get out this way, it's under the ground level. We can at least remain safe for a few minutes.

Adam was following her now, down the back grimy stairs of a cellar. He and Rosie were paving the way for their exit. He could see the endless artwork perched against wooden cargo and the far away door that would lead them into the back court. The flames were spreading into the cellar now. Worse than that, blue and grey smoke now billowed and snaked round them. It wouldn't be long before it would start to fill their lungs.

They could hear the revving of an engine outside. Somehow Adam suspected it would be the departure of their captor and not the arrival of the police.

Rosie pushed down on the emergency bar and opened the door, but it only opened a smidgeon. She pushed harder. 'Shit, he's jammed the door shut with the van,' she screamed.

Adam ran towards it and began to push as well. He heard another engine roar off into the distance. Now, he suspected it was the injured man making his departure.

'What the hell are we going to do now. He's trapped us in here and there's no way we can go back.'

*

Wallace could see the smoke rise from the hotel. If only he had insisted on going there instead of the hoax at the café, he might have been able to prevent the fire from started. He could also see a silver BMW racing towards him. What the hell had taken place up there?

As the other driver shot past him, Wallace noticed straight away that his face looked bloody and that there was a burning fury leering from behind. It was Jason Barr. He recognised him from the few photos he'd managed to see. It became obvious to Wallace that Rosie must be in grave danger.

He was dialling her mobile number now. It went straight to voicemail. The next few minutes felt like a month as his car swept under the row of trees that lined the pathway to the hotel. The most shocking thing for him was that there was no-one on the outside. There was no chaos, none of the fear and panic that might have accompanied such a large fire. Where were all the staff? Hadn't any of the guests arrived? Where the hell was Rosie?

He dialled a different number and heard the soft Irish voice answer.

'Gaby, we know who killed Brian. I think you might be in danger as well.'

'Who was it?'

He wasn't sure he should tell her, but he had to warn her in case she found herself in peril. After all, a threat had been left for her as well. 'We think it may have been Jason Barr or his son, Cammie.'

'No,' she said. 'That can't be right. We know Jason and Carolyn and they're two of the nicest people I've met.'

'I don't know what to tell you, Gaby. Can you go over to Mrs Blyth's? Or go to the hotel and stay with your mum? I really think you should be somewhere safer than your house.'

He ended the call from her and slammed towards

the hotel.

*

Gaby was in shock. She and Brian had dined with Jason and Carolyn. They had lived near the village once upon a time. They also had that awful looking house that had escaped the demolition a few years ago. Why on earth would Jason want to hurt her husband. Her head spun. None of it made sense.

She grabbed Eva up into her arms, wrapped her in her blanket and grabbed the baby bag that was nearly always filled with a spare tin of milk and other necessities.

Detective Wallace was quite right. It wasn't safe for her to stay in her own house. Not if the threat left for her was anything to go by. Why would they be after her though? They'd already killed Brian. What had she and Brian done that had caused this? Surely, this wasn't about a petty drug crime that her husband had been forced into.

She was heading for Mrs Blyth's house now. The older woman was standing in the window in wait. It was as if she knew that Gaby would need her because she always seemed to be there at exactly the right moment.

Mrs Blyth opened the door. 'Come in, pet. You look like you've seen the devil himself.'

Gaby rushed through the door, settled Eva behind a cushion on the sofa and began to cry. 'They know who killed Brian. You know that detective, Jason Barr? Him and his wife used to be around the main village quite often until they moved away. Apparently, it was either him or his son.'

Mrs Blyth had the same reaction as Gaby had had. 'That's ridiculous. I know the young man. He works at the coffee shop in the village. Wouldn't say boo to a goose.'

Gaby realised she didn't know anyone. A week ago, her life here had been perfect. How could it have gone so wrong? 'I know I'm really intruding but I don't feel safe taking Eva back to the house. Could we stay here tonight?'

'Of course,' replied Mrs Blyth. 'You know she's always welcome. You too.'

Gaby sighed with relief. She thought she was going to have to phone her mother who she had been avoiding as much as possible in the last couple of days. She couldn't bear to have to deal with her. Not right now. She also knew she had to go and see Brian's mother. Another task she couldn't face, despite her love for Mrs Houston. 'Thank you so much. You don't know what a support you've been to me in the last few days. I can't thank you enough. I have to collect some things from the house and get Eva some medication from the shop. Would it be okay for me to leave her with you?'

Mrs Blyth looked positively radiant. It was obvious she didn't see much of her own grandkids, who adorned the walls in their droves. 'Not a problem. Take as much time as you need. Be quick at the house. And let the officer drive you into the village.'

Gaby had no intention of letting the officer driver her anywhere. She wanted him stationed outside the house to keep watch on Eva. There was no way she was leaving her child alone with Mrs Blyth, however competent she knew the old woman was. She would speak to the officer and let him know she was only going to pick up medication. It was afternoon. How much danger was she really going to be in if she was in her own car.

'Be careful,' said Mrs Blyth, as Gaby went out the door.

'I will.'

55.

Jason had never wanted people to die. He wanted to destroy their lives. He wanted everyone to know that Detective Brian Houston was peddling drugs into the prison so his brother would receive protection. He wanted everyone to see Detective Rosie Cooper for the slut that she really was. What made her think she had the right to a fresh start when she'd destroyed other people's lives with her incompetence? Still, he hadn't wanted anyone dead.

Now, he'd lost his boy. He knew of Cammie's problems. He'd known about them for years. It still didn't justify someone sticking a knife into his neck and robbing him of his life. Wasn't that what Cammie had done though, he reminded himself. Against his instruction. Nobody was supposed to die tonight. He only wanted to confront them all, tell them all what their incompetency had cost him. Cammie had destroyed that though. He'd taken away Jason's moment and turned it into a bloodbath.

Now, all Jason could feel was unyielding fury. He wanted them all dead. For what they'd done to him, his wife and his boy. They'd destroyed everything he held dear. He could never marry again. Never start a family again. He was middle-aged, layered in pain and now on the run from the very law that he had spent many of his working years upholding. Nobody would understand that his boy had been responsible for those three deaths without his input. He didn't think he wanted them to anyway. As Cammie's father, didn't he owe it to him to protect what people would think of him.

It wouldn't matter now anyway. Jason knew that. He was now going to be responsible for five deaths himself. That didn't even include his own son. Ten people would be dead by the end of today and he had moved well past remorse.

His shoulder ached where the bullet had grazed him. Blood escaped the wound and clung to his shirt. He thought of the house on the lake that he and Carolyn had built together. It had been their dream home. They'd given Cove Cottage to their son to allow him some independence on the proviso that if his mental health dipped, he would come home to them.

Consumed by hatred of Lizzie Hawthorn, he hoped she burned up and died a painful death. It was what she deserved. He slammed down angrily on the accelerator and raced towards Cove Cottage. There wasn't much time. He just needed to take a few things.

The cottage was every bit as dismal as he remembered. It hadn't been remodelled in years. In fact, he now wished he had sold it to the developers and been firmer with Cammie. Maybe he might have saved his life. He was walking inside now, pushing through the squalid door and turning his nose away from the ghastly scent.

There wasn't much time as he suspected that other police detective who'd been in the house with Cooper probably knew everything.

He rushed in, the engine still running outside, and grabbed a few pictures and some of his son's belongings. He rushed to the middle landing and grabbed for a photo of him with his wife and son from the wall. Everything else was replaceable. Those photos weren't. He couldn't leave without taking at least some of them. He could still hear the car roar outside. He then heard the front door creak. Probably caught in the wind. It was only when he was running downstairs and heard a woman's voice that he realised the creaking door he had heard was someone entering the house behind him.

'Jason, I was hoping you would come back here, you murdering bastard.'

*

A group of villagers were heading for the hotel now. They'd heard that it was up in flames and wondered if anyone needed help. That hotel had promised tourism to the village, a growth in business and an increase in jobs. Now it was all going to collapse to the ground. Car's raced, men and women poised for a battle against an inferno. Yet, none of them knew exactly how the fire had started. In the weeks to come, there would be speculation. They wouldn't be privy to the gruelling facts of a murder investigation. The sick young man who had died in the fire would go on to become a figure of both terror and pity. Why hadn't anyone noticed how sick he was? Hadn't Benny noticed something strange about him when he worked with him every day.

Benny had been so shocked and horrified by it all that he'd closed the coffee house for more than a week. Until a friend called him and told him that he was a vital part of the community and that they had to go on. For now, though, the villagers were on route to try and save what was left of the village's newest landmark. It's what they'd been promised when they'd invested their life savings in a life on the sparkling loch. They had to salvage something of their new hope.

56.

Gaby Houston swung the first thing she could get her hands on. The bat had been hanging on the wall, a hangover probably from Cammie Houston's childhood. She'd grabbed it as soon as she heard him coming back down the stairs, having followed him in from the front porch.

He was roaring in rage. He'd obviously already taken some kind of beating as blood was all over his shirt and his shoulder was hunched over. It didn't stop him coming for her.

Gaby didn't run though. She'd lost too much already to let him think he'd beat her. So, she swung the bat again. 'What did Brian ever do to you, Jason? We always got along fine with you and Carolyn.'

'Carolyn's dead. Died in the same car accident as Debra Mullen. Then completely ignored.'

She flinched, shocked to hear it but still too wrapped up in her own hatred of what he and Cammie had done to let it deter her. 'Maybe it's better that than her see what you've become.'

'What I've become is because of what your husband and his cronies did to her.'

Gaby, matching his anger inch by inch screamed. 'Dry your eyes, Jason. You think you're the only one who has lost someone. You said it yourself. It was an accident. Nobody meant to kill Carolyn. Or Debra for that matter. Three men have died, that I know of because of your need for blood.'

She cracked the side of his head with the bat, but it didn't hold him back. He was now grabbing for her, throwing her against the wall and tightening his fist into her face. The bat crashed to the ground.

Gaby felt that her jaw might crack if she didn't

try to get away, so she brought up her knee, caught him in the groin and fled when he arched over in pain.

She ran for the door, into the wilderness of his front path and headed for his car. She had left her own car at the old church and made the brisk walk to his house on foot. Now she knew if he got into the car and made after her, she would have no chance. So, she jumped into the driver's seat, slammed the door just in time to see he was coming in the rearview mirror.

Throwing the car into gear, hitting hte accelerator, Gaby felt the car judder and feared it would stall. Instead, it leapt forward.

It was too late though. Jason was already throwing open one of the back doors. He was leaping into the car and grabbing for her.

The car veered wildly out of control as she felt his hand wrap round her head. Suddenly, her head was being smacked against the front window until it cracked. Finally, on the third hit, the window completely out of the door frame. She could taste the blood on her lips as it started to stream down the edge of her face.

Gaby screamed, revved the engine as she turned the wheel left and right.

Jason was leaning forward now, his face a ravaged mess and blood weeping from his skin. He looked terrifying.

'Let me go,' she roared and clawed at his face. She could feel his blood slip onto her skin and it made her stomach lurch.

The car sped along the side of the loch, the waters lowering as she raced onto the far ridge. Then, when she knew she wasn't going to be free of him, she knew she had to make a decision. It was going to be either her or him.

Gaby moved the car to the edge of the tarmac and when it had finally reached the highest peak above the loch, she threw open her door and turned the steering wheel so sharply that the car instantly careered into the loch.

Jason was thrown around the back seat as he tried to grab for the headrest in front of him. He tried to reach for Gaby as she pushed the door against the rising water.

Gaby was escaping. The car was filling with dirty green water, grit and weeds floating across the dashboard and windows. She could see Jason fighting against the water in the backseat, but he was flailing frantically. Perhaps the pain in his shoulder had finally kicked in.

Daylight was disappearing. The car was floating towards the bed of the loch, taking them both with it.

For a moment, she felt his desperation. Her foot had caught between the door frame and the headrest and she really had to pull to try to get it free. There wasn't much time. For a mere second, she wondered if this was what she really wanted. Shouldn't she help free him, call the police and have him arrested. There wasn't time to think. She pulled once more and managed to free her foot.

He was coming for her. Reaching for her foot as he managed to free himself inside the car.

Gaby lashed out. The moment of guilt had been replaced with a clarity that he'd never allow her to live now. She wouldn't be free of what he'd done to her and her husband. So, she forced her foot against his face, catching it with just enough strength to knock him back down.

Air bubbles escaped him as he tried to grab the

inside of the car door.

Gaby gave him one more kick, straight in the head and watched him hit against the back window of his car. She was swimming now, pushing against the frenzied water that floated around the sinking car. She was fast approaching the surface and thanked god because she was starting to feel as if she her lungs would explode if they didn't get some air soon.

The car was out of sight now. So was Jason. Perhaps he had managed to escape and would be waiting for her on a nearby rock. She still had some fight left in her. So, if he wanted to take her on one more time, so be it. She would fight for what they'd done to her husband until her very last breath.

Finally, she was climbing on to the shore, the skies filled with smoke from the burning hotel. Gaby gasped. She hoped Rosie and everyone else was okay. Just more casualties of Jason and his psychotic son. She wrapped her arms round her breasts and chattered. Her eyes were stinging. She would have to get home and out of these clothes soon or she feared she would catch her death of cold.

Looking into the loch, she searched for any indication of the car or that Jason had managed to escape. There was nothing. No splashing or air bubbles across the settling rapids. No light catching anyone's eyes from the drowning car. Gaby felt relieved. She'd fought the man who was responsible for Brian's death and she had survived. For just a moment, she could hear Brian tell her he was proud. Maybe he wouldn't be so proud of her next decision, but she didn't care about that. Gaby watched for another five minutes to make sure Jason didn't emerge from the water. Once she was convinced that he must have drowned, she scraped back her wet oily hair. She would never speak of this. Nobody would ever know that Jason had returned to Cove Cottage and that she'd been waiting for him. Nobody would know that a murderer's final resting place lay at the bottom of Loch Achray and that she'd denied him his place with his wife. Why should he get a happy ever after when he'd denied her a lifetime with her husband?

Certain that no-one had seen, Gaby slipped away and made her way back to the church. Her car was exactly where she'd left it. As she climbed quickly into her seat, she turned the key and was about to drive off when a rattle on the passenger window made her jump.

She was lowering the window as Father Murphy leaned in.

'Jeez, you'll catch pneumonia girl. It's not summer yet, you know.'

'No, Father. Quite true, I just fancied a swim,' she lied, certain that if he had seen anything he would already be jumping into the loch.

'What happened to your head? It's bleeding. Come into the house and we'll clean you up.'

'I'm fine, honestly, Father. I banged it coming out of the water. I'll dash home and get a plaster on it. Sure, it'll be fine.'

'Well get yourself home and dried off. I'll see you tomorrow as planned, and we'll discuss Brian's eulogy.'

'Okay,' she said, catching her breath and rushing to get away. As she did, she saw Father Murphy become smaller and smaller. There was no doubting the grave expression on his face though. Did he doubt what she was saying? Perhaps he might have seen something that she hadn't wanted him to see. She wouldn't allow her life to become marred by panic. Not now. She'd done what she had to do to protect herself and Eva. She wouldn't regret that. Once Father Murphy was out of sight, she pulled the car over and threw back her head. She checked the mirror and saw the stream of blood down the side. Thankfully he hadn't seen her face full on. She reminded herself of her vow. She would never tell a living soul where Jason's body was. Knowing he would spend a lifetime in limbo would be all it took to allow her to live in a peaceful, happy existence with all the good memories she'd made with Brian.

57.

The cellar was thick with smoke. Rosie had forced the other three to the ground as she continued to try and push against the door. It was a futile attempt she knew. She couldn't just lay down and die. Her only other hope was Wallace. She held her phone above her head and moved it around in circles. She remembered the last time she and Wallace had trespassed here. She was glad now that she'd done that. How else would she have bought time for the four of them?

Upstairs, crackling flames continued to spread, windows breaking in the ferocious heat. Thunderous bangs indicated the building was starting to fall in on itself and it wouldn't be long before the innards might come crumbling to the ground. Rosie didn't want to be here when that happened. They might never be found.

She'd gone over everything in her mind. She couldn't believe that Carolyn Barr was dead. She'd been such a lovely woman, so kind to Rosie when she'd been visibly shaken after Debra's death. It shouldn't have been up to Carolyn to comfort her. It should have been the other way around. Why hadn't someone told her. Perhaps all of this could have been avoided.

Which made her wonder about the state Jason had been left in. What extremes to go to for revenge over a terrible accident. Was he so blind sighted by grief that he couldn't see the truth? Nobody had killed Carolyn. Nor had anyone killed Debra. They were just victims of a terrible crash on a winter's day.

'I wonder if Grey's alright?' Adam sounded genuinely concerned.

Rosie didn't have time to worry about Grey now. She had to get out of here. So she accepted defeat from the mobile phone, tried pushing the door one last time. Finally, it began to creak open and the van began to move. She couldn't believe her own strength. In those final moments before the fire spread into the cellar, she'd been able to save the young couple and Adam Mullen from interminable death.

Wallace appeared in the doorway. 'Quick, everybody out.'

Rosie felt slightly embarrassed by the stroking of her own ego. She was thankful she hadn't announced her newfound strength to anyone else. 'How did you get it moved?'

'Hand brake. I just lifted it and then when I heard you pushing the door, I just gave the van a slight nudge.'

She ushered the other three out and told them to run as far as they could to get away from the hotel. Then, she listened as a melee of sirens filled the air. Following the Hawthorns, Rosie took a deep breath and let the air fill her smoky lungs. She bit her lip because it was the only way to hold back the tears.

'Where's Grey?'

Adam was sidling up to them then. 'I think he's dead. One of the images that were left for me was of him hanging.'

'Images?'

Adam sighed. 'You didn't get any? In the room I was locked in they'd left photos of my wife, another woman and of Grey hanging from a beam.'

'The only thing left in my room was whatever costume that bastard wanted me to wear when I met my maker. I guess he didn't count on how tenacious we could all be.' She looked at Adam and saw he was close to tears. 'Hey! There's nothing wrong with crying for your friend. Whatever anyone else thought of him, you obviously cared deeply for him. And I believe he did for you too.'

Adam let the tears fall but choked back the sound of the sobs. 'I know. All these weeks I've been feeling lousy about him, blaming him. Blaming Debra. Blaming myself. Now they're both dead and I'm left without my wife and someone who was closer to me than my own brother.'

Rosie slapped on his back, gave him a nod of encouragement and then walked towards the Hawthorns. What they must have endured during the past few days didn't bear thinking about. 'I'll need to speak to you both. Get your statements about everything that's gone on, but I think it can wait a few hours until you're both checked out at hospital.'

The fire engines were now in the car park and a pack of fire personnel were dropping out of the front doors to begin their fight against the flames. It pleased Rosie to see that there was a female fire preparing to run into the gauntlet. She turned away from everyone, took a moment to catch her own breath and wondered if Grey's death had been painful. He'd probably burn down with his precious hotel. It would be days before they'd pull him from the wreckage. How sad that he would have met his end in the same terrifying way that his parents had died. Maybe now he might have gained some peace.

58.

The rain came almost immediately after Dave and Lizzie were discharged from the hospital. Their car had finally been released and brought over to the car park by Detective Cooper.

Lizzie loomed in the doorway and watched Rosie run towards her, under the cover of her rain mac.

'If this is the best Scotland has to offer, I'm off back to London,' she said, following with a sharp cackle.

Lizzie threw her arms round the detective and held her tight. 'You've no idea what could have happened to us if you hadn't gotten us out of there. I thought we were going to die.'

'Not on my watch, sweetheart,' she said, tenderly.

Letting go, Lizzie stepped back into under the hood of the hospital entrance.

'Where's the patient? He's not still wimping out on us, is he?'

Dave was walking towards her then, his right arm in a sling. 'I'm afraid Lizzie will be driving for the next few weeks. You'll have to get the traffic police on watch.'

Lizzie would normally have hit him on the arm for such a mark. Today, he was getting a pass.

'There's always a taxi,' snorted Rosie. 'Anyway, I'll be in touch. Here's your car keys back.'

Dave gave her a wink and started towards the car with Lizzie.

However, Lizzie turned back and frowned. 'What about the other man you were talking about? Was it Grey? Did they find him?'

Rosie looked sad. 'They've not found anyone

yet. Jason Barr is still on the run. I'm not sure if they'll catch up to him but we won't stop trying. We believe his son, Cameron and Grey are probably both ashes in the fire. It's too early for the recovery of the bodies.'

'That's sad,' said Lizzie, referring to Grey. She had not an inch of compassion left for Cameron, no matter how bad his father said his mental health was. There was no amount of grief that could excuse what either Cameron, or Jason had put them all through.

'You two take care of each other,' said Rosie before disappearing off into a row of other cars.

*

Wallace arrived just in time to see Rosie walking away from the Hawthorns. He could see the emotions spread across her face. She was experiencing everything now; joy, pain, grief but mostly relief that they'd managed to stop Jason before he killed them all. All they had to do now was to apprehend him.

Wallace was tiptoeing round her today. He hadn't wanted to intrude last night but Rosie had insisted he still stay at the house. There was absolutely no need for him to check into a hotel. Particularly not after the day they'd had.

'You should feel good. Whatever way you cracked it, you still did it.'

Rosie slumped into the passenger's seat, threw back her head and sighed with exhaustion. 'Five people are dead. I don't feel like that's a win in any circumstances.'

'Another five would have been dead had it not been for you being there. None of them would have known how to get out of that building if it wasn't for our snooping and the shifting of that van.'

'I just wish I had looked into the Debra Mullen

case more deeply. You know, I never really felt satisfied that it was over but because I knew it was an accident, there was nothing really left to find out.'

'Except there was,' acknowledged Wallace. 'Listen, you weren't to know. You followed your instincts, but you've also got to follow orders from the heid yin.'

She stared into the sky, a day full of promise and new Spring beginnings. The rain stopped almost as quickly as it had started. 'Will you take me for breakfast? I'm absolutely ravenous.'

He chortled. 'Ravenous. What the hell is that? Can't you just be starving like the rest of us?'

She threw up her arms. 'I can be that later. First, I'll sort out ravenous with breakfast and then I'll be starving by lunch time. Who says a girl can't have it all?'

He turned the key in the ignition, nodded his head and started the drive back to Achray Village. The sun rose just as it did every day. Except today, they'd feel safer than they had. Even if Jason Barr was still out there, they didn't think he'd show his face any time soon. If he did, they would be waiting for him. This time, he'd get more than he bargained for.

Epilogue

He pulled down the white trilby and watched the world go by. The streets were much narrower than he was used to. He didn't really understand many of the words spoken, except for 'Si,' 'Ola,' and 'Gracias.' Maybe he would learn the language himself. What else was he going to do with the rest of his life.

He ordered a second coffee and listened to the bustle of the passing tourists. Once upon a time he'd been here as a tourist himself. Now, he had made it his home. Trevi Fountain was one of the most ornate attractions in a city full of stunning attractions. He had chosen well.

He didn't think much about what had happened at the hotel all those weeks before. That was a part of his life he'd forced himself to leave behind. Going into hiding, being on the run of sorts, had given him a sort of perspective he'd never had before.

Finally, mustering up the courage, he took out the pay as you go mobile from the box and inserted the sim card. He then entered the code for the top-up. There was only one phone call he wanted to make before he threw the phone in the bin and moved on with the rest of his life.

A bead of sweat swam across his face. It was far too warm here. His Scottish complexion would probably struggle when the real heat came. He removed the trilby and placed it on the table beside the coffee cup. Then, he dialled the telephone number written on the piece of paper.

A little girl answered. The sweetest voice and one that he recognised all too well.

He could hear a man scold her for answering the phone when he'd told her not to. 'Who is it?'

'Daddy, I can't hear anyone.'

The man removed the scarf from his neck and ran his fingers across the skin. There was still tenderness, though most of the bruising was now gone. He dared not to think about what would have happened to him if he hadn't managed to get free. He wasn't sure what kept him awake more at night; the thought of hanging, or the thought of burning to death. He listened as Adam Mullen came on the phone. 'Hello, who is this?'

It took him a moment to find his voice. Finally, he leaned into the table and spoke quietly. 'Adam, this is the only call I'm going to make to you. I'll make it quick.'

'Grey?' Adam's voice quivered. 'You're alive. How?'

'It's a long story and I don't have a lot of time. Jason and his son tried to hang me. At first, I thought it was about the fake paintings but then I found out about his wife. The guy's a nutter. Anyway, I don't want anyone to find out where I am. I am just calling because I want you to know I love you, mate. I want to tell you how sorry I am about Debra. It wasn't intentional to hurt you. There's nobody in the world I care about more than you and that little girl.'

Adam took a deep breath. 'Grey, you can come back. You're not in any trouble. Jason Barr is on the run. They don't think he'll come back, and his psycho son is dead. They found his body burned in the fire.'

'Adam, I'm not coming back. Barr will never stop trying to get revenge. None of us will be safe. At least you aren't in his eyeline.'

Adam was silent.

Though, Grey didn't think he'd be surprised. 'I'll wrap this up and you probably won't hear from me for a long time. I opened a bank account in Gracie's name. I'm going to text you the details when this phone call ends. There's twenty thousand pounds in that account. It's not penance money. It's money to help you put your life back together because you deserve to be happy. Promise me you'll accept it and move on with your life.'

Adam sighed. 'You don't have that kind of money to give away, Grey. Everything you owned went up in smoke. Remember?'

Grey laughed haughtily. He wouldn't tell Adam that he would soon be getting an insurance pay out on the destroyed hotel. It seemed callous now to take that money, but he'd almost died himself for it. He also wouldn't mention that he had made a small fortune from selling the original paintings bought by Jason Barr. The fakes were now embers in a small Scottish village. 'It's from the sale of my flat. Most of the money in that account was over and above what I expected to receive. Anyway, I need to go. Just promise me.'

Adam sighed. 'I promise.'

Grey disconnected the phone, text the bank details and asked for confirmation they'd been received. Once he got the text back from Adam, he dropped the phone to the ground, stamped on it until it was completely smashed and then threw a twenty euro note onto the table. With that, he lit a cigarette, returned the trilby to his head and disappeared into the crowd of tourists. If there was one city Grey was happy to get lost in, it was Rome.

Printed in Great Britain
by Amazon